DIRTY LITTLE MIDLIFE DEBACLE

HEART'S COVE HOTTIES
BOOK 5

LILIAN MONROE

Cover design: Qamber Designs
Editing: Shavonne Clarke
Proofreading: Jane Beyer

Published by Method and Madness Publishing PTY LTD
PO Box 168 Subiaco, WA, Australia 6008

Print ISBN: 978-1-922986-45-0

ONE

JEN

I LIKE TO WIN.

Mostly, when I put my mind to it, I do.

But this particular challenge...I'm not sure I can pull it off.

A big farmhouse looms in front of me, imposing with its white siding, black shutters, and gently pitched roof. It would be idyllic, if not for the army of TV-production ants carrying various pieces of equipment and thick rolls of cable currently rushing in and out of every door. To my left a huge barn yawns open, and I can see neat rows of kitchen islands lined up to face in one direction. Scattered around the vast surrounding land, nestled in copses of trees and patches of grass, are a number of guest cabins.

The Heart's Cove Manor Retreat has been repurposed for a televised baking competition—and I let my publisher persuade me to participate.

I may have insinuated I thought I would win.

So, you know. No pressure.

"You must be Jen!" A man in his late twenties wearing a headset with the wire dangling down to a device clipped to his belt comes hurrying toward me. He's thin, with dark navy jeans and a slim-fitting black tee. With a mess of blond curls on his head and a broad, disarming smile, the man spreads his arms. "Welcome, welcome. I'm Gus."

"Hi, Gus," I answer, shaking the hand he shoves toward me.

"I'll be helping you get settled. If you need anything, let me know." He flashes his wide smile at me again, but it doesn't unknot any of the tension worming around my belly.

I have the sneaking suspicion I may have bitten off more than I can chew.

My eyes drift back to the barn. I wonder if Gus will let me back out of the competition, get in my car, and drive far, far away. Maybe he'd let me jump in a time machine and go back to the day I agreed to this stupid idea.

"Amazing, isn't it?" Gus beams, following my eyes to the barn. "We've been working for weeks to get the set prepared. I can't *wait* for you to find out what the judges have planned for you. This show is going to be huge. *Huge*." He spreads his arms wide as if to say, *this big*, then swings his gaze back to me with a decisive nod. "You'll love it."

"What happens to the barn once filming is over?"

"Well, that was serendipity. The managers at the manor have been wanting to offer cooking classes, and we at the show were happy to renovate the space—in exchange for a lower rate for the rooms, of course. We'll leave the amenities when we leave."

"Huh."

"Enough of that, though. Follow me!"

Before I can react, Gus is halfway across the lawn, striding to the farmhouse's front door. I grab my bag from the back seat of my car, which is parked in a gravel area at the front of the house, and hurry behind Gus.

When we reach the entrance, he glances over his shoulder. "I went to Four Cups this morning and tried one of your croissants. Divine." He kisses his fingers. "The crew have a betting pool going, and you're my pick to win this thing."

"Oh, great." I give him a weak smile. Pressure squeezes a little tighter around my chest.

Four Cups is the café that I part-own with my three closest friends. I'm in charge of all things related to baked goods and have made a bit of a name for myself in Heart's Cove, our little Northern California town of artists and eccentrics.

I wish I was in the Four Cups kitchen right now. Being neck-deep in experimental recipes and baking chemistry would be much, *much* preferable, but then I wouldn't get the chance to win the hundred-thousand-dollar prize. My brand-new recipe book wouldn't get beamed to a whole new audience, and I'd stay stuck in the same comfort zone I've been in for years.

So even though all I want to do is bolt, the logical part of me tells me to stay. Staying means opportunity, and opportunity means career advancement. Haven't I already sacrificed a lot to get here? Why stop now?

Plus...I *do* really like to win.

Still, I can't quite shake the feeling that this is a mistake.

I don't do television or public appearances, and if I'm

honest, I mostly avoid social interaction—unless I'm already comfortable with whoever it is I'm supposed to be interacting with. I might as well have INTROVERT tattooed in big, black letters across my forehead.

But hey—a baking show sounds perfect. Stick me in front of a bunch of cameras, ask me to do near-impossible baking tasks that my perfectionist brain will no doubt short-circuit trying to achieve, and watch the fireworks.

This is either genius, or—more likely—a disaster in the making.

Amanda, my publisher, pitched it to me as the perfect way to launch my new recipe book. The book was released three months ago and already shortlisted for half a dozen awards. All those hours I spent in a baking frenzy late at night—and early in the morning—have already paid off. I'm simultaneously elated that my dream is becoming a reality, and worried that everyone will realize I'm a fraud.

It doesn't help that I'm allergic to social interaction. I have the charisma of a bridge troll.

When the book came out, my first interview was over email. The publisher of *Bon Appetit* magazine sent me a list of questions to answer, and it took me three whole weeks to type out a few sentences. My hands shook too much to write out the answers until I got myself tipsy and coerced my girlfriends to type while I dictated.

My second interview was for a local news station. The anchor asked me a grand total of four questions outside the Four Cups Café on a sunny spring morning in Heart's Cove. I puked afterward and refused to watch the news for two weeks.

Look, I said I was a high achiever and a winner. I never claimed to enjoy the spotlight.

Yet here I am, following a spry young man named Gus who has money on me winning the whole competition. Bold of him to assume I won't faint when the cameras start recording.

You know what would be a better bet to take? Maybe one where I run away screaming as soon as someone calls, "Action!"

Deep breaths.

I'm a grown woman. I'm successful. I restarted my career in my thirties, and I can do a silly little televised competition. Piece of cake. Literally.

We walk into a large foyer and past a comfortably furnished living area. Six or seven people are talking animatedly as they sip sparkling drinks, and they all turn to stare at me as I walk past.

I give a little wave.

Gus stops. "A few of your fellow competitors." He sweeps his hand toward the living room.

Two big, burly men stand up to shake my hand.

"Reg," one of them says.

"Call me Tex," the other one growls, his meaty paw nearly crushing my fingers when he squeezes my hand. "Texas born and bred, here to show y'all how things are done." He keeps his hand wrapped around mine as he stares in my eyes. "You're Jen Newbank. I bought your book when it came out."

"Oh." I arch my brows. "Thanks."

They get shoved aside when an old woman butts in. She speaks to me in rapid-fire Spanish and I just stare at her, wide-eyed.

A younger version of her—daughter, probably—hustles up. "Mamá, she doesn't speak Spanish." She flicks her long dark ponytail over her shoulder and sticks her hand out toward me. "I'm Emma. This is my mom, Carla. Big Tex says we're the wildcards." She gives the big man a smile, and her mother just rolls her eyes.

"Wildcards," she huffs, then clicks her tongue before saying something in Spanish that has Emma's cheeks going red as her lips fight to keep a smile down. I'd put money on Carla having a dirty mouth and a love of creative insults.

"Mamá, please. You can't say that kind of thing when the cameras are rolling." Emma gives her mother a loaded stare.

Carla's gaze cuts to me. She winks.

The last two people in the room are a husband-and-wife team from Idaho who introduce themselves as Tori and Hank. They own a cake-decorating shop, and when the woman wraps her arms around me, her whole body is soft and smells like sugar. She gives *amazing* hugs, and I immediately feel better when she pulls away—and that's saying a lot, because I'm not a hugger.

"Okay, okay people!" Gus cuts in. "You can get to know each other once Jen is set up in her room." Gus starts marching down the hallway, and by the time I grab my bag from the floor he's nearly out of sight. "Follow me! Chop-chop—*ha*, get it?" He grins, then ducks around a corner.

I hurry to catch up. We walk past two bathrooms and a huge kitchen teeming with a crew of caterers. A hallway juts out to the back of the house and Gus tells me there are six bedrooms there. "For the crew," he says. "I hope you don't mind, the other competitors have their own guesthouses, but since you don't know your partner very well and the only guesthouse remaining was a one-bedroom unit, well, we thought it would be better to give you your own space."

"Yes." I let out a sigh. "Much better."

I follow him up the creaky, carpet-covered stairs and hike my bag higher on my shoulder. "How many people are competing in this thing, again?" I know Amanda told me about the competition, but I was simultaneously freaked out about being on TV and fantasizing about what I'd do with my winnings, and therefore unable to listen.

"Eight teams of two. We'll film five elimination challenges—one on Week One, two on Week Two, and two on Week Three—until there are three teams left for the finale during Week Four. Production will last one month. You'll get every Sunday off." Gus pauses at the top of the stairs. He turns on the landing and grips the bannister, looming above me on the stairway. "I was really sorry to hear about your partner, by the way."

I frown up at him. "My partner? What happened?" Amanda organized a baking apprentice to work alongside me months ago. A young woman named Mary-Ann, who is apparently very good with chocolate.

Gus tilts his head. "You didn't hear about your own partner pulling out of the competition?"

Uh-oh. "I never even met her."

Gus lets out a long sigh and stares at the ceiling. "That would have been *great* television. Oh well." He turns around and takes a step before I stop him.

"Wait. What happened?"

"Broke her legs in a water-skiing accident, poor girl," Gus says with a wave of his hand. "Got the call this morning right after I finished one of your amazing croissants at the café, which was fortunate, all things considered."

Frowning, I watch him turn around and stride down the hallway. "Why were my croissants fortunate?" None of this makes any sense. I hustle to catch up to him. "Will I be competing alone?"

I'm shuffling behind him, readjusting my bag on my shoulder for the thousandth time and trying to remember what the hell I packed that was so damn heavy.

"No, of course not. We got a replacement. Like I said, fortunate." He stops at a door. "Your room, madam," Gus says with a bow and a flourish, gesturing to the closed room.

The knob turns freely and I push the door open, stepping onto the threshold to get a look at where I'll be staying.

The first thing I hear is a strange ruffling sound, but nothing looks out of place. To my relief, the room is nice and well-appointed, with a neat double bed and sturdy timber furniture. When Amanda pitched this show to me, I was imagining zero privacy, but she assured me the only filmed portions of the show would be the actual baking competition. *It's not a reality show*, she assured me. *Very classy. Very professional.*

At least the production costs cover private rooms. I drop my bag just inside the door.

There are no bunk beds in sight, which alleviates my biggest fear of being on a television competition bunking with a bunch of strangers. Even better, everyone will be out in the guesthouses so hopefully I won't need to interact with them much more than necessary.

Look. I know that sounds bad, but it's the truth. I'm an introvert and a homebody. Simone, Fiona, and Candice—my co-owners at Four Cups—can be the town's social butterflies. I'm happiest when I'm surrounded by baked goods and houseplants.

Another ruffling sound ripples through the room, followed by a snap, like a tea towel being flicked. Frowning, I glance around the tidy space for the source of the noise, then look down at myself and my bag. No stray straps, nothing that would sound like a snap.

What in the world?

The snapping sound rings out again, twice in quick succession. I glance back at Gus, who looks horrified by something inside the room. His eyes are angled toward the ceiling.

I take a single step inside, look up at the exposed roof rafters, and freeze.

Dozens of crows are perched on the beams. As soon as I cross the threshold, the cawing starts. The nearest crow cries and I just stare at it, then look forward at the wide-open window.

"Oh, dear," Gus whispers behind me.

Then the swooping starts.

The crow nearest to me dive-bombs, swooping near my head as I double over.

I scream, throwing my hands up to protect my face. Without my hand holding onto the doorknob, the door swings open wider and more crows start their attack.

The noise is deafening. The swoops are never-ending. Crow

after crow after crow attacks my head, with their talons and beaks pecking at my hair, my neck, my shoulders. I fall to my knees with a yelp, then flop forward onto my front.

Gus screams for help. I'm breathless as I try to protect my face from the swooping crows. They're vicious as they attempt to rip apart my face—or at least that's how it feels. Most of them just swoop close but don't touch, but the noise of the wings and the intensity of the swoops has me screaming. My hands are clutched over the back of my head as I lie on my stomach on the floor, the insistent cawing of a murder of crows resonating from all corners of the room.

This is an omen. I don't believe in omens, obviously, but a literal murder of crows attacking me as soon as I step foot in my room? Come on.

I quit. I'm going home. I'm locking myself in the Four Cups kitchen and baking for the next seventy-two hours straight just to wipe the memory of this from my mind.

Screw winning. I don't care about the hundred grand. This isn't worth it.

But first, I need to get the hell out of here. Gus is still screaming, and I hear the sound of his retreating footsteps as he runs away. Wonderful. I'm on my own.

I take a moment to peek over my shoulder, only to see a huge crow diving for me. I scream, shielding my head just in time to protect it from a sharp peck. Pain lashes across the back of my hand.

Get out get out get out I need to GET OUT.

Army-crawling backward, I feel the threshold under my

toes. Good. Only a few more steps and I can close the door on this nightmare—

Where the hell is the door?

I glance up and scream as six crows swoop me at once. I need to close this room *now*. Another crow dive-bombs my face, cawing loudly in my ear. They're angry. There are a dozen angry crows attacking my head and I need to *close this damn door*.

Is this why the collective noun for crows is a murder? Because homicidal crows enjoy killing hapless TV-baking-show contestants? I knew this stupid show was a mistake. I knew it would be a capital-D Debacle.

I didn't think it would end with me getting my eyes pecked out.

Wings flap all around me as I try to protect my head, crawling around the floor to grab at the door. A bird lands on my back and something hard whacks down on my spine. I grunt, falling flat on my face.

"Sorry!" Gus shouts. Then he screams like banshee. "Away! Get away! *Ahhyiiiiiii!*" Something whooshes above me as he swings—yep, he's swinging a broom—in the doorway as the crows flap angrily just out of reach.

My hand finally finds the doorknob and I start shuffling back, still on my knees as I use my other hand to protect my face.

"Hurry!" Gus swings the broom again. "I'm dropping back. Close the door. Jen, what the hell are you doing, *close the door!*"

"I'm trying, damn it!" I shout into the arm shielding my face, moving back one knee-length at a time as I try to get this stupid door closed on these stupid territorial crows.

The biggest crow—the one by the door that first warned me when I entered—uses Gus's retreat to make one last desperate attempt to kill me. It swoops at my head, its beak pecking at my skull as I screech, diving backward and pulling the door closed with me. My back slams onto the hard timber floor as I fall down and smack the back of my head, groaning as the world whirls around me.

I blink, staring at the ceiling. My heart is a drum beating inside my chest, my breaths short and sharp.

What. The. Actual. Fuck?

I lift my head and see Gus leaning against the wall, panting, the broom clutched in his hands like a lifeline. He lets out a hard breath and shakes his head. "I hate birds." He closes his eyes and rests the back of his head against the wall.

The noise of cawing and flapping wings is only slightly muffled by the door. I wonder if I should lock it, then shake my head to dispel the thought. Crows are smart, but they can't open doors.

...Can they?

Huffing, I lift myself up to my elbows and survey the damage. My hands are full of red scratch marks, with blood beading along two particularly deep gouges. Twin black feathers cling to my pants, and when I reach up to touch the matted mess of hair on my head, I groan.

Blood smears on my fingertips tell me the final attack on my scalp did some damage.

Pounding footsteps on the stairs make me turn my head to

see two paramedics—one man and one woman—rushing up with all their gear. They kneel next to me and start asking me questions and inspecting my injuries.

"I'm fine." I groan as I sit up. "But you'd better call the local Audubon society to take care of those crows."

"The what society?" Gus pulls a nearby chair over and sinks into it.

"Bird people," I answer with a sigh as the female paramedic starts cleaning the wound on my head.

Gus just shudders.

"Crows get a bad rap, but they're supposedly really intelligent," I say.

Gus stares at me. "Why are you defending them? They just tried to kill you." Gus gives me the oddest look, like he might be regretting his choice to bet on me.

I close my eyes as the paramedic cleans the cut on my hand. "True."

Once I'm tidied up and the paramedics are sure I'm not going to keel over and die, I push myself to my feet and stare at the door, then swing my eyes to Gus. "What now?"

He taps the headset and jerks his thumb to the stairs. "Just got confirmation to move you to a guesthouse. It's on the other side of the barn. Apologies, Jen, but you'll have to share. The team is organizing a cot." He looks at his watch. "We're supposed to start the pre-competition interviews with all the contestants in ten minutes, but I think we can delay that to allow you time to shower and get yourself settled on account of the crows." He pauses and shakes his head. "I've worked in television for eight years, but that is *not* a sentence I ever thought I'd say."

I nod, already exhausted. The competition hasn't even started yet, but I'm already feeling like this was a bad, bad idea.

GUS IS STILL HOLDING the broom as we walk across the lush green lawn, wielding it like a sword in case of swooping crows. His eyes dart to every roof eave, every treetop, body tensing at every unfamiliar noise.

I glance back at the farmhouse, seeing the open window to my assigned room and wondering how the hell the showrunners are going to get the crows out. My eyes dart to my car, and the urge to drive far away grips me—but I manage to tamp it down. I'm here; I might as well compete. I might as well win.

Even if I have to bunk with someone.

Beside my little white car is a black Jeep. Frowning, I squint to get a better look at it. I could have sworn I saw that Jeep in town when I drove here. It reminds me of—

"This way!" Gus angles down another path and the parking lot moves out of view. We walk past the huge barn and I take another peek at the state-of-the-art kitchen appliances inside, a knot of nerves tightening in my belly.

What if I fail? What if I embarrass myself?

Closing my eyes for a step, I take a deep breath.

Those fears have been my constant companions since I was a little girl. I grew up with a surgeon for a mother and a Fortune 500 CEO for a father. Needless to say, they expected a lot from me. When I told them I wanted to go into computer science, the disappointment radiating from them was palpable. It tasted rotten on my tongue.

Over the course of a decade, when they saw how fast tech was growing as a field and how successful I was, they came around.

Then I quit and became a baker.

Let me tell you, even though I was in my thirties and more than capable of making my own decisions, that was *not* a fun conversation.

Jennifer Newbank was supposed to *be somebody*. She was supposed to do her parents proud. At the very least, she was supposed to marry somebody who was a somebody. Unfortunately, Jennifer Newbank decided she wanted to make muffins for a living.

Perfectionism doesn't quite cover how I feel about myself. It's somehow too big and too small a word. There's no amount of success that could ever be enough. No wins that make me feel satisfied. I should have been more. Done more. Achieved more.

Anyway, I'm here now, competing on a televised baking competition and being swooped by homicidal crows instead of being a brain surgeon like my mom wanted.

Gus and I find a little dirt path on the side of the barn and he gestures for me to follow. "I have confirmation that there are no crows in this cabin. I promise."

"So why are you still holding that broom like a weapon?"

"Just in case." He grins over his shoulder.

The woods open up to a clearing where a tiny log cabin sits nestled in tall grasses, a beam of bright sunlight shining across the front of the house. Charming—except my eyes are searching the trees for angry black birds.

I'm just as bad as Gus.

"We've done so much shuffling of accommodations in the past few hours. This guesthouse was supposed to be for the host, Carrie, who asked for privacy from the contestants and staff, but she got here and didn't like the isolation. She said it was creepy." He snorts, looking at me with a flat gaze. "You know what's creepy?" He doesn't wait for me to answer. "Crows."

I can't quite help the smile that tugs at my lips.

Gus hurries ahead and knocks on the door to the cabin.

I hear a muffled male voice say, "Just a minute," from the other side, and let out a tired sigh. After all those assurances that I won't be bunking with anyone, here I am.

I can survive a few weeks of sharing my space with someone else...right? Never mind that I'm now officially in my mid-forties and I haven't lived with anyone else since college.

Maybe they'll let me stay at my own house in light of the whole crow thing. My contract requires that I stay on site, but these are extenuating circumstances...right? I know there was some clause about *force majeure*. If a murder of crows isn't an unforeseen circumstance preventing me from adhering to the contract, I don't know what is.

But Gus is standing on the doorstep, holding that broom like he's Gandalf back from the dead, and the words die on my lips.

I can do this. If I can start my career over in my thirties, publish a successful recipe book, and survive those damn crows, I can sleep in the same room as whoever is inside this cabin.

That is, until the door swings open and I see the man on the other side.

TWO

JEN

FALLON RICHTER IS STANDING in the small, one-bedroom cabin, a half-emptied suitcase lying on the bed in the corner. That Jeep in the parking lot? It's his.

My heart squeezes hard at the sight of him, breath leaving my lungs in a whoosh. Words fail me.

Six and a half billion people in the world, and it had to be him.

The one who, a year ago, kissed me like a man starved. Six months ago, he quit his job at Four Cups and left without a word of warning.

My lips tingle at the sight of him, so I pinch them together to chase the feeling away.

Fallon and I didn't just *kiss*. We made out like two horny teens on the floor of the Four Cups kitchen. Then, right after Fallon told me he liked me, his ex-girlfriend showed up in town.

At his invitation.

Her name? Amanda Bailey. The woman who would become my publisher. He wanted her to meet me, which was great, but she was staying at his house—and was obviously angling to get back together with him, which was less great. I could see the lust in her eyes whenever she looked at him, the way she lingered in the kitchen when she was done meeting with me just to get the chance to talk to Fallon.

I often wondered if my recipe book was just an excuse for her to keep visiting Heart's Cove. That thought has niggled at me for a year—am I really good enough to have my own book, or was this all just piggybacking on some poor woman's unrequited love?

Her arrival presented me with a horrible, difficult conundrum: if I chose to pursue things with Fallon—and get more of those knee-weakening kisses—I had to get between Amanda and Fallon. It was either romance or my career.

I chose my career. Of course I chose my career. What's one kiss in the face of a published book? What's one man compared to my lifelong dream?

I win. It's what I do. I choose a path and I crush whatever obstacles stand in the way.

But the past year has been torture, and the success of the book feels like ash on my tongue—especially since Fallon quit his job at Four Cups and left without looking back.

Fallon's eyes move from Gus to me, but unlike me, he doesn't look surprised. "Hi, Jen."

Complicated emotions swirl inside me, and I do my best to tamp them down. So what if I kissed this man over a year ago?

So what if I haven't kissed anyone since? So what if pushing him away felt like my own chest was being shredded to pieces?

I feel confused, excited, nervous. Terrified.

Happy. I'm happy to see him again, even though he left without warning. Without ever giving me the chance to mend things between us.

But he's here, in this cabin, and he's...competing against me?

I stare. "What are you doing here?"

Gus glances from Fallon to me and back to Fallon again. "Oh, right. We were talking about this before the crows. Fallon is your replacement partner."

My mouth goes dry. "My partner?"

Wait—Fallon is competing *with* me? I'll be spending the next four weeks cooped up in a little guesthouse, working side by side with the man who hasn't been able to look me in the eyes since I told him I didn't want to date him? The man who quit his job because I rejected him?

Fallon rubs the back of his neck, eyes flicking to me. "Um... surprise?"

"No." I drop my bag and cross my arms. "No way."

A crow caws in the distance, and Gus flinches. He looks up at the sky, then back at us. "I'll just...leave you two to get comfortable." Gus turns, surveying the trees suspiciously, still gripping the broomstick with both hands, then marches off and leaves me on the doorstep.

Fallon faces me fully, and the world suddenly feels smaller. He reaches for me and takes my bag from the ground, dropping it inside the door. "Come in, Jen. I'll explain everything."

"Explain...everything?" My feet betray me by taking a step inside, and Fallon closes the door behind me. His presence is a warm wall beside me, and I close my eyes as I catch a hint of a woodsy male scent. He's always smelled divine. I remember the way it felt to be wrapped up in his arms—

No. That was over a year ago. I need to get a grip.

I need to focus on winning this competition, getting a hundred grand, and starting my own bakery. *That* is what's going to happen here—nothing else.

But getting a grip is hard when a man like Fallon is involved, because another thing I haven't mentioned about Fallon is that he's drop-dead gorgeous. Not in a male model kind of way, but in a big-burly-man-who-could-throw-you-over-his-shoulder-if-he-wanted-to kind of way. Pin-you-against-the-wall kind of way.

Screw-you-till-you-forget-your-own-name kind of way.

Not that I've imagined it, or anything.

He's got thick black hair, full lips, and a neatly trimmed beard. Brown skin, brown eyes, drool-worthy body. His biceps are the size of melons, but he moves like a dancer, especially in the kitchen. Watching him cook is one of the sexiest things I've ever seen. He's totally in control. Masterful.

He makes amazing chai tea, courtesy of his mother's Indian heritage. I discovered this when he made me a thermos full of the deliciously spiced drink, unprompted, simply because he noticed that I liked drinking chai more than coffee.

So, not only is he beautiful, burly, and unimaginably sexy, he's also thoughtful, his kiss made my knees weak, and at one point, he thought it was hot that I'm a nerd who likes to bake.

Me, the nearly celibate ex-computer scientist who has an

unhealthy obsession with being a high achiever. He thought *I* was sexy.

But he also invited his ex-girlfriend to town, let her stay at his place even though she was clearly pining after him, and called me a coward when I refused to date him. Then he walked away.

So...I'm not sure where that leaves us.

Fallon clears his throat, his eyes on the timber floorboards beneath our feet. "I went to Four Cups this morning."

"Why? You don't work there anymore."

He lets out a huff and lifts his gaze to the ceiling. "Maybe I wanted a coffee, Jen." His eyes drop to mine, brow arching.

I nod, chewing the inside of my lip. "Fair point."

"Maybe I wanted to see you," he grates.

My head jerks. "Did you?"

"Would that be so surprising?"

"Um..." I tilt my head. "Yes?"

The aggression in his stance softens, and Fallon does something I don't expect. He *smiles*. His eyes gleam, and it looks like he's about to say something. Maybe tease me the way he used to before the kiss. Before Amanda. Before the whole mess between us.

But instead, he just clears his throat and the glimmer fades from his eyes. "Anyway, Gus was in line behind me. I overheard him saying your partner broke both her legs." Fallon is staring at me, eyes serious, chest just a few inches from me. "I volunteered to take her place."

"You...volunteered?" I'm just repeating his words, but I can't manage much more than that. A murder of crows just tried to kill me. I'm about to embarrass myself on television. Fallon is standing in a shaft of sunlight and he looks like a god. Give me a break, okay? I can't quite seem to focus on a single thought, especially when Fallon reaches over and takes my hand. His palm is broad, warm, and it feels like magic against my skin.

Then he pauses. "What the hell happened to your hands?" He grips my chin and tilts my head to the side. "And your head?"

"Crows."

"Crows?"

I close my eyes. "Yes. A murderous murder of crows. It was an omen." My head throbs as if in response to my words.

"You don't believe in omens." His voice slides over my skin like silk, thumb making slow sweeps across the back of my hand.

It takes me a few moments to find my voice. "Now I do. I'm going to leave. I'm going to quit this thing. It was stupid of me to agree to this competition anyway."

"Jen," Fallon says, and my knees wobble at the sound of my name. "Look at me."

I open my eyes.

"You're not going to quit. You're going to win, you'll expand your bakery, and you'll fulfill every dream that ever entered that thick-skulled, rational, logic-oriented head of yours."

A spasm grips my heart. No one—and I mean *no one*—has ever given me that kind of blind, unwavering support. Then I tilt my head, frowning. "That last part kind of sounded like an insult."

Fallon huffs a laugh and squeezes my hand. "Jen." His eyes warm, and my stupid, unreliable knees start wobbling again.

When he says my name like that, it makes me want to tear my clothes off, spread my arms, and scream, *TAKE ME NOW!*

Nope, nope, nope. We're not having another kissing incident. I'm not opening myself up to feelings for him, only for another ex-girlfriend to show up, or for Fallon to decide he's had enough of me and leave again. The past year was torture enough for me, thank you very much.

Fallon is one thing and one thing only: a distraction.

I pull my hand away. "You don't even like me anymore. I rejected your advances and chose the book instead of you. You quit because you couldn't stand to work next to me. You haven't spoken a word to me in six months. Why are you here?"

A pained sort of expression crosses Fallon's eyes. "That's not why I quit, Jen."

I open my mouth to ask for an explanation, but there's a banging on the door. "Yo!" Gus calls through the door. "You're needed on set."

Fallon's eyes are still on mine, and he gives me a serious look. "This conversation isn't over."

Why did my stomach just tighten at the way he said that?

Never mind. Doesn't matter. Right now, I need to stay focused on winning this competition, if only to avoid thinking about all the feelings swirling inside me that don't make any sense.

I pull open the door to find Gus leaning against his trusty broomstick.

He straightens up, glances behind me at Fallon, and nods. "Good. You're ready. Follow me!"

. . .

THERE'S a camera pointed at my face. I shuffle in my hard plastic seat, which causes my arm to brush against Fallon's. In response, he shifts to drape his arm across the back of my chair. A flush creeps up my cheeks as my heart flutters.

It's just the cameras. That's why I'm nervous. Not the weight of Fallon's arm or the fact that I can smell his cologne.

"We're here to win," Fallon says. "Jen is the most talented baker I've ever had the pleasure of meeting, and I intend to support her all the way to the finale." He glances down at me, those lush lips tugging into a smile.

The interviewer, the show's host named Carrie, crosses her legs as she shifts her gaze. "And you, Jen? How do you feel about being here?"

"I'm terrified," I tell her.

Interest sparks in her eyes. "Go on."

"Well, I'm not sure how else to put it. I'm here to win, obviously, but this whole experience is terrifying. Baking is usually something I do alone, often late at night or early in the morning, when the whole world is quiet. But now I have to somehow shift that to a high-pressure situation in front of cameras—"

"Not to mention the live audience."

"—and..." I snap my mouth shut as Carrie's words sink in. "The what, now?"

Fallon shifts in his seat, his fingers brushing my arm in what I assume is supposed to be a comforting movement. Except all I feel is ice water jetting through my veins.

Carrie tilts her head, blinking those long, false lashes at me.

"You know that for each elimination challenge, the final hour of baking will be filmed in front of an audience, right?"

I'm frozen. My muscles must all be malfunctioning, because I can't move from my spot on the chair. I stare at Carrie, at her long blond hair pulled into a high ponytail with the ends curled, at her perfectly flicked eyeliner, at the heavy makeup that supposedly looks normal on camera. She tilts her head and blinks again. I wonder if those lashes are too heavy to hold up for long periods of time.

Focus, Jen.

Fallon's arm moves closer again, his fingers curling around my shoulder. "Did you not know the audience would be live, Jen?"

I part my lips as I glance at Fallon, then close them again. My throat is too dry to speak. "I'll be baking in front of people?" My voice squeaks. Then I turn, but I can't bear to look at Carrie's beautiful, showbiz face, so I look at the only other thing that happens to be directly in front of me. The camera. "I'm so screwed."

Carrie waits a beat, then exhales and claps her hands. "Oh, *you* are going to be a fan favorite. I can already tell!" She glances over her shoulder. "Gus?"

"Amazing. Breaking the fourth wall there at the end— genius. You're a natural, Jen."

"A natural?" I repeat, an edge of panic creeping into my voice. "Can we go back to the part where you revealed the audience will be live?"

Instead of answering, Gus taps his watch. "You're done. We need to get Tori and Hank in here. Next!"

Fallon helps me stand and keeps his arm around me as he leads me out of the room. It's a comforting weight across my shoulders, and when he pulls me closer, the twist in my stomach unknots. Damn my body for reacting to him without my permission.

His breath is warm near my ear. "Did you really not know about the live audience? Simone was telling me about her plans to come to every live shooting. She said she discussed it with you."

I squeeze my eyes shut as he leads me to a door. We're inside the farmhouse, in one of the ground-floor rooms repurposed for filming one-on-one interviews. I take a deep breath. "You know the adults in *Charlie Brown?*"

Fallon hums. "Yeah. What about them?"

"Well, any time someone mentioned this competition, that's all I heard. Just '*wah wa wa wah wahh wa wa.*'"

Fallon stops, his arm tightening around my shoulders as he pulls me close and ducks his face into my neck to muffle his laugh. His other arm comes to wrap around me as his chin lifts, eyes twinkling as he meets my gaze. "The worst part is, I know you're telling the truth."

I frown. "Why is that a bad thing?"

"It's not." His eyes are warm, and the corners crinkle as he smiles. "You only ever speak the truth. No white lies, no pleasantries, no polite conversation just for the sake of small talk."

"Small talk is pointless and a waste of time."

His smile widens. "I rest my case."

As I open my mouth to answer, Fallon just tugs me toward a door, and we end up in a large lounge room filled with comfortable chairs. All the contestants I met earlier are chatting excitedly, including a few new faces. Fourteen people that will all expect me to interact like a normal human being.

Would they look at me weird if I ran away screaming?

Two women, both dressed in what I can only describe as matching Daisy Duke outfits—complete with big hair, cowboy boots, cutoff jeans, and shirts tied off at the waist—jump up from their chairs and come rushing toward me. "How was it?" one of them asks, then sticks her hand out toward me. "I'm Nikki."

"Jen," I answer. "It was fine."

"More than fine," Fallon cuts in. "They said Jen was a natural."

Does he sound...*proud?*

Daisy Duke number two tilts her head. "Do you do television often?"

Ha! I cover a self-deprecating laugh with an awkward clearing of my throat. "Uh...no."

"Oh." She titters, then introduces herself as Sonia. "I'm so nervous I could puke."

"Just don't do it on camera," I say, and everyone laughs, as if they think I'm joking.

Fallon's arm tightens around my shoulders, and when I glance at him, I can tell he's fighting a smile.

He does that a lot around me.

Fallon leads me to a seat and asks me if I want any food from the buffet tables, but I just shake my head. I can't eat right now. Not until we get the first event out of the way.

But Fallon still comes to sit next to me with a plate piled

high with all kinds of food that he holds in one hand, shifting it over to me every few minutes until I pick off a few carrot sticks, a piece of pita with hummus, and a few other bites of what's offered. Before I know it, the showrunners are calling for us to move to the barn, and I've somehow eaten enough to settle my stomach and my nerves. Fallon just winks at me, then puts the empty plate in a bin of dishes.

Sneaky bugger. He fed me without me even realizing.

THE BARN HAS BEEN KITTED out with eight baking stations, all facing the front of the room. When we enter, I notice the mezzanine level, which surrounds the entire baking space and has been filled with long wooden benches. There's enough space for a hundred or more people to watch. I gulp, following the directions to stand behind one of the stations.

Fallon's hand brushes the small of my back. "You okay?"

"I still can't believe I agreed to do this," I tell him.

He grins. "For what it's worth, I'm glad your partner broke her legs."

"That's an awful thing to say."

"At least it's not small talk," Fallon says quietly, his hand warm against my spine.

"True," I mumble. "Small talk *is* horrible."

His deep chuckle resonates in my chest. It sends something warm unfurling in the pit of my stomach. There's something about Fallon that's just irresistible. Always has been. He's like a rock, a quiet, strong presence—until his hand starts sweeping up and down my spine, and heat gushes through my body.

His touch scrambles my brain, so instead of trying to talk, I turn to the front of the room.

Carrie and the two judges stop on their marks, and someone else calls for silence.

My stomach twists. "That's Bernard Franco," I whisper, seeing the brown-haired judge on the left. The man is a world-famous pastry chef who lives in Paris, and he happens to be my hero. "Oh my God. No. I can't do this."

I start turning away, and Fallon's strong arms wrap around my waist. He pulls me tight to his body, my front mashed against his side. Despite myself, my hand flies up to rest on his chest.

His very hard, very warm chest.

Have I mentioned that Fallon is sex on legs?

"You *can* do this." Fallon's breath is warm on my neck, and a shiver travels down my body. "You can do anything, Jen." When he says the words, it actually sounds like he means them. His hand brushes the small of my back once more before he allows me to pull away. I do, but mostly out of habit. My body screams for me to get close to him again. To have those comforting arms wrapped around me. To press myself against his broad body.

I feel the whisper of his touch in the pit of my stomach and lower, between my thighs. I don't understand how Fallon can have this effect on me. He *shouldn't* have this effect on me. I should be focused on what's going to happen next.

The second judge is a woman younger than me with warm blond hair pulled back in a single, thick braid. She has a lilting Irish accent when she speaks, and my eyes widen when I hear her name. Heather Brennan. The Pastry Prodigy.

I'm going to vomit. Truly. I start scanning for a bucket, then calculate the distance between me and the sink. Three steps. Maybe four.

Fallon's hand makes slow sweeps up and down my spine, moving up to squeeze my shoulder. His strong, warm fingers start kneading my neck, and despite myself, I soften. A rumble sounds in the back of his throat, as if he's enjoying touching me, too. His hand does something magical to the stiffness in my muscles. The nausea in my stomach subsides the tiniest bit.

The heat between my thighs, on the other hand, does not.

For the briefest moment, I wonder what else Fallon's hands could do. How would they feel against my bare skin? Would he be rough with me, or gentle? Would he take control?

Then I squeeze my eyes shut, because now is *not* the time.

"Welcome to *Boss Baker*," Carrie says to the camera with a sweep of her hands. One of the staff members gets her to say it again, and then they set up a teleprompter so she can run through a few lines.

I shift my weight from foot to foot, nervous energy bubbling through me.

Fallon's hand slides from my back to my hip, his fingers taking a strong grip. "Relax, Jen."

"Oh, right. Easy. Just relax," I hiss without rancor. "No problem. I'll get right on that."

His lips tilt, eyes glimmering. Damn it, I love that look on him. He's the only person besides my girlfriends that doesn't look at me like I'm a total weirdo.

"Quiet, please!" one of the crew members calls out, and I zip my lips shut.

Fallon's hand squeezes my hip once more, then drops away. I miss his touch as soon as it leaves. My body feels bereft, untethered without his hand on me.

Sucking in a breath, I try to regain control over my own body, ignoring the imprint of Fallon's fingers branded on my flesh.

The host and judges film another version of the introduction, then have to do it again, then someone comes over and powders Carrie's face, and they do the introduction a third time, and finally our attention is directed to a box on the edge of each team's station.

We're filming online segments now, or "bite-sized" baking challenges, which will be offered to subscribers on the show's online portal. I heave a big sigh of relief when I hear no one will be eliminated.

"This is your chance to make a strong first impression," Bernard intones, his eyes landing on each and every one of us in turn. When they land on me, they seem to linger. Or is that all in my head? His gaze moves to Fallon. "Make it count."

"The first challenge is a mystery box," Heather Brennan announces, her eyes scanning the room. They land on Fallon. Something like heat sparks in her eyes. Feminine interest.

The urge to vault over my counter and punch her in the throat rises within me.

Um.

It's the nerves...right?

She stares at him for a moment longer, then shifts her gaze away. "You have one hour to create one sweet and one savory muffin from the available ingredients."

Carrie, with her straight, white teeth and her perfect television face, smiles wide for the camera. "Your time starts...*now*."

THERE'S nothing sexier than a woman who knows what she's doing. Watching Jen work is the most unexpectedly erotic thing I've ever seen. She flicks the white sheet off the mystery box and immediately starts cataloguing ingredients. A camera is pointed at us, and Jen either ignores it or is in such a deep zone that she doesn't notice.

"Start chopping this bacon. We'll make…" Her eyes roam over the ingredients she lines up on the counter. "Bacon and chive for savory."

A pack of bacon slides across the counter toward me. "Yes, Chef."

Jen glances at me, and I wink. Her cheeks flush pink, and I immediately wonder if the rest of her skin would react the same way. Maybe her chest would warm if I ran my lips over her neck? Her collarbone? Her breast?

How many times have I imagined her body reacting to me

over the past couple of years, knowing I had no right to find out? I've wondered if she'd ever let me kiss her again, if she'd ever melt into me the way she did last year. I've wondered if her nipples would pucker if I ran my tongue over them. If the honey between her legs tastes as good as I imagine.

Tearing my eyes away from her, I try to pull myself together. *Now is not the time, Fallon.*

Jen turns back to the ingredients. "They haven't given us any oil or butter. *Hmm.*" She leans her palms against the counter, staring at the ingredients. Then she glances at me. "Save the bacon fat. We'll either have to make fat-free sweet muffins or use bacon fat for both recipes." She taps her chin and glances at me. "What do you think?"

"I think you already know what you want to do, and you shouldn't waste time asking me my opinion."

Then, for the first time since before I left Heart's Cove, I see Jen's face crack into a smile. She nods. "Bacon fat it is. I'll play around with a filling if I have time—maybe something like my apple pie muffins. Bacon and apple sound kind of weird together, but if we get the balance right it could taste amazing. We can do a candied bacon topping, maybe?" She bites her lip and looks at the countdown timer on the wall. "No time to hesitate. Let's just go for it." She glances at me, that smile still lingering on her lips.

God, she looks good right now. The barn doors are thrown open, the summer sun framing her in a golden glow. Her blond hair is pulled back in a low bun and she's wearing a white chef's jacket with her name embroidered on the breast. High cheekbones, sharp eyes, and lips that are thinner than average with an over-defined cupid's bow. Slight crinkles around her eyes that I find unbearably sexy for some reason. That concentrated frown that makes me want to kiss her brow until she relaxes.

I don't know what it is about the angular nature of Jen's face, but it's always attracted me. It matches her personality. Sharp, to the point, efficient. Like there's nothing extra added to her features beyond what's strictly necessary to make her beautiful.

Then the host and judges appear beside us, and they ask Jen what she's making.

Jen tells them in her usual no-nonsense voice, all while sifting dry ingredients without looking. She looks like a rock star, and she doesn't even know it.

"You seem very confident," Bernard says, piercing blue eyes intent on Jen.

I don't like the way he's looking at her. My body stiffens as his gaze roams around her face and down her body.

"I am," Jen tells him. "I've made a lot of muffins in my life."

I was telling the truth this morning when I said I was in Four Cups to see her. After staying away for six months—all those months spent facing the skeletons in my past—I needed a glimpse of her to feel something good, for once.

And when I overheard Gus on the phone? I volunteered for this job before I could stop myself. How could I resist? I signed the contract at once, with only one small change to the clause regarding the prize money.

"And you think you can complete all that work in only one hour?" Heather asks. Her thick braid falls over her shoulder as she leans over to watch what I'm doing.

"Yes," Jen answers simply.

My lips twitch. That's so perfectly Jen. No explanation; no excess words. Yes, she can do all this work in an hour, and yes, it's going to be amazing.

"Well, good luck," Bernard says, his bright blue eyes intent on Jen. "I like your confidence."

That flush returns to Jen's cheeks, and an unholy hatred for Bernard fucking Franco rises up inside me. So he's a famous chef and Jen admires him? He has no right to make her blush the same way I do.

Reeling myself back in from the edge, I focus on my work. *I have no right to be with Jen—I sure as hell have no right to dictate who she talks to.*

But Jen just gives him a curt nod, and the judges and Carrie move on to the station behind us. She lets out a long sigh and glances over at what I'm doing before giving a satisfied dip of her chin. We've always worked well together at Four Cups, and in the months that I've been gone, I've missed her.

I mean, obviously. Last year, when she told me she didn't want to pursue anything with me because of Amanda and her book, it was a hard rejection to take. But can I really blame her? I'm a forty-six-year-old chef who's never going to amount to anything. With my history, working in kitchens is all I have to offer. I'll never be on her level.

Jen, on the other hand, is a brilliant computer whiz who was, by all accounts, amazing at her job until she decided to quit to pursue her pastry baking dream. She's all class and education and brilliance, and I'm just the piece of shit who chops her bacon.

When she told me she had been working at a Michelin-starred restaurant under Guillaume Boucher, one of the most famous French chefs in the world, but quit to become a co-owner of the Four Cups Café, I thought she was crazy.

She's got guts. She acts like her decisions are the most natural thing in the world, and I don't know if she realizes that most people would never have the courage to quit a good job to pursue a dream with so few guarantees as becoming a pastry chef. Then, quit a great job at a renowned restaurant to strike out on her own.

She's *brave.*

When we started working together, her talent was obvious. The fact that her new book is shortlisted for so many awards hasn't surprised me.

And yes, I googled her after I left Heart's Cove. How could I not?

It's hard not to feel inadequate around someone like that. Someone who can create things that are so incredibly perfect, who's intelligent and educated and driven. Talented beyond measure.

Is it any wonder she didn't want to date me? What can I possibly offer a woman like Jen?

I chop half the bacon into small pieces and start rendering the fat before moving to make candied bacon with the rest of the meat. To be completely honest, apple-bacon muffins sound a bit weird to me, but judging by the fact that I've tasted all of Jen's recipes and not one of them has been bad, she has my complete confidence.

As she should. We end up winning the first bite-sized

competition, with the judges calling her sweet muffin "inspired." Jen smiles again, and the sight of it makes me need to adjust the waistband of my pants. There's just something about this woman that turns me on. She has no idea how hot she is. Or maybe she knows, but she doesn't care.

There are more interviews and promo sequences to shoot, and by the end of the day we're both wrung out and exhausted. Jen and I return to our room without speaking. It's silent in the woods as we enter the cabin.

The cabin consists of one big room with a queen-sized bed, a dresser, and a closet in the corner. Opposite the bed, there's a couch, an armchair, and—as of this morning—a single cot shoved in the corner by the big bay windows overlooking the lawn. Finally, along the wall shared with the bathroom is a small kitchenette. The bathroom is spacious. It's probably designed for couples or honeymooners vacationing in Heart's Cove.

Jen runs her fingers through her hair and casts a glance toward her bag.

"You nervous about filming in Heart's Cove tomorrow?" I ask. We were informed by Gus that in the morning, we'd be shooting the last of the *get-to-know-you* sequences featuring Jen in the Four Cups Café. All the other competitors were visited in their hometown over the past few weeks.

Jen's eyes lift to mine. She's got a streak of dried batter in her hair and her eyes are hazy, and she's never looked better.

"No," she answers simply.

"No?"

She flops down onto the armchair by the window, looking up at the darkening sky. "Four Cups is where I feel most comfortable. It'll be nice to be back there, even just for an hour or two."

"I get that," I answer quietly, moving to my half-unpacked suitcase on the bed and picking up where I left off this morning. "It was nice to go back there today. Felt like coming home."

"So why did you leave?" Her eyes are still directed out the window, but her question feels pointed. Heavy.

And I can't tell her the truth.

I can just imagine how that would go. How would I word it?

—I was in Nevada.

—What were you doing?

—Oh, I was going to prison every day to teach cooking classes.

—Huh, that's weird. Why would you quit your job to do that?

—I wanted the men on the inside to learn some skills they could use to start over when they're released. It's a cause near and dear to my heart, because well, here's the thing: I'm a convicted felon.

Yeah. That would go over well.

Instead of answering, I just change the subject. "You did well today, Jen. It was great to be cooking with you again."

She blinks over to me, looking like she wants to say something. Finally, she just nods. "Thanks. You want to shower first while I unpack?"

I just fucked up. I can tell by the shuttering of her gaze, the way she angles her shoulders away from me. I had a chance to open up to her, to make her understand who I am, why I left, and how I feel about her...and I wasted it.

Big fucking surprise. Screwing up is what I do best.

I hold her gaze for a moment, conflict roiling inside me. If I told her the truth about my past, my family, my troubles...would she judge me like everyone else does? Would she look at me differently? Would she reject me the same way she did when Amanda showed up?

Probably.

Finally, I nod. "Sure."

I watch her thin, angular body unfold itself from the armchair and stand, her clothes clinging to every slight curve. I still remember how it felt to have my arms around her, my hands buried in her hair. She tasted sweet as honey, so fucking delicious I never wanted to stop kissing her. I didn't think it would be the only chance I'd get. I watch her walk to her bag and lift it onto the bed, then I turn around and head for the bathroom.

As soon as the door closes behind me, I release the breath I'd been holding. I've been on edge all day. When I opened the door to see Jen on the stoop, all I wanted to do was drag her inside and crush my lips to hers. I wanted to push her up against the wall and claim her, make her see exactly what she does to me.

Stripping my shirt off, I look in the mirror. I turn to stare at the huge tattoo that spans the width of my back, the tails of two snakes coiling over the sides of my ribs. My biggest mistake inked into my skin forever. The pledge I made to a brotherhood when I was too young to understand the consequences.

And that's why I can't tell Jen where I was, or who I used to be. Because she knows me as the happy chef who worked at Four Cups—not the ex-con who ended up in prison when he was too young to know any better. The guy who's relegated to kitchens and construction laboring jobs forever, because he'll never amount to anything more.

Tearing myself away from the mirror, I turn the shower on and tilt my head into the stream. My skin feels too sensitive, and when I hear Jen humming to herself on the other side of the door, blood starts flowing between my legs. Did I really commit to four whole weeks of this? Four weeks of being close to Jen and not being able to touch her? Four weeks of feeling my cock twitch every time Jen gives me one of those rare smiles?

Turning the shower to cold, I do my best to chill my heated blood. I wash quickly, ignoring the insistent throbbing between my legs, and exit the bathroom to find Jen tucking her empty duffel bag away in the closet. She's got the shelves color-coded and organized, with honeycomb-shaped organizers for all her socks and underwear. Of course she does.

I fight a smile at the sight of it, then point over my shoulder. "Bathroom's all yours. Go for it."

She nods, grabs a towel, and shuffles past me. The bathroom door snicks shut, and I find myself sinking down onto the edge of the bed.

It's amazing how natural it feels to share a space with Jen. It was like this when we started working together too. We just fell into a rhythm without much effort—well, I *did* bribe her with masala chai tea to get her to stop coming in at the crack of dawn to avoid me. And I did stop playing my music whenever she was around because I learned she likes silence. And I might have kept her multitude of kitchen scales stocked with fresh batteries to stay in her good graces.

But after that? Working with Jen was a dream.

I missed her. I didn't want to leave—but I had to.

Being back here—seeing her little sock organizers and her perfectly folded clothes—it reminds me of all the reasons we can't be together. We come from different worlds.

Women like Amanda Bailey like me because I have sharp edges. I'm just trouble enough to feel dangerous for a night, but not so much that they get hurt. Amanda didn't want to get back together with me—she just wanted me to fuck her.

I wasn't interested, because there's only one woman I've wanted for the past three years, and she's currently showering in the next room.

Night has fallen. It's dark in the room, so I stare out the window as the sounds of the shower fill the space, Jen gently humming a song to herself.

Then, something moves outside the window. It's barely a shadow in the woods, but I freeze, squinting. I stand up and move to the side of the window, peeking outside, trying to tell shadows from branches.

More movement. My blood freezes as the hairs on the back of my neck prickle. There's someone out there. Another shape darts in the trees, and my blood starts pumping.

They fucking followed me. I should never have gone back to Nevada, back to prison. The guys that got me arrested just couldn't let it be, and now they're here, outside a cabin while Jen is singing in the shower. Adrenaline dumps in my veins as my aggression roars to the forefront, my mind screaming *protect her*!

It only takes me three steps to get to the front door. I throw it open and call out, "Hey!"

Stillness answers back. I scan the woods where I saw the shape and I wonder if I'm going crazy. The paranoia is getting to me. The past six months have ridden me hard. I thought going back to face the worst years of my life would allow me to move on—but it feels like it's only dragged me into the quagmire of my past.

"Who's there?" I yell out in the night, and the breeze ruffles the trees. Standing on the stoop for a few more moments, I shake my head.

There's no one there. I'm losing my mind. Scraping my nails over my scalp, I squeeze my eyes shut and try to calm my racing heart.

When I re-enter the room, Jen has her hair wrapped in a towel and is wearing loose pajama pants and a hoodie. As soon as I see her, my latent aggression turns to lust. Her nipples poke through the fabric like two little beacons begging to be sucked.

I'm so fucking screwed. A month? I signed up for a month of this torture?

She frowns at me. "What's going on?"

I shake my head, tearing my eyes away from her chest. "Nothing. Thought I saw someone out there, but it must have been the wind."

Jen nods, then glances at the two beds. "I'll take the cot."

Oh, hell no.

"Uh-uh." I walk up beside her and cross my arms. "You're the whole reason we're doing this competition. You need your sleep. You take the bed."

Jen arches a brow. "Fallon, you're huge."

I can't help the tugging of my lips. "I get that a lot."

She rolls her eyes, which makes me want to kiss the sass right out of her, and points to the tiny single bed that looks like it'll collapse under my weight. "That thing is too small for you. I'll sleep in it."

"No."

Jen huffs. "Fallon."

"Jen."

"I'm not letting you sleep on the cot."

As if she could stop me. "I'll sleep on the floor." A smile twitches at my lips. I love when she argues, when those lines appear on her brow and her jaw sets in a hard line. My eyes drop to her chest again, to those small breasts that would fit perfectly in the palm of my hand.

Her cheeks are red. "Why are you being so stubborn?"

"Because I'm right."

"I didn't know 'right' was a synonym for 'overbearing.'" Jen moves to the bathroom door and starts unwinding the towel from her hair. She hangs the towel up on a hook without looking at me.

Overbearing, huh.

I lean a shoulder against the bathroom doorframe. "I'm not budging on this."

"Fallon, be logical." She grabs a wide-toothed comb and starts untangling her hair, her eyes meeting mine in the mirror.

When she glances away, my eyes drop the length of her body. Even in sweats, I can't resist the sight of her. "I am logical. You deserve the bed."

She frowns. "Deserve? I don't deserve the bed any more than you do."

Oh, but she does. She's a college-educated genius from a good family. I'm lucky I'm not still in prison.

I point to the bed. "You're sleeping on the bed."

"No, *you're* sleeping on the bed. I'm taking the cot." She puts the comb down and turns to face me. It takes all my self-control not to stare at those taunting nipples.

I push off the doorframe. "Absolutely not. You need to rest for the competition." I walk into the main room, heading for the cot.

"Fallon, stop." She gives me a glare, fists clenched at her sides, then grabs a pillow and shoves it on the end of the tiny, nearly child-sized cot. "Try it. Lie down and see how comfortable you are."

"Fine." I plonk myself down on the cot and drape my legs over the end, my feet sticking out in midair from mid-calf down. I rest my head against the pillow and spread my hands. "See? Perfect."

Sort of. My legs hang off the end, and my feet will probably go numb if I stay like this, but there's not really enough room to roll onto my side. There's nowhere comfortable to put my arms, but still. It's only temporary. Jen should have the bed. Worst case, like I said, I'll sleep on the floor.

"You'll give yourself back problems." She arches a brow. "Take the bed."

"This discussion is over." I close my eyes and cross my arms.

"You look ridiculous. It looks like you're on a toy bed, Fallon."

"I'm comfy," I lie. My eyes are still closed. "Sleepy."

"You know what? Fine. I'll take the bed." She stomps over to the other side of the room and slips under the covers. I hear her huff as she turns off the bedside lamp.

When I crack an eyelid to peek, Jen has an eye mask on with her own blankets pulled up to her neck. I smile at the sight of it, and my heart does another one of those spasms.

My smile fades.

This is as close as I'll get to her.

The truth is, Jen is much better off without me. What can a guy like me offer a woman like her? A woman whose life has been one straight, consistent upward trajectory?

I spread a blanket over the cot and punch the pillow, glancing one last time out the window. When I see no movement beyond the leaves rustling on the trees, I lie down and close my eyes. Sleep doesn't come easy.

FOUR
JEN

I WAKE up to a loud bang and a groan. Pushing my sleep mask to my forehead, I sit up and see Fallon on the floor beside the cot. He rubs his shoulder and glances at me. "Fell off. Had a dream I was skydiving without a parachute. Shit." He rubs the heels of his hands in his eyes.

Sighing, I flick the blankets on the other side of the bed. "Get in, Fallon."

To my surprise, Fallon only hesitates for a moment. There's a rasp of fabric as he gets to his feet and grabs his pillow. I put my eye mask back on before feeling the bed dip beside me.

My heart thunders. The last time I shared a bed was a couple of decades ago, with the one and only boyfriend I've had after college. The heat of Fallon's body soaks into my side and I turn my back to him, grateful for the dark, the eye mask, and the blankets pulled up to my chin.

. . .

WHEN MY ALARM STARTS BLARING, the first thing I notice is a hot, heavy weight draped over my body. Fallon's leg is thrown over both of mine, and it must weigh a hundred pounds. His arm is pinning me to the bed. I groan, wiggling away from him to smack the button on my phone to stop my alarm. I hit it with the tips of my fingers, then pause.

This feels...nice. For a few glorious moments, I find myself snuggling into Fallon's warmth. His hand tugs me into his chest while his leg curls over both of mine, as if he wants to drag me as close to his warm, hard body as possible.

I close my eyes for a few seconds. Fallon's breath ruffles my neck, his body curled protectively around me. His scent is everywhere, his body pressed up against the length of mine. I'm being lulled back to sleep with every breath. Nuzzling into my pillow, I curl my arm around his and hold it against me.

He's sleeping anyway. He won't know. It's just one little snuggle. It can't hurt anyone.

When my alarm goes off again, I jerk fully awake, then use all my strength to heave Fallon's arm off me. He tumbles to his back, with his lower body twisted so it's still covering mine.

With a grunt, I pull my leg free and stumble out from under him to stand up next to the bed. Panting, I put my hands on my hips and stare at the man starfished across the sheets.

Maybe him taking the cot *was* a good idea.

"Fallon."

No answer. The man doesn't even move.

I poke his arm. "Fallon."

A snort—but zero movement.

This is ridiculous. I shove his shoulder which, predictably, barely even budges. Fallon turns his head and mumbles something into the pillow.

"*Fallon.*" This time, I use both hands to shake him awake.

Nothing.

Something skitters in my peripheral vision, and I look down to see a palm-sized spider inches from my foot. Screeching, I hop onto the bed and land on all fours. I don't know if it's my scream or the weight of me on the bed, but Fallon jerks awake.

He sits up so fast I don't have time to move out of the way, and his forehead connects with my temple. Pain explodes as I flop onto my side, sprawled on the bed over his legs.

"Shit, Jen, shit!" He drags me by the armpits and holds me to his chest, broad palms spread over my face. "You okay? What the hell happened?"

"Spider," I groan, clutching my head.

Fallon freezes, his head tilting. "You're...scared of spiders?"

My eyes cut sideways to glare at him. "It's a natural evolutionary mechanism, thank you very much. People have grown afraid of spiders out of fear of venomous bites."

"Uh-huh." His hand is still splayed over my cheek as he uses his other hand to move my hair out of the way. He inspects my temple, then, to my surprise, brushes his lips over my skin. Heat blooms low in my stomach as my heart thumps. Fallon must not notice, because he just says, "All better."

"I'm not a child who needs to be kissed better, Fallon," I say, wriggling off his lap. "I'm a grown woman." Fallon goes very, very still as I do, but I don't have time to decipher his reaction because I'm already gripping the edge of the bed and peering

over on all fours. I click my tongue. "Damn it. Spider disappeared. Now we have to burn down the whole cabin."

"What were you saying about being a grown woman?"

I glance over my shoulder to see him grinning, then sit back
down and cross my arms. "Well, if you're such a macho man,
why don't you get out of bed and kill it!"

"I'm not going to kill a spider," Fallon says, swinging his legs
over the edge of the bed. "But I'll catch and release it if it makes
you feel better."

Still sitting on the bed, I pull my knees up to my chest. "It
would, actually."

"Your wish is my command." He jerks his head to my eye
mask. "Didn't take you for a Beverly Hills housewife."

I pull off my silk mask and frown. "Sleeping in total darkness is important. This place doesn't have blackout blinds. The
only logical solution is a mask."

Fallon's lips curl. "Of course it is." He gets on his hands and
knees to check under the bed, then makes a noise at the back of
his throat. Then, he's grabbing a broom and dustpan from the
cupboard and heading back to the corner of the bed. With
gentle movements, I watch Fallon coax the spider onto the
dustpan as he covers it with the broom.

Jerking his head to the door, he asks me to open it up for
him. When I do, Fallon gently releases the spider onto the grass
before standing up and brushing his hands off. "There," he says.
"Better?"

I rub my temple, already knowing it'll bruise. "Yeah."

When we get inside, Fallon checks his phone for the time

and arches his brow. "We have to get to set. Call time is in half an hour."

Obviously. "That's why I was trying to wake you up, but I didn't know I'd be putting myself at risk of death by head-butting."

Brown eyes glitter. "And I didn't know I'd be seeing the first illogical facet of your personality."

"Fear of spiders is not illogical." I cross my arms with a huff.

When Fallon laughs, I tilt my head. He seems to do that a lot—laugh when I'm around.

People have been laughing at me since I was a kid. I was the punchline of a lot of jokes. But with Fallon, it feels different. He's not laughing *at* me. He actually thinks I'm *funny*.

Ducking away to hide the redness of my cheeks, I do my thing in the bathroom, then get dressed while Fallon is in the bathroom. It gives me time to inspect the guesthouse for more eight-legged intruders, then take a few deep breaths to calm myself down.

A few minutes later, we meet Gus in front of the barn. The other contestants will be filming interviews and miscellaneous promotional shots while a cameraman accompanies Fallon and me into Heart's Cove.

I'm glad I didn't give this too much thought last night, because I might have lost my nerve. When we enter the café, Fiona is behind the till while Clancy, her stepdaughter, busses tables. Through the opening to the kitchen, I can see our new chef, Kyle, who was hired to fill Fallon's very large shoes.

Fiona brightens, and when she sees the camera she immediately reaches for her phone. I bite back a groan. No doubt everyone in town will know there's a camera crew with me here.

"We want shots of you two baking in the kitchen," Gus says, consulting his tablet. "We also need to stop by your house and do a quick interview there."

I freeze. "In my house?"

Gus looks up and frowns. "Is that a problem?"

"No," I answer, then let my eyes dart to Fallon. He'll be in my house. *In my space*. Where I've fantasized about him for the past year. In the same building as my vibrator, which I've also used while thinking of him. Often.

I *knew* being partnered up with him was a bad idea. How am I supposed to win when I have a big, six-foot-something attractive beast of a man beside me all the time! Fallon is the mother of all distractions, but having him in my space might be a step too far.

My palms sweat as I nod to Fiona and head to the kitchen. The cameraman follows, hiking his camera onto his shoulder while Gus asks Fallon and me to position ourselves.

"We'd like to get a shot of you baking together," he says, waving his hands for us to move closer together. "Just like you used to. You worked together, yeah?"

I shuffle toward Fallon, then shake my head. "We didn't bake together. Fallon was usually standing over there with his back to me." I point to the grill, where Kyle is flipping a few strips of bacon.

"Well, you're baking together today," Gus announces. He sweeps a hand in an arc. "Showbiz, Jen."

"Should I check the space for creepy-crawlies before we begin?" Fallon asks near my ear.

I glare at him, which only makes his lips twitch.

Gus and the cameraman position themselves, then look at me expectantly.

I blink. "Well, what do you want us to make?"

"Anything, Jen! Literally anything. You can stir flour around in a bowl for all I care." Gus waves me forward with an encouraging smile.

"I can't believe I'm doing this," I mumble, reaching under the stainless-steel countertop to grab a few mixing bowls. I point to the pantry area. "Get me some bananas. We'll make banana bread."

"Yes, ma'am," Fallon says with a salute, and I know he's only doing it to annoy me when he glances over his shoulder to check my reaction. When he sees me with my hands on my hips and thunder on my brow, he starts laughing.

"This is great," Gus says. "Keep doing this."

"You're filming already?" I screech.

"Relax, Jen. You're a professional, remember?"

"Am I?" I ask under my breath, then reach for the dry ingredients and start mixing. My shoulders immediately drop. Banana bread is really a one-person job, but Fallon mashes the bananas and gathers the wet ingredients. We have it mixed and in the oven in record time, and I only realize after a few minutes that Gus has been asking me questions about myself the whole time.

"So you quit your successful tech job to pursue your dream to be a pastry chef?" Gus tilts his head.

I close the oven door and brush my hands on my apron, suddenly self-conscious. "Um, yeah."

"Jen is a rock star," Fallon cuts in.

I frown. "My bedtime is eight-thirty."

Fallon's lips twitch as he glances down at me, as if I just made a hilarious joke. I don't understand this man at all. My bedtime is *literally* eight-thirty.

He turns back to Gus while hooking an arm around my shoulders. He's getting real comfortable tugging me close to his body, and I'm still telling myself I hate being manhandled by him. I glower at him while he speaks, even though my hand *does* rest on top of his very solid stomach.

Fallon gives me a squeeze. "She's the best baker I've ever met. Working with her was a privilege, and I have no doubt we'll go far in the competition."

As soon as Gus wraps up the unending questions, I pull away from Fallon. "I'm not a cuddler."

"Could have fooled me." Fallon's voice is low, his eyes twinkling as he looks down at me. I know he's talking about this morning.

"I thought you were asleep," I hiss from the corner of my mouth, moving to the sink to wash the few dishes we made.

"I was. Mostly."

My cheeks heat, and I scour the bowls I used with more violence than necessary. Once everything's done, with Kyle on duty to remove the bread from the oven, I follow Gus out to the front of the café.

And freeze.

Nearly every single resident of Heart's Cove is crammed in

the small space. Every chair is full. Every wall is lined with people. The chatter is a loud hum as we walk out, and it immediately cuts off when I walk into the space.

"There she is!" Candice says, climbing up to stand on top of a table. "Our very own Jennifer Newbank."

Applause erupts and all eyes turn to me. Including the camera, which is back on and pointed at my face.

Deer. In. Headlights.

This is literally my worst nightmare. I force a smile, heart beating a million miles an hour in my chest. Everyone is here. They're all looking. Waiting.

"We know you'll win," Dorothy says. The elderly, animal-print-loving woman owns the Heart's Cove Hotel along with her twin sister Margaret. She slings an arm around my shoulder and pulls me into yet another hug. "You're the town's pride and joy, Jen."

"I can't believe you'll be on TV!" Allie, Candice's daughter, screams in my ear.

"Go, Jen! Go, Jen! Go, Jen!" Simone, the fiery redhead who co-owns the café with Fiona, Candice, and me, starts chanting.

To my abject horror, everyone joins in. The dozens and dozens of people in the café are all looking at me, cheering for me, chanting my name, expecting...*something*. I don't know what they want! I don't know what to do.

So, like the lump I am, I just freeze. I stand in the middle of this big crowd, feeling the temperature of my body ratchet higher and higher, while panic starts swirling around and around and around in my head.

Too many people. Not enough air. Too much attention,

expectation. They want me to do something, but all I can do is stand here. What do I do? What do I say? How do I—

My body is hauled up with two big, broad hands clamped around my waist. I vaguely register that those hands belong to Fallon as I'm flung over his shoulder, his strong arm banding over my thighs.

"Coming through!" he bellows. "Move over, people!"

Breathless, panic still sizzling inside me, I glance over my shoulder to see a thin slice of space forming between us and the door. Fallon shoulders his way through the crush, not stopping until the door opens and sweet, sweet fresh air fills my lungs.

I breathe deep, expecting Fallon to put me down.

He doesn't. He keeps going. And going. And going.

We walk all the way down the block and around the corner, where Fallon finally sets me down with steady, careful movements. His head ducks down so his eyes can meet mine, searching my flaming face. "You good?"

"The people," I push out with a breath.

"You looked stressed."

"Too many people," I manage.

"I figured." Fallon moves one hand from my waist, and I immediately miss the comforting warmth and weight of it. He doesn't go far, though, sliding his palm behind my neck and tugging me into his chest.

It's not until a few shuddering breaths make their way in and out of my lungs that I realizing I'm clinging to him, hands curled in his shirt, tears wetting the jersey fabric.

"I can't do this," I say, voice muffled in his broad, safe chest.

I inhale the clean scent of detergent and that musky cologne that smells like Fallon.

"You can." His hand nestles into my hair while the other slides around my waist and starts making slow, comforting circles over my back.

"There's too much pressure." My voice cracks on the last word.

Fallon's hand freezes, and he pulls away a few inches to look down at my face. "Do you really want to stop? Quit the competition?"

He doesn't say it judgmentally. He's just...*asking*.

The earnestness of his expression hits me hard. I gulp, mind whirling, trying to find the words.

I've always been told that I need to do something with my life. Be someone. Make something of myself. I grew up in the shadow of my parents, who had enough degrees between them to cover an entire wall in our house. They were titans of their fields. Forces of nature.

It was never a question of whether I'd be successful, only a question of what I'd sacrifice along the way.

And I've always done my best. I won scholarships to college and rose like a rocket in my tech career. I finished pastry school with a job offer from none other than Guillaume Boucher. I *am* successful. I'm a winner.

But...I'm *tired*. What if this competition is just too much?

I'll be fifty before I know it. I've basically had two full careers in my life, and I still have more to give—but when will it be enough?

I don't know what I want. I want to win the competition. I want to feel that rush when we made those muffins yesterday, the timer counting down while I entered the flow that only happens when I'm baking.

I want to win a hundred grand and start my own bakery. I want my book to be a success...but I also want to feel Fallon's arms around me and see him laugh when I say something he doesn't expect.

So, when I meet Fallon's gaze and shake my head, it's not because I feel like I need to compete in order to be successful. For the first time in a long time, I'm doing it because I want to.

"No," I tell him, my voice gaining strength. "I don't want to quit. I just...don't like crowds."

His lips quirk. "Then I'll keep you away from them. I'll be your official personal-space-implementer and spider-catcher. I'll take care of you, Jen. All you have to do is win."

For the briefest moment, his eyes drop to my lips, and fire roars to life in my core. I want him to kiss me. Even after the past year, even after he left. Even though he's the biggest distraction ever, and kissing would only mess with my head, I'm still desperate to taste his lips again.

Then Fallon's eyes slide to the end of the alleyway, where Gus is standing with the cameraman. His cheeks are flushed, his blond hair wild around his head.

"We got some great shots in there, guys. *Great* shots. Let's go to your place for a quick interview, then break for lunch. Amazing. Fan favorite in the making, Jen. I knew I was right to bet on you!"

Fallon drops his hands from my body, but his palm finds

mine. He gives it a squeeze, and an injection of strength courses through me.

I glance up at him through my lashes, and let my lips slide into the first real smile I've had all day.

Yeah, I can do this—as long as Fallon is by my side.

FIVE
FALLON

I'VE NEVER SEEN Jen's house. In the years we worked side by side every day, I never even drove her home. So when we roll up to a small apartment building on the outskirts of the town center, I'm not quite sure what to expect. Militant neatness, perhaps? Spartan decor? Something super organized, minimalist, Pinterest-worthy?

Well, it's not what greets me on the other side of the door.

Jen lives in a damn jungle. There are plants everywhere. Every windowsill. Every flat surface. Every corner. There's an entire bookcase filled with cacti and succulents, and through the windows to the balcony, I see dozens of planters full of herbs. Looking closely, I see little stickers on every single plant, color-coded by section with neat, square numbers handwritten on each of them.

I blink, surprised, then turn my attention to Jen. She's dropping her purse on a little table by the door—which, no doubt, was bought for that exact purpose—and sucking those irresistible lips between her teeth. She lets them fall out with a long breath. "Well, this is it." She spreads her arms. "I can, I dunno, give you a tour of my house plants?"

Gus frowns, eyes sweeping over the hundreds of bits of greenery in the room. I can almost hear the gears gnashing in his head, calculating how long a tour of this rainforest would take. "Uh, that's...not necessary. Maybe we could see the kitchen?"

"Right, right." Jen nods and starts walking toward the kitchen, which is visible through a doorway with no door, then pauses at one of the plants near the closest window. It's got stiff green leaves which are maybe a couple inches across, three feet high. She pokes the dirt and frowns, then rotates the pot a hundred and eighty degrees. On her way past another plant, she prunes a few dead leaves off before finally making it to the kitchen.

I fucking love this woman.

I mean, I've known I liked her for a while, with her weird quirks, big fat brain, and thousand and one moods. But this? This is so exactly Jen that I can't even put it into words. Obsessive, talented, oddly charming. There's literally nothing she's not good at.

Well, maybe public speaking. And small talk.

Still, as I follow everyone into the tight kitchen and lean against the doorway, I can't help but watch the way she moves. She always has efficient, calculated movements. No extra energy to spare, because she's probably analyzing the angle of the sun hitting her plants and how that'll affect their growth. She leans against a counter, finally meeting my gaze.

Her cheeks are that shade of pink I love so much, eyes still a bit wild from the events at the café. Gus directs her to sit in a chair, then pulls one beside hers and tells me to take a seat. Unable to resist, I hook my arm across the back of her seat and lean my body into hers.

She doesn't pull away, which makes warmth flood my chest.

I never should have left. I should have fought for her. Yes, I have a messy history that to this day still follows me like a shadow. But Jen would understand...wouldn't she? She wants me just as much as I want her...unless my leaving was the last straw. I have to wonder—is it too late for us?

"We're just trying to get to know the two of you," Gus says as the cameraman unfurls a tripod and starts setting up lights. "If you make it far into the competition, we'll be editing some of these clips throughout the show so the audience can see what you're all about."

White radiates from each of Jen's knuckles as she clenches her hands into tight, tight fists. I use the hand I've got slung across the back of her chair to start drawing shapes on her shoulder with my fingertips until her muscles relax and her palms flatten on her thighs.

A deep breath leaves her lungs, her body melting into mine ever so slightly. Then she nods. "Okay. I'm ready."

WE MAKE it back to set in time for lunch, then are thrust into another bite-sized baking challenge. We're given sugar cookies and bags of royal icing, and told to decorate the cookies as best we can in fifteen minutes. Jen kills it, obviously. I stumble along beside her, as usual.

We do a few more promo shots for advertisement and social media, then are fed a hearty dinner at the farmhouse, and finally dismissed for the evening. I hold back a growl when smarmy Bernard Franco comes to put his hand on Jen's shoulder to congratulate her on the first couple of challenges. Jen just thanks him with a nod, not giving him any more attention. Her response pleases me more than it should.

Jen is quiet when we make it back to the guesthouse. Her face is drawn, pale. I close the door behind us as Jen pauses in the middle of the room before making a beeline for the kitchenette. She puts some water to boil and hunts through her belongings for a teabag, finally leaning against the counter with her arms crossed.

Gnawing on her nail, Jen stares at a spot on the floor like she's trying to burn a hole in it.

I take a seat on the couch near the window, arm stretched over the back of it, watching her. "You did really well, Jen."

Instead of accepting the compliment, Jen deflects. "I messed up that one cookie. We could have come in first place."

"We came second. First and second place in the first two bite-sized challenges isn't bad."

She huffs. "Still."

"And your interview was great."

"It was awkward."

Chuckling, I cross the room to lean against the counter,

hands placed on either side of her. She's like a magnet to me; I can't resist moving close to her whenever I get the chance. I duck my head, staring into her eyes. "Jen, just try to accept these compliments, okay? You were great today."

She opens her mouth, then closes it again. With great effort, she lifts her eyes to mine. "Thank you," she says with deliberate precision.

I grin. "Was that so hard?"

"Yes."

Smile widening, I can't help but lean into her body. I remember the way it felt to have my arms around her, my hands on her curves. I remember how it felt to kiss her like I had a right to.

I want that again. I want it every day until I die.

My eyes linger on her lips, heat lashing across my body. My fingers grip the counter so hard I'm worried it'll crumble to dust in my hands. The urge to kiss her almost overwhelms me. I could lift her up and notch myself between her spread thighs. I could tear her jeans off and bury my face between her legs. I could make her scream my name as she rides my mouth. I'd want to see her come apart as she let go of that control she wears like armor.

But I'm not going to.

Jennifer Newbank is not the type of woman who sleeps with a man like me. Or she wouldn't—if she knew the truth about my past.

Finally, stifling a groan, I tear myself away.

That night, I sleep in the cot. I wake up on the floor, achy and sore, but it's better than having Jen wrapped up in my arms when I know I won't be able to keep her.

TWO MORE DAYS are spent like this—filming small challenges, chatting with the contestants, getting to know the judges. One evening, at dinner, when Bernard pulls out a copy of Jen's book and flips to one of the recipes to compliment her on some special cake technique I've never heard of, I hold back the urge to throttle him. He smiles at Jen, eyes roaming over her face, dipping to her chest, and I can almost taste his interest on my tongue.

My hands clench into fists under the dinner table, breath sawing in and out of my lungs.

The worst part?

Bernard Franco is exactly the type of man Jen should be with. He's successful, charismatic, and famous. Even I can tell he's handsome with his stupid, perfectly styled brown hair and stupid piercing eyes. He looks at Jen and sees talent, so he's obviously not totally clueless.

And he wants her.

But no matter how much I *know* that Bernard would be a better match for Jen, I can't help wanting to punch him in his stupid handsome face.

Because Jen is *mine*. At least for a month.

THE NEXT MORNING, I wake up with a stiff neck and tingles in my feet. The cot is far, far too small for me, but Jen deserves the bed. I certainly don't—and based on how much I enjoyed waking up next to her that one morning, I already know that's a dangerous path to take.

She walks out of the bathroom holding her toothbrush, watching me rub my eyes as I try to rouse myself. "We only have an hour until the first elimination challenge," she says, glancing at the time on her phone.

I stifle a yawn. "You nervous?"

She snorts. "Obviously. What's a bigger word than nervous? Apprehensive? Anxious? Scared shitless?"

I lean back on the cot and fold my arms behind my head, noting with more than a bit of satisfaction that Jen's eyes linger on my shoulders, my arms, my chest, then drop down to my stomach where my tee has ridden up to show some skin. The blanket is gathered over my hips, and I lift a knee to hide the pulsing erection that grows under her perusal.

Her gaze is hot, and—me being the horny, keyed-up asshole I am—it makes me want to toss her on the bed and ram myself into her. When she tears her eyes away from me and turns back to the bathroom, I press my palm on my crotch and stare at the ceiling, willing my hard shaft to go down.

I should never have volunteered for this. When I saw she wasn't at Four Cups, I should have left town again.

The truth is, our situation hasn't changed. I'm still the washed-up chef who hasn't done anything with his life since his misspent youth. I'm the guy who tried to move on but ended up right back where I started.

She's still the brilliant baker who's on a never-ending upward trajectory. Even world-renowned pastry chefs are congratulating her on her brilliance and salivating at the sight of her.

But when Jen exits the bathroom and pours herself a tea, I watch her grab a mug for me and fill it with coffee. She hates coffee, but she must have made a pot before I even woke up. My heart squeezes, because I don't deserve her. She's far too good for a guy like me.

Jen perches at the end of my cot, and I sit up and accept the steaming mug. All the reasons we can't be together seem to fly right out of my head. I ache to tug her close, to feel her back resting against my chest, to run my fingers through her hair and feel her soften against me. No matter how many times I tell myself I don't deserve her, it doesn't change the fact that I crave her twice as badly.

Movement out the window catches my eye. I squint at the swaying trees, body stiff, trying to see what the hell is out there.

"What's wrong?" Jen shifts closer on the couch, and her knee touches my thigh. I glance down at the contact for a brief moment, loving how easy it is for her to get close to me. When I look back at the window, all I see is greenery.

I shake my head. "Nothing. There must be an active deer population out there. I keep seeing shapes moving in the trees and thinking they're people."

"Maybe they're birds." She shudders.

I grin. "Still scarred?"

"What do you mean, 'still?'" She rears back. "That was trau-matizing."

I grin just as her alarm goes off. "Time to start our first elimi-nation challenge."

Jen releases a long sigh, and I slide my hand over her thigh to give it a comforting squeeze, loving the feel of her body beneath my palm. Craving more—always more.

If my touch has any effect on Jen, she doesn't show it. Her mind is already on what's ahead. She squares her shoulders, jaw clenched. "Let's do this."

SIX

JEN

FIRST ELIMINATION CHALLENGE:
CROISSANTS

WE MAKE it to set with three minutes to spare, finding a seat next to the Daisy Dukettes. There are sixteen chairs set in a semi-circle facing the front of the barn, with the kitchen stations behind us. Fallon and I are on the far left.

"Hi." Sonia squeezes my forearm. "Are you excited for today? You two have been doing so well all week! I heard the Texas boys say you two were the couple to beat."

A bolt strikes my chest at the thought of Fallon and me being a couple. I glance at the opposite end of the semi-circle, where two big, burly Texans are sitting with their arms folded and wide, friendly smiles on their faces.

Reg catches me looking, his face morphing into a scowl. When I jerk back, he winks.

Okay, then. Maybe everyone in this competition is insane.

Fallon squeezes my thigh, almost in the same spot he did

this morning. "They got nothin' on us, Jen." His lips brush the shell of my ear as my eyes flutter closed.

That feels way, way too good.

Heat floods through me, and when Fallon takes his hand away it feels like he's taking all the warmth in the room with him. The imprint of his palm stays burned into my jeans, and I find myself clenching my hands into fists to stop rubbing the spot he touched. I could trace the outline of his fingers by memory, because it feels branded on my skin.

Over the past three days, I've come to crave Fallon's touch. How he puts his hand on my hip when he's walking by, or the way he slings his arm over the back of every seat I'm in. For someone who's never craved contact with anyone, enjoying his touch is...unexpected.

It's distracting me from my ultimate goal of coming home with a hundred grand and a trophy, but I can't quite bring myself to care.

Then the host and judges walk up, the cameras start rolling, and my nerves explode.

Especially when Carrie says we're doing pastry.

Now, I'm good at pastry, but it's finicky and it can be hard to get right. So when the judges tell us we have to make thirty-six perfect, flaky croissants, twenty-four of which need to be filled with two separate flavorings of our choice, my palms start to sweat.

Gus, who's standing off-camera, meets my gaze and gives me a hidden thumbs-up. He tasted my croissants at Four Cups and was impressed—but doing the same in a competition setting is different.

Since croissants are a multi-step process, we'll start them today, let them proof in the fridge overnight, then do the folding, shaping, final proof, and baking tomorrow—in front of a live audience.

My nerves are writhing snakes in my belly. Pain lances through my fingers as I squeeze my hands together, trying to get a grip on myself. I am *not* built for television. The camera lenses placed all around the room seem like big, black, looming eyes drilling into me, making my heart race so fast I might fall off my seat.

I don't know if I can do this. What if I fail at the first hurdle? This is the first challenge that the TV audience will see—the rest of the bite-sized competition was only for online viewers, and there was no threat of elimination. What if I fall flat on my face when this is supposed to be my specialty?

What if my friends, parents, publisher, and budding fan audience all see how terribly I perform? What if I get knocked out in the first round?

Anything less than perfect just isn't good enough.

But Fallon is a steady presence at my side, and the two of us use our allotted hour to put together the dough, the butter block that's so important for the flakiness of the pastry, and one of the two fillings we've decided to use in our croissants. Fallon encourages me when I suggest a classic almond croissant, and dismisses my fears it'll be too cliché.

"Classic is good, Jen. Trust your instincts. Hell, I trust your instincts better than my own." His roguish grin melts my panties, which isn't helping the whole distraction problem.

By the end of the hour, I look around at the elated faces of the other contestants and let Fallon sling an arm around my shoulders, tugging me into his massive chest.

"You did good, Jen," he says in my ear. His thumb lifts up to brush flour off my cheek, the featherlight touch sending a spear of heat through my middle.

My arms hook around his waist, head tilting to look up at his gorgeous face. "So did you." I glance up to his eyes, which crinkle at the corners, the laugh lines around his mouth growing deeper.

I don't know if it's the magic of being in this weird, intense competition environment, but I find myself thinking I could get used to that look on his face.

THAT EVENING, we have dinner with the rest of the contestants. Everyone is on edge. I sit beside Tom and David, two British bakers who met in pastry school. They seem confident, even surprised Fallon and I didn't get both our fillings done. Across from me, a mother-and-son team from New York—Mary and Tony, who run a family bakery—are just as surprised we left our second filling until tomorrow.

"You'll be cutting it close tomorrow," Mary tells me.

"It'll be fine," Fallon says with complete confidence.

"We only got one done," Hillary, the woman across from me, says. "If you're behind schedule, then so are we." She smiles at her husband, who gives her a chaste kiss. I find out they're from a small town in Virginia and they own an at-home cake-decorating business.

Looking at all the contestants, my nerves start to build.

Everyone is so *competent*. Some of them have been baking three times as long as I have. I only started less than a decade ago!

Before I can panic, Fallon puts his hand on my thigh and gives me a searching look. Then a commotion at the other end of the table draws me out of my own thoughts. I quickly discover that Carla is as sharp-tongued in English as I suspected she was in Spanish. Creative insults are being flung with ferocity as Emma doubles over laughing. Carla has the big Texans cowed within minutes.

Sonia and Nikki have delicate, tinkling laughs, and I find out they've been friends since they were three. They're often confused for twins, even though they're not related. When I comment that it's probably because they dress like twins, they just laugh.

Tori and Hank, the cupcake couple from Idaho, are lovely. They have four kids—two girls, two boys—and met in pastry school thirty years ago.

To my absolute shock, after I get over the nerves, I realize I'm...*enjoying* myself. Fallon sits next to me, his leg warm against mine, arm slung across the back of my chair, and I end up laughing with a group of people I barely even know.

It's completely unheard of.

By the time Fallon and I make it back to the guesthouse, I feel tired, yet happy. Fallon insists on taking the cot again, and when I wake up to him falling out of it, I just flick the covers back without even removing my eye mask. He hasn't come back to bed with me since my first night, so for a few seconds, I hold my breath.

When I feel the bed dip beside me, my heart thumps a little bit harder.

WHEN WE RETURN to the barn to finish the croissant challenge the next morning, all happiness and levity is gone from my mood. It's time to compete. Time to show everyone that I *can* do this.

The judges spring another challenge on us, asking us for six perfect, identical danishes to be made with puff pastry, which means Fallon and I need to split our attention. I make a snap decision when I find out Fallon doesn't know how to make puff pastry without a recipe. He can fold the butter into the croissant dough, finish the fillings, and I'll work on the danishes.

Things start going off the rails pretty quickly—right around the time the live audience shows up.

Somehow, the filling ingredients for our almond croissants end up way, *way* too salty. It needs to be made again. Once that's done, the red timer is counting down, down, down—so I go to check on the folded croissant pastry in the fridge. Beside it, my carefully prepared butter block is still wrapped in plastic.

I pull it out, frowning. "Fallon?"

He's prepping our onion-and-goat-cheese filling for the other croissants we're making—we decided to go savory—and glances over his shoulder as his hands keep chopping. "Yeah?"

"What butter did you use for the croissants?"

He jerks his head at the end of the counter. "The stuff over there."

My stomach bottoms out. "The room-temperature butter?"

He yelps, then looks down at the fresh line of blood on his finger. "Shit. I cut myself." Glancing up, he nods. "Yeah, the soft stuff. I spread it over the dough and folded it like you said."

As a medic rushes over to tend to his finger, I almost start to cry. Croissants need cold butter. You need to have thin sheets of cold butter sandwiched between thin sheets of dough. If Fallon didn't laminate layers of butter in between the dough, that means the pastry won't be flaky. We won't have croissants.

And it's too late to start over—especially since Fallon needs to make the onion mixture again on account of the blood.

By the time the timer has counted down to the last hour, I know our croissants haven't proofed long enough. Without the butter laminated properly, they won't end up flaky. They're going to turn into a dense, soggy mess, and there's nothing I can do about it.

My danishes have fared a little better, but the fillings aren't anywhere near perfect. I cut them crooked, too, and I forgot to egg wash them until they were already in the oven a few minutes, so they're not as golden-brown as they should be, and the filling has run out and burned around the edges.

It's a complete and utter unmitigated disaster. Not one single thing has gone well.

I'm close to tears and my hands are shaking so much Fallon has to take over pulling the danishes from the oven. His lips are pinched, jaw set in a grim line.

Glancing up at the bleachers in the mezzanine level, I see my best friend Candice leaning against the railing. She's shouting and cheering me on while Simone and Fiona are waving signs with my name on them in glittery writing.

Behind them, I meet a man's eyes for a brief moment before he ducks away. Did he look familiar? I glance again, but I can't see anyone. My eyes are too blurry to tell, anyway.

Dread twists in my stomach. Everyone will see me fail.

I should be happy they're here, but all I feel is deep, overwhelming embarrassment. I've made thousands of croissants in my life, and none of them have been as bad as this.

When Fallon pulls out the croissants from the oven, I brush a hot tear away from my face. They look like they were made by a child. An amateur. Soggy, with butter melting out the edges, dense, and I can already tell the bottom is doughy.

Fallon sets the tray down and leans against the counter, looking at the little nuggets of unrisen dough in crescent shapes. He glances over at me, looking miserable. "I'm so sorry, Jen. This is on me."

I pick up one of the ruined croissants and turn it over, dropping my chin to my chest. My bottom lip wobbles.

Look, somewhere in my mind, I know it's only a TV show. I know it's some stupid competition, and in the grand scheme of things, it means nothing.

But the thing is...it means a *lot*. This is going to be broadcast to thousands—maybe *millions*—of people. My parents could see it! How will they react when they see me making a fool of myself on national television? How could they possibly be encouraging of my career as a pastry chef when *this* is what I produce?

Congrats on the new book! I heard you can't even make a croissant.

"Hey, don't cry," Fallon says, moving closer to shield me from the nearest camera.

I put my palm on his chest and gently push him away. "Stop, Fallon. It's fine."

His face twists. "I'm sorry. It was my fault. I didn't know about the butter."

"I should have paid closer attention," I say, and it's true. How could this be Fallon's fault when *I'm* the supposed pastry chef?

I'm ashamed of myself. It's *pastry*, for crying out loud. But, but... Oh, I'm such a loser, because I *do* care. I wanted this to be perfect. I wanted to do well. I wanted my friends and family— my parents—to be able to watch this show on television and finally, *finally* understand why I quit my "real" job to pursue this dream.

I wanted to *prove* something.

I don't even know why I care what anyone thinks. Logically, I know I'm a grown woman and I know it doesn't matter. But I wanted this very public display to be something I could be proud of. It's so far out of my comfort zone that I almost *need* to be successful just to show myself that I deserve this book deal, I deserve this success.

Amanda didn't just give me this opportunity because she was pining after Fallon. She gave it to me because I'm *good*.

But...am I? How can I claim to deserve my success when I can't even do a stupid TV show?

I open my mouth to apologize, because really, what excuse do I have? I failed the man who dropped everything to be my partner in this competition.

But the buzzer goes off, the crowd in the mezzanine goes wild, and I lift my gaze to my friends. Candice's brows are arched high. She gives me a sad smile as Simone does a thumbs-up, but by the looks on their faces, they can tell the greasy, dense mess on my platter isn't anything to be proud of.

I failed.

Fallon has his palms flat on the counter, his head bowed. I hate that he feels bad for this when I'm the one who should have known better.

Carrie calls for quiet, and the tension in the room grows thick. When the judges start making the rounds, praising Reg and Tex for their flaky, near-perfect croissants, Fallon puts his hand on my lower back.

Instinctively, I pull away.

It's not because I don't want him to touch me—it's because I feel ashamed of this failure. So embarrassed that all my friends saw how badly I performed.

"We're going home," I say to Fallon, my voice flat.

He doesn't deny it. It's stupid to be this upset about a competition, but I grew up under so much pressure to perform that *any* failure feels like an attack on my character. Losing is a heavy, suffocating weight on my shoulders.

I'm a perfectionist. I don't fail. I don't come in last place. I don't *lose*.

Fallon's face screws up, and he combs his fingers through his hair. "This is my fault."

That weight on my shoulders sinks lower, and suddenly I can't bear that Fallon's blaming himself. I can be hard on myself any day of the week, but him? This isn't Fallon's fault. He used the wrong butter because I didn't tell him the right instructions. He's not a baker. He's not a pastry chef. He's an amazing chef and I respect his skills, but the fact that he didn't know how to laminate pastry properly is entirely on me.

Instead of saying anything, I reach down for Fallon's hand and give it a squeeze. He meets my eyes, and something softens in his gaze. The blackness recedes ever so slightly inside me.

I've spent so, so many years being hard on myself. Being exacting. Thinking that success was the only way to be worth something.

But what if there was another way? What if I could be happy without putting so much damn pressure on myself?

"We've entered the sudden death elimination round," Carrie says, a serious expression on her face. "Jen, Fallon"—she looks at the two of us, then shifts her gaze to the two cake decorators from Virginia—"Hillary, Nate. You'll each have to choose one competitor from your teams to go head-to-head. Please make your selection now."

You know, when you watch these shows on TV, they seem kind of silly. All so serious and emotional, and for what? For some stupid competition?

But let me tell you, in real life, the pressure is *intense*. You could hear a pin drop in this barn. Fallon squeezes my shoulder and gives me a nod. "You got this, Jen." His full lips curl into a smile, and everything inside me tightens—because he looks like he's telling the honest truth.

He believes in me. Even after the last disastrous few hours in the kitchen. Even after I pushed him away and chose my book instead of him. Still, after all that, he's got my back.

I don't deserve him.

Fallon steps aside, and it's me against Nate, the big-hearted man who made me laugh at dinner last night. We have to produce a dessert containing three elements, at least one of which has to be baked. We have limited ingredients and only half an hour.

The time starts, and I sink deep into my own meditative zone. My hands work fast as my mind grows calm, my movements sure as I whisk, mix, sift, and fold a new dessert into existence. I make a quick shortbread with strawberry reduction and fresh whipped cream. The skills I learned with Guillaume come into play when I plate the dessert up in a delicate, artistic way that would be worthy of a Michelin-starred restaurant.

When the buzzer sounds, I step back, and even though I can hear the girls cheering me on from the other level, the first person I look at is Fallon.

His eyes are shining, his lips are spread into a wide smile, and before I can even say anything, he strides over to me and wraps me in a big, warm, beautiful bear hug.

And there's nowhere else I'd rather be.

THE REST OF THE COMPETITORS, Jen, and I end up in the main farmhouse after it's announced that Jen and I are safe from elimination. Nate and Hillary are eliminated, but they'll be staying on site until the competition is over. We all had to sign non-disclosure agreements—and everyone in the live audience, too—and we're expected to stay in Heart's Cove for the full month to avoid leaks about winners and losers.

Jen ends up sitting next to me on a couch in one of the big living rooms, her body nestled against mine with my arm draped around her shoulders. It feels right. So, so right. She rests her head against my chest and lets out a quiet sigh, and the thumping of my heart gets louder.

Is it any wonder I came back to see her? Even if I haven't suddenly changed where I come from, who I am? Even if I'm still not worthy of her? How could I resist someone as masterful as she is in the kitchen, who then turns into a soft, sleepy kitten in my arms?

I've longed for this for more than a year. Ever since I tasted her lips, my arms have felt empty without her in them.

As the other competitors drink and celebrate being safe from elimination, Jen looks up at me. "I'm sorry for snapping at you."

My shoulders drop, hand skimming her jaw. "You didn't snap at me."

"I did. What happened today was my mistake. You're not a baker. It wasn't your fault you didn't know about the butter."

I shrug, then crack a smile. "I didn't exactly learn about French pastry in my house growing up."

"What was it like growing up at your house?" she asks, head resting on my shoulder. "You said your mom taught you to make chai tea."

"She did," I answer noncommittally. A lump forms in my throat at the thought of saying anything else. I could tell her that my father died when I was twelve, and I didn't know how to deal with the loss. All I had to remember him by was his old hunting knife with the bone handle, the etchings on it worn down from years of use. It'd been passed down to him by his father, and then it went to me.

That fucking knife ruined my life.

Widowed and alone, my mother worked herself to the bone and never accepted help from anyone. She had to work two or three jobs and was never home, leaving my sister and me to fend for ourselves.

I could tell Jen that I fell in with the wrong crowd, that I thought I'd found a brotherhood—but all I found was trouble.

My past is a black hole. My childhood was one trauma after another, and it wasn't until I was in my mid-twenties that I started cleaning up my act. By that time, I had a reminder inked on my back of all the mistakes I'd made. I had no skills and no education beyond a high school diploma I'd barely managed to earn.

I've been working in kitchens ever since.

Lungs squeezing so hard I can barely breathe, I just lean my chin against Jen's head. "My life was boring up until about a year ago," I tell her. "I'd rather hear about your childhood."

Jen snorts. "No, you wouldn't."

"I would."

She pulls away from me to search my face, eyes narrowing. "You're being serious right now."

I nod. "You're much more fascinating to me than almost anything else."

"Has anyone told you that you might need to get your head checked?"

The tension gripping my chest eases as my lips curl. "No, but I'm sure you're about to."

"'Fascinating' is not a word I'd use to describe myself." Jen sits up and stretches her neck from side to side. I watch the way the light plays on her hair, how her slim neck moves, how her shoulders bunch and relax.

"Agree to disagree," I say quietly.

"Well, if you must know, I grew up with a surgeon for a mother and a CEO for a father," she says matter-of-factly. "My brother got a degree in business and ended up in executive management at one of the fastest-growing companies on the eastern seaboard, so of course he's my parents' pride and joy. I'm doing this"—she sweeps her arm at the room full of contestants —"so you can imagine how proud they are of me."

Prouder than they would be if they knew you were sitting beside me.

Forcing a smile, I stand up. "Come on. I want to do something." Mostly I want to get away from this conversation, this constant reminder that I'm not good enough for her. I grab a plate full of food—piling it high with nuts and seeds and a few pieces of fruit—and duck out the front door.

Jen trots after me, frowning. "What are you doing?"

"Making an offering to our overlords."

"What?" Jen twists her head to frown at me, then follows me around the side of the farmhouse.

When we get under the window she pointed out to me when she told me about the crows that attacked her, I look up to see the window closed, but a big black bird perched on the gutter above.

"Looks like they got the crows out," I say, then drop the plate on the ground.

"What are you doing?" Jen hisses, eyes darting to the bird as she clings to my arm. "They'll never leave if you feed them."

I put my arm around her—can't help myself—and tug her against me as I back up.

The bird on the roof looks at us, then down at the plate, and swoops down to inspect. Pretty soon, there are four crows around the plate, pecking at my offering.

"Fallon, that wasn't a good idea. They'll stay now and attack everyone until they get fed!"

I grin. "Or they'll become our friends and apologize for putting those scratches on your hands."

Jen glances at me and frowns.

I can't quite hide my smile. I love it when she looks at me like that—like I'm some problem that needs to be solved. Like if she only *thinks* hard enough, she'll be able to figure me out.

She might be right about feeding the crows. But as soon as Jen glances at the birds and her lips twitch at the corners, I know I'd do it a hundred times over just to see her smile.

Then my phone buzzes in my pocket, and I pull away from Jen to see my baby sister's name light up my screen. Swiping to answer, I put the phone to my ear. "Nora?"

"Fallon, I need help." My sister sniffles, and I freeze.

Jen notices and looks at me, doing that puzzle-solving frown of hers again.

"What's wrong?" I start walking toward the guesthouse cabin, if only to start moving. I don't like the sound of my sister's voice. Not one bit.

"Slim is out of prison. He showed up at my house to ask about you."

Those words hammer a spike of fear in my chest. Harvey "Slim" Miller was my best friend at seventeen years old. He's also the guy who ruined my life.

I grip the phone so hard I'm worried I'll crack the screen. "What do you mean? How did he know where you live?"

"I don't know. Someone must have followed me." She sniffles. "You need to talk to him, Fallon. He's been to my house three times already. I don't feel safe."

Here it is. My past, rearing its ugly head. That shadow I can't quite shake.

The man who put that tattoo on my back is harassing my sister. I'm the one who brought that sack of garbage around *my family*. I'm the one who put her in danger. All those shapes I saw in the trees? They were probably Slim's cronies looking for me.

I'm halfway to the guesthouse now, with Jen hurrying by my side. She hasn't said a word, but I know she's listening. Usually I'd be pulling away from everyone around. I'd be lowering my voice so no one can hear. But Jen slides her hand into mine, and I slow my gait so she can walk comfortably.

I want her beside me—but will she be in the same position as Nora? Am I poison to everyone around me?

Taking a deep breath, I turn my attention back to my sister. "I can't leave right now, Nora. Not for another three weeks. Can you find somewhere else to stay?" We've made it to the door and Jen hurries ahead to unlock it. I close my eyes and lean against the wall. "I can send you money, Nora, but I don't have an apartment of my own anymore. I've got nowhere for you to crash. I can book a hotel for you for a few nights? Give us time to figure something out?"

"She can stay at my place," Jen cuts in. "Whoever Nora is, I can meet her in town and give her the keys. When do you need them?"

The woman has no idea who I'm talking to, and she's

already rifling through her bag to find her keys. She pulls them out and holds them in her cupped hands like an offering.

"One sec," I tell my sister, then put my hand over the mouthpiece. "Jen, it's okay. You don't have to do that. It's my sister. She's just... There's a guy..." I drift off.

Jen lives in a world of surgeons and CEOs. A world where bad croissants are the worst part of her day. This is... The shit I'm potentially bringing to her doorstep isn't even in the same universe.

But this is my sister.

"I'll send Nora some money right away, book her a hotel, and call her when she's calmer."

Jen lets out a little sigh and shakes her head. "Does she need somewhere to crash? Use my place. No one is there. She can water my plants. It would be doing me a favor." She pauses, then frowns. "Actually, don't have her water my plants. They're on a strict watering schedule and Candice is taking care of it. I wrote out the instructions for each plant and she promised she'd follow it to the letter. I'm not sure I trust someone else to do it."

Despite myself, my lips curl into a smile. Of course she has a strict watering schedule for her jungle. Her hand is soft and warm when I reach over and squeeze it.

"Is she in trouble?" Jen asks, those intelligent eyes searching mine.

I give her a sharp nod.

"An ex?"

I shake my head. How do I explain this?

"It doesn't matter. You said she's not safe? So put her up in my place." She thrusts the keys toward me, the look on her face telling me she knows her logic will win.

Shoulders dropping, I give in. "Thank you. It's only temporary." I put the phone back to my ear. "Nora?"

"Yeah?" Her voice is so fucking small and it makes me want to *kill* Slim for doing that to my baby sister. How dare he find out where she lives.

"I'm sending you some money. Can you make it to Heart's Cove?"

"Yeah. I've got a car. If I leave tonight I can be there by tomorrow. I've got enough money, Fallon, I just didn't know what to do. I feel like I'm being watched."

"Okay. Pack everything essential. Assume you're not going back. I'll meet you in town and you can crash at my..." What is Jen to me? *Co-worker* isn't accurate anymore. *Friend* seems wrong. "At Jen's place."

After solidifying our plans, my sister and I hang up, and I let out a long sigh, rubbing my thumb and forefinger over my forehead.

Look, I know this sounds so selfish, but it seems like any time I try to do something for myself, some emergency happens and I need to divert all my time and energy away. I was hoping to have one month—just *one, single* month—to spend time with Jen. But I'll be paying for my teenage mistakes until I'm old and gray.

Well, old*er* and gray*er*.

With a sigh, I resign myself to this. I love my sister, and it's *my* fault she's having to leave her own house. Wrapping my arms around Jen, I inhale the scent of her fruity shampoo and let my nerves settle ever so slightly. I'm not sure if I'm thanking her or if I just need the comfort of her in my arms. "That was really generous of you, Jen. I'll find somewhere else for my sister to stay once I know what's going on."

"It's fine," she says, her voice muffled against my chest. She pulls away and looks up at me, the air between us shifting slightly. The panic from my sister's call ebbs, and my heartbeat takes on a different timbre. I tighten my hold on Jen's body, loving the way she fits against me. Loving the way her hands slide up my chest.

I could kiss this woman every day of my life and never get sick of it.

Jen's fingers drift over my beard, tickling the skin where I've shaped it along my cheeks. "I think it says a lot that your sister knew she could call you in a crisis, and you'd sort it out without question."

My gaze slides to the side as my throat grows thick. "I'm her big brother."

"My big brother hasn't spoken to me in three years apart from my birthday and Christmas."

Your big brother probably didn't bring a man like Slim Miller into your life.

I stare into her eyes, wishing I were someone else. Someone worthy of her. "And yet you have enough heart to give up your house to a stranger."

She cracks a smile, and my hold on her tightens. "Your sister is hardly a stranger," she says softly. Her eyes drop to my lips, and all my blood rushes south.

But before I can dip my lips to kiss her again, to relieve that ache in my chest that hasn't gone away since the day my parents got in that accident, Jen pulls away. And I let her.

Because, really, she deserves more than what I can offer.

EIGHT

JEN

FALLON and I do the whole *I'll-sleep-in-the-cot-no-you'll-sleep-in-the-bed* thing, until he ends up on the floor and I invite him into the bed in the middle of the night. I wake up to a blanket of Fallon once again. This time, he blinks his eyes open when I move, and I feel something, um...*stiff*...between us. Fallon shifts his hips away from me and rolls off me with a sleepy groan.

And I'm...disappointed?

It's Sunday, which means we have the day off today. I sit up and lean against the headboard, scrubbing my face to wake myself up. I need to forget how it felt to have Fallon's hard shaft against my butt—and how much I liked it.

"My sister should be in town around five or six." Fallon turns his head on the pillow, and warmth spreads through me.

He looks good like this. He's wearing an old T-shirt that was soft against my skin when he wrapped himself around me. With slitted, sleepy eyes, he looks deliciously undone. His beard has grown out a bit in the last few days, the silvery strands in it stark against the coarse black hair. My eyes slide down to where the sheet has fallen down and his shirt has rucked up, to that dark line of hair below his navel. The sight of it makes my heart thump, and my fingers curl into the sheets to stop myself from reaching over and touching it.

Blinking, I shift my gaze up...to a tattoo? I just spy the edge of a black shape on his rib. "I didn't know you had a tattoo."

Fallon goes rigid beside me, pulling his shirt down with a hard yank. "Yeah. I'll use the bathroom first." He gets up with a swift movement, not looking at me as he crosses the room.

Um...okay.

The silky, hot feeling that had been weighing me down like a blanket is ripped away—and I remember that this is temporary. All of it. The competition, the guesthouse, Fallon's presence. I shouldn't get used to it. Once the competition ends, Fallon will leave. Like he did before. Like everyone does. Why wouldn't they? It's not like I have much to offer a man besides too many plants and obsessive baking tendencies. I'm not exactly a catch. I'm the woman that gets passed over. The one that is memorable for all the wrong reasons.

What I need to do is stay *focused*. Fallon's happy trail and secret tattoo need to be relegated to the section of my brain that only gets visited when I've had too much wine.

His scruffy, handsome head pokes out of the bathroom, and he speaks around his toothbrush. "Are you sure it's okay for my sister to stay at your place?"

"Of course," I answer. My eyes drop down to his torso,

hands itching to remove his shirt. Why didn't he want me to see his ink? Does he think I won't approve? I'm uptight, but I'm not *that* uptight.

Plus, anything Fallon does is ridiculously sexy.

Blinking, I meet his eyes again. "I mean, as long as Nora doesn't kill my plants or wreck my house, obviously."

Fallon chuckles. "I'll warn her not to poke the dragon."

I arch a brow, eyes drawn back to his. "The dragon?"

"You're slow to anger, but once you go off"—he makes an explosion sound—"run for cover." Eyes glimmering, he returns to the bathroom to finish up.

I huff, insulted. That's not true...is it?

He reappears, and when he sees my face, Fallon laughs harder. "See? The dragon. I can see it waking up already." He picks up a pillow from the ground and tosses it on his side of the bed. "I got a stern talking-to from you last year and I'm still reeling. I distinctly remember you waving a spatula around like you wanted to smack me across the face with it."

Hmm. I did do that.

He yanks the blankets up to make the bed. "I was afraid for my life."

The twinkling in his eyes tells me he's joking, but I still cross my arms with a huff. "You asked me to choose between you and my book. What was I supposed to say?"

The laughter in his eyes fades. He gives me a sad smile. "I don't blame you, Jen. I was wrong to push you. You had every right to reject me when you did. I didn't read the signs of what Amanda wanted from me. I thought she was just being her usual flirty self. She's like that with everyone."

Everyone, huh. Didn't know Fallon was delusional.

Fallon's ex-girlfriend was very, *very* obvious in her intentions any time Fallon was around. I'm not sure if he's just being dense because he's a man and he truly didn't realize she still wanted him—or if he's trying to downplay what happened.

"My turn in the bathroom," I announce. At least if I'm busy, I don't have to think about how good it feels to wake up next to Fallon—or how awful it'll feel once the competition ends and we go our own ways.

UNBEKNOWNST TO ME, there's some sort of party going on at Four Cups when we arrive. Through the big windows at the front of the café, I notice that the tables and chairs are set up facing one wall, where a big screen and a projector are beaming a massive image of my face.

Wonderful.

I cast my eye over the assembled crowd. Of course, Simone, Fiona, and Candice are there with their partners Wes, Grant, and Blake. Blake has his arm around Candice's shoulders and his mouth near her ear. She's blushing, and something like jealousy pierces my gut. Not that I want *Blake* to do that to me, but I'd like to have someone's arms wrapped around me like that. And by someone I mean Fallon.

Candice's sister, Trina, is off on a romantic two-week vacation with her man, Mac, to enjoy her time off while her kids are with her ex-husband. No doubt when she gets back, she'll be loved-up as well.

I glance at Fallon, who's scanning the space through the window, probably looking for his sister.

In the opposite corner to Candice and Blake, Dorothy and Margaret are huddled around a table with their partners Eli and Hamish. Candice's mother, Lottie, is wearing a T-shirt with my face on it, and she's sitting to Dorothy's left. Beside her are Blake's parents Gina and Merv. There's some kind of highly animated debate going on between the seven of them, until Margaret spots me through the doorway and points, and then they all jump up and cheer.

Candice opens the door and ushers us in, hooking her arm in mine. "We're celebrating! We just watched your interview with the local news station. Trying to figure out a format for viewing parties for when the competition is aired. Your television appearances so far are pure comedy, Jen."

I blink. "They are?"

Simone appears from the kitchen with a tray of snacks. "You should have had a career in TV, Jen. I'm not even joking."

"Uh, no," I answer. A career in television sounds like torture.

Simone just laughs, and Candice grabs me by the elbow to drag me in.

Fallon floats in afterward, and when I glance at his face he looks almost uncomfortable. I pull myself away from Candice and touch his arm. "You okay?"

He shifts his gaze to me, and I note with some satisfaction that his shoulders instantly relax. The smile he gives me is slight, but it makes my heart beat something fierce. "I'm good. It feels weird being back in here with everyone."

"Good weird or bad weird?"

The smile widens. "Good weird."

"Damn it!" Lottie tosses a napkin at us, which flutters uselessly to the ground a couple feet in front of her. "Dorothy was right."

Dorothy plucks a piece of lint from her leopard-print scarf, her lips pursed in a self-satisfied smirk.

I frown. "About what?"

"About this not taking long!" Lottie thrusts her arm toward Fallon and me. "I was sure it would be another few months at least."

Ice freezes every single muscle in my body. "What, exactly, is not going to take long?"

"You and Fallon, honey," Margaret says, pouring fresh tea into her mug from a steaming teapot on the table. She arches her brows at Hamish, who—looking completely smitten—gives her a nod and a smile. She fills his cup with precise, graceful movements. When she places the teapot back down, she meets my panicked gaze. "Oh, come on, Jen. Don't pretend you don't know you'll end up together."

Dorothy cackles. She's drinking wine instead of tea, and she lifts her glass to me. "Enjoy the ride, Ms. Newbank. And I do mean that literally."

A suspiciously mirthful cough escapes Fallon's throat, who covers his mouth with a fist before putting his hand on the small of my back. And damn it, it feels good. "Let them have their fun," he murmurs in my ear.

"I give them a week," Dorothy stage-whispers.

I don't have time to glare at her, because the bell above the café door is ringing, and the most beautiful woman I've ever seen walks through the door. She's curvy in all the right places, with long dark hair and the same brown-black eyes as Fallon. Where Fallon's features are rough-hewn and masculine, she's delicate. Wide-eyed, full-mouthed, and totally gorgeous.

Nora—Fallon's sister.

As soon as she spots her brother, her bottom lip starts wobbling. A thump sounds as she drops her small overnight bag to the ground, and her arms are already around Fallon's waist in a tight hug. He curls his strong arms around her and says soft things I can't hear until Nora starts sobbing in his chest.

My heart squeezes.

Silence settles over the café as we all witness this teary reunion.

It doesn't surprise me that Fallon is close with his sibling, nor does it shock me that she feels like everything will be okay now that she's here. It's the same reason Amanda kept coming back here and fawning over him. It's the same reason I sleep better when he's beside me.

Fallon is a rock. He's a steady, warm presence that anchors everyone around him, and you can't help but feel that if he's here, everything will be okay. His presence is addictive.

"I'm sorry," I hear Nora say, her voice muffled. "I'm embarrassing you."

"You're not," Fallon's warm, rumbly voice says. "You're fine, Snotface."

She snorts, pulls away, and punches her brother in the arm. Hard.

He laughs, and my heart just cracks into a million pieces

right there. I haven't heard him laugh like that since before the book. Before Amanda.

Then Nora blinks, and notices the crowd behind her brother.

Fallon steps away and jerks his thumb at his sister. "This is Nora. She's my baby sister. She's going to be staying in town for a while."

And that's all it takes for the dam to break. Fiona, ever the mother hen, is the first one to jump up and hug a shellshocked Nora. She introduces herself and immediately offers coffee, tea, iced coffee, iced tea, juice, water, beer, whiskey, bourbon, until Nora blurts out, "Water," and Fiona rushes to get a glass with a smile. There's a veritable procession of hugs and greetings as Nora is indoctrinated into the Four Cups posse.

I meet Fallon's laughing eyes over the crowd. He scrapes his fingers through his hair and winces. "Maybe meeting here wasn't such a good idea."

"You shut your mouth, Fallon Richter," Simone snaps. "Now, Nora, where are you staying? I have a few extra scented candles upstairs. I'll grab one for you. You can have a nice bubble bath with a candle and some wine, and whatever made you cry will be okay. Okay?"

"Um..." Nora glances at Fallon, who just grins.

"She's staying at Jen's place."

Silence crashes down, and all eyes turn to me.

Candice blinks. "She's staying at your place?"

I shrug. "What's the big deal?"

"You won't even let *me* stay at your place, Jen," Candice

says slowly, as if I'm dense. "And I've known you since we were toddlers."

"You already have a home." I frown. Why would she want to stay at my house?

Candice's lips twitch. "Yeah, but you basically gave me an hour lecture on plant care before you'd even give me your spare key. You sent me a spreadsheet with dates and times with every plant. You numbered your pots for me!"

"Yeah, because I have a lot of delicate plants on a strict watering schedule, and you wouldn't be able to tell them apart without a system." I don't see why that's so hard to understand.

Candice grins, then shifts her gaze to Nora. "You don't know Jen, so you don't know what a big deal this is, but no one— I mean *no one*—gets admitted to her space unless she trusts them."

Nora's eyes widen. "Um…"

"Fallon vouched for you," I cut in. "And Candice is being dramatic. Her movie-star boyfriend must be rubbing off on her." I stick my tongue out, because I'm a grown woman.

Blake just laughs.

Nora stumbles back. "Is that Blake Harding?" Her voice comes out as a raspy whisper just as Fiona appears at her elbow with a glass of water.

"Just go with it, honey," Fiona says. "You'll get used to it."

NINE
CANDICE

FALLON'S SISTER IS A DARLING. She allows herself to be ushered to a table and does her best to answer the bombardment of questions hurled at her from everyone in the café. Then, Dorothy has the brilliant idea of restarting the clip on the screen so we can all watch Jen frown at the reporter's inane questions.

Comedic. Gold.

At one point the reporter asks her, "What's next for you, Ms. Newbank?" and Jen, instead of talking about her career, replies, "Next? Well, I'll have to check, but I think it's lemon-raspberry squares."

As if he'd been talking about her to-do list. Cracks me up every time.

Jen, predictably, doesn't want to watch herself. She shuffles to the kitchen, her happy place, which also happens to be far, far away from the massive screen projecting her face onto the café wall.

Nora accepts another glass of water and a mug of tea as Fallon fusses over her—adjusting her jacket, pushing food toward her, taking her bag—until she gives him a stare that screams Death by Little Sister.

I grin when Fallon throws his hands up and backs off.

My mother, Lottie, pulls up a chair. "So, Nora, tell us about yourself. What brought you to Heart's Cove?"

"I, uh, needed time away," she answers flatly.

"From a man?" Dorothy asks, leaning forward with her wine dangling between her thumb and forefinger.

Fallon's jaw hardens.

Nora tilts her head from side to side. "Something like that."

"That *ass*." My mother huffs, then glances at the crew of elderly ladies leaning in to hear every word. "Get the pitchforks ready, ladies."

Nora's lips twitch. She flicks her gaze to Fallon, who's scrubbing his forehead with his broad hand.

"Don't worry, honey, we'll sort him out," Dorothy says. "If all else fails, we can ask Agnes to go speak to him. Lord knows being in *her* presence would scare him straight." The older woman shudders.

"Who's Agnes?" Nora asks, her shoulders relaxing ever so slightly. She breaks a piece of cookie off and pops it in her mouth, her eyes widening in surprise and delight.

Yep—Jen's creations. They have that effect on people.

"Agnes is the town hag," Dorothy says with a pleasant smile on her face.

When Nora's brows tug, I glide over to them. "Don't mind

them, Nora. Welcome to Heart's Cove. Do you know how long you'll be staying?"

She bites her lip. "That depends on Fallon."

"No, sweetheart." My mother pats her hand. "It depends on *you.*"

Something crosses Nora's eyes—surprise, or maybe revelation. As if she hadn't considered that she could be in charge of her own future. But before she can respond, the bell above the door rings, and the last person I ever expected to see enters the café.

"Iliana?" My mother straightens in her chair, her head tilting to the side. "Lily, baby?" Her voice breaks on my sister's nickname.

My youngest sister puts her big travel backpack down beside her, eyes sweeping over the assembled crowd. She's wearing loose, drawstring sweatpants with a cropped patchwork sweatshirt of a thousand colors. Her dark, near-black hair is piled high on her head in a messy bun, face lined with tired lines. Streaks of silver shimmer in her hair, as if she hasn't been to the salon in ages. Damn her, but gray hair looks good when Iliana does it. My sister's bright-green eyes meet mine, and she gives me a half-smile. "Surprise."

I jump when my mother shrieks, then launches herself at Lily. The top of my mom's head only reaches my sister's chin, but she still manages to nearly bowl her over. They crash into the wall as my mother grasps Lily's cheeks and lays a thousand kisses all over her.

"My baby's home!" Mom pulls away, her hands on my sister's upper arms. "You didn't tell us you were coming."

Lily's eyes slide to the side, and warning bells start ringing in my head. Something's up. "It was...unexpected."

"Well, you're here now." My mother turns around and starts jabbing her finger at people. "You remember Dorothy and Margaret? This is Fiona and Simone; I think you met them at Thanksgiving a couple of years ago. They own this café with Candice and Jen. That's Fallon's sister. You remember Fallon from before, yeah?" Her arm is hooked tightly around my sister's as she drags her around to various people, making introductions.

When they reach me, my mother reluctantly pulls away from Lily and allows me to hug my sister. Lily clings to me, hard.

Something's definitely wrong.

But when I pull away and search her face, my sister just paints a smile on her face and glances around. "Where's Trina? Last I heard she moved here to be with all of you."

"She's having a sexy two-week vacation with her new motorcycle-riding hunk of a boyfriend," Simone supplies, grabbing empty mugs and plates from a nearby table. "Back in a week."

Lily's eyes widen. "Katrina has a new boyfriend?" Her gaze lands on me, shock written over every line of her face. "And her boyfriend rides a *motorcycle?*"

"I know." I grin. "I'd expect that from you, but not from Trina."

Lily's face shuts down. "I'm done with men."

"Oh, that's what they all say." Dorothy nudges my sister

with her elbow. "Won't take long for you to find someone of your own."

Lily grimaces, and I bite back a smile. A year and a half ago, I would have thought the same—then I met Blake. Meeting my man's eyes, I extend a hand toward him.

He closes the distance between us and slides his arm across my shoulders, extending his other hand toward my sister. "I'm Blake."

Lily's eyes widen. "Blake Harding."

"The one and only." He gives her his most winning Hollywood smile, and my sister nearly has a heart attack.

I roll my eyes. "Don't encourage him," I tell Lily.

Her eyes swing to me. "You're dating a movie star? Since when?"

"Uh...a year, give or take?"

"Officially one year since our first kiss next Saturday," Blake provides, squeezing my shoulders. "And I have video evidence."

I blush, grinning at the man I love. It's not like I'd forget *that* first kiss.

Lily's brows lower over her eyes. "Why didn't you tell me?" She seems...hurt?

I clear my throat. "Well, Lily, you haven't had a phone in five years. We get postcards from you once every six months or so, and I never know what country you've traveled to. You don't even have social media."

"I have an email. I'd like to know when my sister shacks up with a literal Hollywood movie star!"

I flinch. "I'm sorry, okay? You've been jet-setting around the world for over a decade. I didn't think you'd be interested in my boring little life."

The hurt in Lily's eyes disappears when she drops a blank mask over her face. She shakes her head and takes a deep breath. "You're right."

"If only Trina were here, we'd be all together for the first time since your thirtieth birthday." She shakes her head. "That's *ten years*." My mother puts her hand around Lily's waist, as if she can't believe my sister is really here. "Tell me you're staying more than a few days."

Lily bites her lip, eyes darting from me, to my mother, to the rest of the assembled crowd. She lets out a huffed laugh and spreads her arms. "I was kind of planning on staying...for good."

Her smile is wide, but there's something dark in her eyes. My sister is hiding something—and it's big.

But before I can ask her anything, Jen walks out of the kitchen, and my sister moves to greet her. Then Dorothy insists on restarting the video *again,* since we haven't actually gotten through a full viewing without interruption. Jen takes that as her cue to leave, and glances at a wide-eyed, exhausted-looking Nora and her protective older brother hovering nearby.

"We're leaving," Jen proclaims, not leaving any room for discussion.

Nora's face relaxes, and she nods. "Okay."

Fallon glances at me, Lily, then at his own little sister, grabs her bag, and says his goodbyes. The three of them walk out the door and I turn back to Lily, but she's already collapsed on a chair looking close to exhaustion.

Giving her the third degree will have to wait—but I'll find out what she's hiding sooner or later.

TEN

JEN

NORA LETS out a long sigh when we get to my place. It looks like she's only holding on by a thread.

While Fallon busies himself carrying her bags to the spare bedroom, I turn to her. "Do you need to be alone, or do you need us to stay? Either is fine."

She blinks, then lets out a huffing laugh. "I think...alone, if you don't mind. I won't mess with your plants."

I give her a sharp nod, then turn to look at Fallon as he enters the living room.

My mouth waters.

He's just so...*big.* Over six feet tall, with shoulders nearly the width of a standard door. My apartment looks like a hobbit home with him in it. His hair is tousled from the thousand times he's run his fingers through it. A threadbare tee clings to his muscular shoulders, and I wonder what it would feel like to nuzzle into its softness.

Is it wrong that I *want* him to fall out of the cot tonight so he has no choice but to sleep in the bed with me?

He stalks out of the guest bedroom, eyes on his sister for the briefest moment before flicking to me. Fallon must see the hungry expression on my face, because one eyebrow arches ever so slightly.

"We're going," I blurt.

His head tilts. "That so?"

"Yeah. Nora wants to be alone, and we need to get back."

His gaze drops to my lips when I speak, and heat gushes through me.

This is bad. Really, really bad. If we go down that path again, it'll get messy. I have proof! The last year of my life is irrefutable evidence that getting involved with Fallon is a Really Bad Idea.

He's my partner in the competition, nothing more. We kissed once, a year ago. There's no need for me to be obsessively replaying the memory every chance I get.

At the end of it all, he *left*. Didn't even warn me. Didn't even tell me if he'd be back. I know myself, and I know I'm not strong enough to go through that all over again.

What if he kissed me again...but there wasn't an ex-girlfriend who showed up to break us up?

Then, if he left, it would simply be because he didn't want *me*.

No, Fallon is a distraction, and I can't afford to go down that path. I need to focus on this competition. On my goals.

His long legs eat up the space between us, eyes burning

with something I don't understand. At the last moment, he turns to his sister. "You don't want us to stay?"

She lets out a long sigh, sounding exactly like her brother. Then she shakes her head. "I just want to shower and go to bed. I haven't had a good night's sleep in months."

A muscle feathers in Fallon's cheek. He cares about his sister—a lot. But he gives Nora a nod, squeezes her shoulder, then we say goodbye.

We don't say a word in the stairwell as we descend, or when we spill out into the cool evening air. I suck in a breath, my skin overheated for reasons I don't want to admit.

"I'll drive," Fallon says, his low voice rumbling through me, his eyes searching mine before dropping to my mouth, my shoulders. I'm so flushed I know my chest is red, and I wonder if he can tell in the darkening night.

It seems to surprise Fallon when I don't protest, choosing instead to hand him my keys without a word. In some corner of my mind it surprises me, too, because I'm not the type of woman who likes to give up control. Any type of control. But with Fallon, it feels easy to let him take the lead. I *like* when he's in charge.

His fingers brush mine as he grabs the keys, a step bringing us nearly chest-to-chest. "Thank you, Jen," he rumbles.

"For what?"

He jerks his head to my apartment building. "What do you think?"

Breath stays caught in my lungs as I watch the moonlight play on his skin, his hair. When I meet his gaze, something smolders there. He gulps, watching me, then jerks his head. "Let's get back."

I nod, throat suddenly tight.

There's tension between us. Some sort of energy that's making my skin feel tight, sensitive. My clothes are rough against my body. When I put my seatbelt on, it presses my bra up against my breasts and I know my nipples are hard.

My body is out of control. Is this perimenopause? Some sort of physiological change in my body making my libido go haywire?

...or is it just the fact that Fallon is the first man I've ever met who makes me fantasize about every dirty thing I've never had the chance to do?

As we start driving, I let out a sigh. Wondering if Fallon feels the tension between us, I glance over at him and see his jaw clenched, his hands tight on the steering wheel.

"You okay?" I ask.

Fallon flicks his eyes to mine, to my lips, and then back to the road before dipping his chin. "Yeah. I'm good."

"Worried about your sister?"

A pause stretches, then Fallon nods again. "That too." He clears his throat. "Thank you for offering up your place."

"It's fine." I can't seem to tear my eyes away from him, from the white of his clenched knuckles as he kneads the steering wheel. His hands are so big and strong—so different from my own. Would they feel good sweeping over my curves?

One of those hands moves to adjust the collar of his tee, then rakes over his scalp before returning to the steering wheel.

"You don't seem fine." I state the obvious, knowing I'm entering dangerous territory.

Fallon's warm chuckle makes my insides clench. He concedes a nod. "Fine." We turn onto the long, winding, wooded road that will eventually open up on the *Boss Baker* compound. "I was having very selfish thoughts that I'm ashamed to say out loud."

Another thrill stabs me through the middle. Is he thinking about me? Does he feel the electricity in the car? Does he feel the night pressing in on us, shrouding us in this little bubble inside the vehicle?

My voice is scratchy when I finally manage to speak. "You should say them out loud, then."

Fallon pauses, his body tense. As if he's holding himself back. When he speaks, his voice is low. "That seems counterintuitive."

"If you say them out loud, they're usually not as bad as you think."

He snorts, shooting me a quick glance. "I can assure you, what's going on in my head is very, very bad."

Heat spears through me. I gulp. "Oh."

The car has slowed, and I wonder if he did it so the drive would last just a bit longer. "Okay, Dr. Jen. You first. What thoughts are you ashamed of?"

"That's easy," I answer immediately. "My constant failure. The fact that I can never quite live up to my potential, no matter how much I try. The fact that my perfectionism is like a cancer inside me, and it pretty much guarantees I'll never be happy with anything I achieve. I'm ashamed of the fact that I'm in my mid-forties and I've never had a long-term boyfriend, apart from one guy at college. Which was literally more than twenty years ago." I stare at the passing trees as my eyes grow unfocused.

"Jen..."

I blink, glancing back at him. "See? Easy."

"Why haven't you had a boyfriend?" Did his voice just get deeper? He looks almost...*pleased?*

I snort. "Look at me."

He looks at me—and doesn't snort. His eyes flick from my face down my body, and heat flows wherever his gaze lands.

Oh, my.

"I'm not seeing anything wrong," he growls.

My mouth grows dry, and when Fallon turns back to the road, I try to release the breath I'd been holding without him noticing. Being in his presence is becoming too much. How am I supposed to focus on the competition when all I can think about are his lips, his body, the way his voice skates along my skin like silk?

I force myself to look out the window. There's so much that I could say. How about the years and years as a child that I tried to be *enough*, only to be torn down by the two people who were supposed to prepare me for the world? How about the fact that in my mid-forties, I still feel inadequate?

This is my life. I'm good at baking. I'm good at taking care of plants. I have a deep need to be the best at what I do. I hate failure. I hate compromise.

Does that sound like nothing is wrong with me? Does that sound like someone a man like Fallon would be interested in?

"I'll never be the woman you think I am, Fallon."

The car swerves onto the shoulder and jerks to a stop. Pain snaps across my torso where my seatbelt catches me. In an instant, Fallon is unlatching his seatbelt, then unlatching mine. Hands wrap around my waist, and Fallon is dragging me over to sit across his lap.

I freeze, eyes wide.

I'm sitting across Fallon's lap, my side to his chest. My feet are stretched out across the center console, the gear shift between my knees. And he's so close I can feel him *everywhere*. His hands around my waist. His strong legs beneath my ass. His impossibly broad chest against my shoulder.

Fallon's hand moves from my waist to my cheek. The roughness of his hands sends tiny shivers racing over my skin, down my neck. I gulp, my hands having somehow moved to cling to his shirt. His touch feels so damn good.

"You're already the woman I think you are, Jen," he growls. "And I wouldn't change a damn thing." His eyes are dark, searching mine.

I swallow. "Oh."

"I should never have left," Fallon rasps. His fingers tighten over my cheek, sliding back to tangle into my hair. My own hands curl into his shirt, feeling the tenseness of his shoulders beneath the soft fabric. I'm pinned between him and the steering wheel, and when he slides his other hand up under my shirt, I nearly come apart.

"Why..." I gulp, trying to gather my wits enough to speak. His hand starts sweeping across my bare skin, and it's hard to push out the words. "Why did you leave?"

"I left because I needed…" Fallon inhales sharply, his hand gripping my waist for a moment, as if he doesn't want to let go. "There were things I needed to do. I'm sorry, Jen."

I shake my head. "Don't be. You didn't owe me anything."

The hand on my waist tightens, and heat lances my core. I realize that I like this—being here, in his lap. I like Fallon's hungry eyes roaming around my face, flicking from my gaze to my lips and back again. For the first time in my life, I *like* being pinned here against him, giving up control.

"You ruined me when you kissed me, Jen," he rasps. "It was over a year ago and I haven't been right since."

"Oh," I say. "I'm…sorry?"

His lips tilt. "I happen to like being ruined."

"Well, that makes one of us."

When a deep chuckle rumbles through his chest, I can't help the clenching of my core. His eyes are dark, almost black, and they promise dirty, dangerous things.

It's been a long, long time since I've been with a man—and even longer since I've felt on edge as I do now. But all it takes is Fallon's thumb to sweep a few inches over my back, and my whole body wants to melt.

"We shouldn't do this," I whisper.

"Do what, Jen?"

"Whatever it is we're doing."

"When was the last time you broke the rules?" Fallon leans his head back against the headrest, surveying me through half-lidded eyes.

"Ten minutes ago," I answer.

His eyebrow arches. "How so?"

"Well, you're not on my insurance and I let you drive my car."

His lips twitch. "Does that stress you out?"

"I gave verbal consent for you to drive it, and it's a relatively short distance back to the farmhouse, so the risk was low enough for me to take it."

His hand tightens around my waist, smile widening. "What a rebel."

"I know you're making fun of me, but I don't care." I jut my chin out, challenging.

"I would never."

I roll my eyes. "You constantly make fun of me, Fallon. For drinking tea. For liking to work in silence. For having four kitchen scales. For baking late into the night. For baking early in the morning. For caring about the correct temperatures for tempering chocolate—which, by the way, is the whole *point* of tempering chocolate." I huff. "You make fun of me for talking about protein content of various wheat flours and their effect on recipes, which again, is *important*."

His smile stretches all the way across his face, and I try my best to ignore the hard thumping of my heart. "Fine. Maybe I poke fun at you once in a while."

"Once in a while? It was honestly a relief when you left. At least I could get a bit of peace." My hands are still clinging to his shirt, twisted into the soft, black fabric. His shoulders shift beneath my hands, and I can't help my soft exhale at the feel of his warm, strong body moving against mine.

The leather seat creaks as he shifts his weight forward, pulling me tight to his chest. "I don't believe you."

My breasts crush against his chest as he holds me tight, but I do my best to look unaffected. "Well, you should."

"I think you've missed my comments. My making tea for you. My showing up at Four Cups in the middle of the night to pull you back from the brink of baking mania."

"Nope," I lie. "Didn't miss you for a minute."

His arms tighten, that sinful smile tugging. "You're lying."

I gulp, and Fallon sees it. The hand curled around my nape tightens as he exhales slowly, caging me in his strong arms. "You missed me, and you can't stop thinking about kissing me."

"Patently untrue."

"So why are you staring at my lips?"

Damn it. I flick my gaze back up to his laughing eyes, but I know I've already lost.

How did this happen? How did we get here? I was supposed to keep my distance. I was supposed to treat him like a professional partner in this competition, then move on. Somehow, his sister is staying at my place and I'm wrapped up in his arms on the side of the road.

And I *like* it.

Then the pressure of his hand on my nape increases, and without giving me a moment to process what's happening, Fallon pulls me in for a hard kiss.

I'd forgotten what it felt like to kiss Fallon. To have his firm, unyielding lips on mine. To feel him groan against my mouth as his body grows tense around mine. To be so wrapped up in him that I forget the world exists beyond the confines of his arms.

Once my lips are thoroughly ravished, Fallon pulls away and looks at me through heavy lids, satisfaction curling his lips.

"What was that for?" I ask, breathless.

"Two reasons," he says, his hand cupping my face. "First, as a thank you for everything you did for my sister tonight." A gentle kiss on my lips. "And second"—another brush of his lips, like he can't help himself—"because I've wanted to kiss again for a whole damn year."

We pause, tension stretching between us. I gaze into his brown-black eyes, realizing I'll get lost in them. In him.

And maybe...I want that.

Pulling him closer, it's my turn to kiss Fallon hard—because the truth? The truth is, I've been dreaming of this for a year too.

Fallon crushes his lips against mine, his kiss claiming. Possessive. He nips at my bottom lip, his hand sweeping higher under my shirt to my mid-back. When Fallon kisses me again, his tongue delves into my mouth and another groan is ripped from his throat. I answer with a whimper.

That's when the hand around my waist moves to my front, palming my small breasts with his big, hot hand. I gasp, my nipples going hard in an instant, my body on fire.

This is what kissing Fallon does to me. It cranks me so tight I can't think. Can't breathe. All I can do is shove my hands into his thick, black hair, parting my lips to kiss him harder. His beard feels rough against my skin as he breaks the kiss and nips at my earlobe, my neck. When his tongue slides out to taste my skin, I let out a shaking breath.

His hand kneads my breast, his thumb making delicious, mind-melting circles over the stiff peak. When I shift my body, his steel-hard shaft presses against my hip.

"Missed this," Fallon says, pushing me down so I'm leaning

against the door, my legs stretched out toward the passenger seat. He shoves my shirt up to expose my plain white bra. "Wanted you for years."

"Me too," I pant, hands still tangled in his hair.

When Fallon dips his head toward my chest, I close my eyes. The window is cold against my shoulders, my neck, but Fallon's heat is a blaze all around me. My bra is shoved down beneath my breasts in an instant, and his mouth is on my skin.

I moan.

He sucks my breast into his mouth, his tongue laving my nipple until I'm in a frenzy. "Make up...for lost time," he grunts between nips of my breast, his hand cupping my flesh as his mouth drives me wild.

I could come like this—sitting across his lap in the car, my body awkwardly shoved against the door, my shirt shoved up to my neck while he teases my breasts like a man starved.

Hand scrabbling for purchase, I grip the steering wheel and arch into his mouth. He answers with a groan, his hand sliding down to wrap around my rib cage, holding me right where he wants me. Sharp jolts of pleasure pierce me with every flick of his tongue, every squeeze of his broad hand.

Sex has always been awkward for me. Something I'm supposed to do a certain way, with certain men that have been vetted and approved ahead of time. I had my first one-night stand at the tender age of forty-one, when I signed up for a dating website for a grand total of two weeks. His hands were clammy and I never called him again.

I've only ever had sex in a bed, with the lights off. Until Fallon kissed me last year, I hadn't even realized that it could be anything other than uncomfortable. That pleasure could be so intense it would drive me out of my mind.

My hips grind wantonly, and I feel so intensely, painfully empty.

Fallon lifts his head from my chest, his lips glistening, eyes glazed. His hand moves from my ribs to my breast, as if he can't stop himself from touching me, feeling me.

For the first time in all my life, I feel sexy. Sensual.

Chest heaving, he palms my breast and shakes his head. "Better than I imagined."

Before I can answer, headlights appear behind us. I jump, my elbow hitting the horn. The noise startles me and I yelp, then shove my bra back up and my shirt down, but Fallon's hand tightens around my waist to stop me shuffling back to my seat. We wait in tense silence as the car passes us, slowing as it goes by.

My cheeks flame.

"They won't be able to see anything, Jen. It's dark."

"I'm not the type of woman who makes out with strange men on the side of the road."

That makes him smile. "Am I a strange man?"

"Extremely." Wrenching myself from his grasp, I shuffle across to my own seat and let out a huff. It's awkward and difficult and damn it, when did I get so old and creaky? Climbing across a car seat shouldn't be this hard. Once I make it across, I slap my palm against my forehead and squeeze my eyes shut.

This is bad.

Very, very bad.

The kiss was great. Wonderful. Earth-shattering.

But the consequences?

Devastating.

I already want Fallon more than I can say. It's clouding my mind, pushing all other thoughts to the side. Everything else that has happened over the past week fades to nothing. The competition? What competition? His sister? Iliana's unexpected arrival? My career prospects? My book? My plants?

None of it matters, because my swollen, kiss-bruised lips are throbbing for more. Every heartbeat pulses through me and reminds me of all the places Fallon touched—and places he didn't. Damp fabric clings to the space between my legs as I clench my thighs to ease some of the pressure.

I want him so desperately it aches in every part of me. I'm so far gone already, and it only spells trouble.

Because what happens next time Fallon leaves without warning? Next time he has "things to take care of" out of town and disappears for six months? What happens next time an ex-girlfriend shows up to stay at his place?

What happens when he gets bored of me?

Because if there's one thing I've learned over the four-and-a-bit decades of my life, it's that I cannot keep a man entertained. I'm too neurotic. Too unyielding. Too stuck in my ways.

I have obsessions that my friends call quirks—and men call annoying.

Fallon said he's been waiting years to feel my breasts, to kiss me like that—but what happens once he gets what he wants? The heat spearing my core tells me he'll destroy me. Maybe he already has.

"Hey." Fallon moves my hand from my brow with a gentle,

firm touch, then hooks his hand around my neck. His lips are tender when they press against mine. "Whatever's going on in your head right now, it needs to stop. I can't have the best pastry chef in town panicking on me."

His beard scratches against my jaw as he kisses my cheek, then my nose, then back down to my lips. I shiver, loving his touch far, far too much for my own good.

"We should get home," he says quietly. "Big day tomorrow."

"Yeah," I croak. "Sounds good."

What happens after we get home might sound even better... if I can get out of my own head.

ELEVEN

JEN

SOMEONE WAS IN OUR ROOM. The housekeeping staff, for one, but when I step inside the guesthouse, the hairs on the back of my neck stand up. All the heat from my car ride with Fallon seeps out of me, replaced with cold dread.

"Does that look like the imprint of someone sitting on the bed to you?" I point to the slightly rumpled sheets near my pillow.

Fallon straightens from where he'd been bent over one of the drawers containing his clothing, his brows tugging together. "Maybe the maid needed a break when she was cleaning."

I've stayed in a few hotels in my life, and I've never seen anything like this. Crossing to the closet, I glance at my shelf and freeze.

Has someone been rummaging in my stuff?

I color-code my clothing—have done for years. It's all Marie-Kondo'ed within an inch of its life, and I made sure to bring shelf organizers for my stay. They're honeycomb-shaped, with each little hexagonal section available for a perfectly folded item of clothing. Every single pair of socks and underwear should be folded precisely and slotted in its own little section of my shelf. But some of my underwear is *rumpled*.

My heart thumps. I whirl on Fallon. "Were you rifling through my underwear?"

He rears back. "What? No!"

I stare at him for a beat, searching. Did he? *Would* he?

My eyes dart around the room, searching for something— anything. A clue. The window is cracked open, just how we left it earlier, and I cross the room to glance outside. The window is the type that opens two ways: it either swings fully inward, or it can be latched and tilted from the top to let in some air. We tilted it. Outside, I scan the trees, the grass, the underbrush, but I see nothing.

Until I look directly at the ground near our guesthouse. A single black feather rests on the grass just outside our cracked window. A *crow* feather.

Did—how—*what?*

I press the heels of my hands to my eyes and take a deep breath. I'm going crazy. There's no way a crow rifled through my underwear. Literally no way.

Fallon walks on soft feet to approach me, stopping just inches from my back. When he puts his hands on my shoulders, I flinch. "Talk to me," he rumbles.

"The bedsheets are mussed."

Something crosses his eyes. Real worry—maybe even fear. But his face is blank in an instant. "Barely."

"My underwear was tampered with."

There's slight pause, as if Fallon is trying to compose himself. When he speaks, his voice sounds calm, casual. "Is it possible you did that when you got dressed this morning?"

I glance at the closet door, biting my lip. I *was* frazzled this morning when I woke up wrapped up in Fallon's arms. Is it *possible* that I messed up a few items of clothing when I got dressed?

Yeah, it's possible.

Is it *probable*?

I'm going with *hell no*.

But what's the alternative? A freaking *crow*?

I'm going insane.

"I need to call the Audubon society. I need to know just how smart crows are, and whether they can squeeze through"—I glance at the window—"two or three inches of space." I straighten my shoulders, but Fallon doesn't drop his hands.

A deep, rumbling chuckle sounds as his hands slide down my arms and wrap around my waist. "Jen." His voice is quiet, his breath ruffling over my neck.

"What?"

"Is it possible you're deflecting from the real issue?"

I frown. "What's the real issue?"

"The fact that we made out like two horny teens in your car a few minutes ago, and now we're back in our private guesthouse with nowhere to be until tomorrow morning?"

I stiffen.

He lets out a long sigh, his arms still wrapped around me— and damn it, I like the feeling of him curled around me like this.

The hardness of his muscle. The warmth of his body. The rasp of his beard against my neck, my chin.

"I'm not going to push you to do anything you don't want to do," he says quietly.

Of all the reactions I could have to something so thoughtful, so gentle, I have the worst one. I get *embarrassed*. How humiliating is it that I've been on this earth nearly half a century, and the thought of being intimate with a man still fills me with dread? I still feel like I should be alone. I don't deserve someone as thoughtful and kind as Fallon.

Breath fills my lungs as I spin around in his arms, placing my hands on his chest as I lift my gaze to his. "I want you to sleep in the bed tonight, but I don't want... I'm not ready to do anything." I'm grasping at straws here, wanting to take things slow with him. Ever since the first day of the competition, we've been getting closer and closer.

But I can't afford the distraction. I need to focus on winning.

"Okay," he replies, tucking a strand of hair behind my ear.

"That's it? Okay? Aren't you going to try to convince me to sleep with you?"

His lip quirks. "Is that what you want me to do?"

"No."

"Well, there you go."

"You're too nice. It's weird."

Fallon's eyes grow shadowed. He gives me a sad smile, then jerks his head to the bathroom. "I'm going to get ready for bed."

When we finally climb into the fresh bedsheets together, Fallon doesn't even pretend to stay on his side. He hooks his arm around my waist and tugs me close, shifting his hand up to rest just under my breast. Behind me, his cock throbs, but he makes no move to do anything about it.

I blink, staring out in the darkened room, heart thundering.

There's too much going on. I gave up on Fallon a year ago, when his ex showed up in town and I had to choose. Now he's here, and it looks like he never gave up on me. He kissed me like the world was ending, and now he's holding me like I'm precious.

I've never had this.

My one, singular boyfriend was a biomechanical engineer who had his life planned out in a spreadsheet. I ticked the boxes for the woman he wanted—literally, he had a checklist—but there was none of this heart-racing, body-heating reaction to his touch.

His name was Will, and he never proposed to me. He just... assumed we'd get married. One day he started talking about the tax implications of marriage, and how it made sense for us to head to the courthouse.

I almost agreed, until he started talking about me staying home with the kids. Frowning, I asked him what he meant, because I'd been very clear that I didn't want kids. I wanted to focus on my career in tech.

And he *laughed.* I remember his exact words. He said, "If you won't have my kids, what the hell is the point of all this?"

We broke up the next week, and he was married with a baby on the way a year later.

I know I'm not some incredible catch in the romance department. I'm neurotic and obsessive and hate compromises. My body has never been amazing. I was too skinny as a kid, and

I grew into a pretty flat-chested, bony adult. Now, things have started sagging, wrinkling, and graying around the edges, and it's even more obvious that I'm past my prime.

But having someone dismiss me and replace me so easily? That stung.

Fallon's breath deepens, and I know he's asleep. He huffs, his breath flicking a strand of my hair over my neck, then shifts to press his body along the length of mine. His hand slides up to cup my breast and he mumbles something unintelligible in his sleep, tightening his hold on me.

Is it completely pathetic that even that simple touch makes my body feel like a live wire? When I'm with Fallon, I don't feel gray and wrinkly and old. I don't feel like I'm past my prime. He makes me feel beautiful and attractive and wanted.

But how long will that last? How long until he sees me for who I am and decides that I don't tick all *his* boxes?

Fallon's hand gently squeezes my breast, sending a jolt of arousal down between my legs. "Sleep, Jen," he murmurs. "I can hear your thoughts from all the way over here."

"That doesn't even make any sense."

He huffs a laugh, nuzzling his face into my neck. "*Shh.*"

"Did you just shush me?" The nerve!

When Fallon's thumb brushes over my nipple in a slow, torturous sweep, my eyes nearly roll back in my head. His voice is a growl when he says, "I can think of other ways to stop your mind from running away with you."

I manage a huff. "You're unbelievable."

His teeth rasp against my earlobe, and I feel an unmistakable throb from his crotch. When he rolls me onto my back and props himself on his elbow above me, his eyes are dark, his face shadowed. "Do you want me to sleep on the cot?"

Throat tight, I shake my head.

He stares at me for a long moment, as if he's trying to read me. Figure out if I'm telling the truth. "You'll hate yourself if you don't do well in tomorrow's elimination challenge because you're tired."

I blink. That's...very true.

His lips are soft when he lays a tender kiss on my mouth, shifting his hand to my jaw as he deepens the kiss. With a low growl, Fallon pulls away. "I'd do anything to have my way with you right now. To taste you. Have all of you." He rests his forehead against mine. "But I'd never forgive myself if I was the reason we got eliminated tomorrow. You need to shut that big brain of yours off and try to sleep."

My heart spasms. Gulping, I nod. "Okay."

Rolling me back over, Fallon shoves his leg between mine and tucks me into his chest, wrapping me up in his warmth and weight. He wants me, but he knows how important doing well in this baking competition is to me.

When was the last time someone gave up what they wanted for me? I can't think of a single time.

So, blood humming, lips curling as warmth settles over my body, I close my eyes and do my best to sleep.

OUR NEXT ELIMINATION challenge involves bread. We have to make thirty-six perfect dinner rolls. Fallon and I work fairly well together, landing somewhere in the middle of the pack. Our bread was well-baked, but the texture was a bit too chewy for the judges' tastes. Reg and Tex win that round, and Carla and Emma end up going head-to-head against Mary and Tony, the mother-son duo from New York. The Latinas come out ahead, and another teary hug-fest ensues. I...don't hate it.

Over the course of the week, Fallon and I spend a lot of time together. We don't kiss again, but the tension is there. Bite-sized challenges go well for us, including focaccia so good Reg asks for the recipe. The days are busy, and by the time evenings come around, we both end up stumbling to shower before falling face-first into our pillows.

I do enjoy waking up wrapped up in Fallon's warm body, though. Mornings are my favorite time of the day.

Before I know it, Saturday morning dawns and it's time to head back to the barn for another full day of cooking. Our third elimination challenge is upon us.

TWELVE
FALLON

THIRD ELIMINATION CHALLENGE: CHOUX
PASTRY

"A CROAK IN WHAT?" I say out of the side of my mouth as
Carrie introduces the challenge.

This week was a revelation. It made me regret letting Jen
push me away last year. I should have spoken to Amanda and
told her about my intentions with Jen. I should have pursued
her harder, told her how much she meant to me.

I should never have left—but then I think of my sister being
harassed, my criminal past, all the shit I've done in my life.

Jen deserves better.

"*Croquembouche,*" Jen whispers. "It's a tower of *choux*—
cream puffs—with threads of caramel wrapped all around it."

Bernard Franco surveys the assembled crowd, his pale eyes
assessing. "We are looking for perfectly uniform *choux,* which
need to be filled completely with at least two different fillings.
Your caramel should be golden-brown, not burned. We're
looking for structural stability in the tower, so make sure you

137

adhere the *choux* to each other properly with your caramel. They should not, however, be impossible to take apart when it comes time to taste them." He grins. "A hint—use a candy thermometer, or risk disaster."

When Jen's hands clench the side of the counter, I know we're in trouble. She's gnawing on her bottom lip, eyes darting over the other competitors as if she needs to check that they're as nervous as we are.

The only people that look unworried are the judges. Everyone else is freaking out.

Pastry Prodigy Heather spreads her arms. "You have two and a half hours."

"What?" Jen claps a hand over her mouth as a cameraman shifts to catch her reaction.

Bernard grins. "We're looking for perfection, folks."

"Of course they are." Tex crosses his arms over his barrel chest, glancing back at Jen and me. "You look nervous, Blondie."

"Shut up, Tex," Jen grumbles.

The big man grins. "Finally, she looks shaken. You were flying through our bite-sized challenges. I was worried you were a robot."

"You wouldn't be the first person to think that." Jen arches a brow. "My nickname in high school was the tin man." She glances at me. "No heart."

"We both know that's a lie," I say softly, unable to resist putting my hand on her lower back.

Reg nudges his partner and jerks his head forward.

Carrie flicks her hair over her shoulder and angles her face to the camera. "Your time...starts...*now*."

Jen snaps into action. She grabs the recipe provided to us, scanning it with a pen shoved in the side of her mouth.

I admit, I take a moment to take a mental snapshot of her like this—elbows leaning on the counter, ass pushed back, legs spread wide—before I sidle up beside her and lean a palm next to her elbow. "What are we doing?"

"This recipe gives measurements but no real instructions. It just says, 'Make the choux pastry.'"

"I'm hoping you know how to do that," I say, "because I sure as hell don't."

Jen glances at me, brow arched. "What do you think?"

I lean in close to her ear. "I think you know exactly what you're doing, and it's hot as hell."

A flush sweeps over her cheeks, but she brushes the compliment off. "Do you know how to make *crème pâtissière?*"

"Uh..." I cringe.

Jen sucks in a breath and jots down a few things on a paper. "It's a type of custard. Here, heat this much milk and measure out the flour and sugar. I'm going to get started on the dough. We need to get the choux in the oven and cooled before we can fill and assemble, and the filling needs to be chilled, too."

I nod. "Yes, Chef."

She grins at me, and then we get to work.

As I babysit the heating milk, Jen works like a madwoman. I'll never get over how impressive it is to watch her do her thing. When I first invited Amanda to town with the intention of introducing her to Jen, I hoped it would help Jen's career. I hoped that I could have a small part in seeing her achieve the success she deserves.

I didn't know Jen would end up pushing me away as a result, but it's hard to be bitter about that when I'm standing next to her, watching her hands move like magic.

She throws directions at me for the custard, telling me to split the milk in two so we can flavor one of them with chocolate. "We're going to make raspberry coulis to add to the chocolate ones, and maybe some lemon curd for the vanilla," she tells me. "Cut the sweetness a bit." Her eyes brighten. "We could swirl them together before we pipe the filling into the choux, so you bite into it and you get streaks of color in the center."

That sounds like genius. But—

"Do we have time for that?" I glance over at whatever she's doing on the stove—mixing some sort of flour, butter, and egg mixture like her life depends on it.

Jen just shoots me one of her rare, radiant smiles. "Of course we have time. Who do you think I am?"

Grinning, I turn back to my work, and we fall into a groove. I manage not to mess up the pastry cream, and when Jen tastes it she gives me a quick nod. "It's good, Fallon."

Those three words mean a lot to me. More than I want to admit. After the disastrous croissants, I'm glad I can actually contribute.

Jen pipes the dough onto a waiting baking tray, and has dozens of little balls of choux in the oven within minutes. She's incredible.

The two women in the head-to-toe denim outfits are at the station next to ours. Nikki glances over, her hair mussed, flour streaked all over her face. "I'm never eating cream puffs again! Ever!"

Her teammate, Sonia, rushes over from the bank of freezers holding a bowl. She's got tears in her eyes. "Look, the filling is all separated. It curdled somehow."

Jen glances over and, thrusting a whisk into my hand with the stern order to not stop agitating whatever's on the stove, she flies over to the next station. "What have we got?" she asks, wiping her hands on her apron.

"Separated fillings. Flat choux pastry." Nikki shoves her hand in her hair. "And I don't even know how to make caramel!"

"Give me a pot," Jen says, pointing. "And sugar. No, the white sugar. Thanks."

I steal a glance over to see Jen's brow drawn in concentration. She starts coaching the Denim Ladies on caramel, giving them her usual no-nonsense instructions. Then she's back at our station, tasting, mixing, checking.

A screech sounds from Sonia. She pulls out a baking tray from the oven in a puff of black smoke.

"Oh, dear," Jen mumbles. "I'm not sure they'll come back from this."

The two women look shellshocked. Jen rushes over again—even though I'm whisking three different mixtures like my life depends on it—and counsels Sonia and Nikki on what they should do. Prognosis: start again.

The competitor in me wants to tell Jen to get back over here and work on our own croquembouche, but the man in me admires her. Even in the midst of a high-pressure situation, her heart is big enough to help a struggling team. These are the things that first made me notice Jen when we worked together.

She notices so much about how other people feel. For Simone's wedding, she made a hazelnut and chocolate cake at the last minute because she noticed Simone eating Ferrero Rochers all the time. She quit her job at a Michelin-starred restaurant under a world-renowned head chef to step into the unknown with the Four Cups Café—and I suspect a big part of that was wanting to support Candice in her new project.

On the outside, Jen seems like a hard ass. A logical, rational kind of person. But she's deeply, incomparably empathetic. And I love that about her. I love a lot of things about her—maybe more than I want to admit to myself.

Because in what universe could a woman as incredible as Jen want an ex-con like me?

She makes her way back over to our station under the judges' watchful eyes.

"Are you sure you've left yourself enough time?" Heather asks with an arched brow, eyes flicking to the Denim Ladies. "Assisting other competitors won't help you win."

"We've all been there," she says, setting up a pastry bag to be filled with our swirled pastry cream and lemon curd. "Fallon has saved me more than once from a breakdown." She glances over at me, a smile tugging at her lips.

I saved her from a ruined-cake-induced mental breakdown the first time we kissed. I didn't mind her chocolate-covered hands being shoved into my hair—still wouldn't mind if we got that messy again. My cock throbs at the memory, and I'm glad I'm wearing a heavy apron.

Jen glances at the judges, her eyes landing on Carrie's assessing gaze. "I want to be able to look at myself in the mirror by the end of the competition and be proud of myself—and not just because of my baking."

"Well, good luck," Bernard says. He's the only one who seems to approve, and a flare of jealousy lights up inside me. I can't explain it, but I just hate the way he stares at her.

While I start on the raspberry filling, I watch Jen crouch down to check on the oven. She grabs one of the choux, tests the weight, then pulls the tray out.

Jen doesn't stop for a minute. She orders me around, and I'm happy to oblige. When the dough is out and cooling, we check our fillings and assemble the sugar for the caramel. Jen tells me we'll make two batches, since it's quick to make and we don't want it to harden halfway through assembly.

"Whatever you say, boss." I mean the words seriously, but Jen just arches a brow at me, her lips quirking.

"I don't remember you being this docile when we worked together at Four Cups," she notes.

"Docile, huh?" My hands move without me watching as I glance over at Jen, loving the flush in her cheeks, the sparkle in her eyes.

This is where she belongs, and I'll be damned if I ever let anything stand in her way. It's almost awe-inspiring to be in the presence of someone so talented, when my whole life has been an exercise in survival, in mediocrity.

In the last hour of baking, the live audience starts filtering in. Jen gives them a quick glance, flashing a smile at her posse. We work down to the wire, our hands sticky, the choux stuffed and caramel'ed and set in an impossibly tall tower.

When Jen starts creating spun sugar, it looks almost like a

dance. Her hands sweep and swirl as lines of caramel dangle down from her spoon, encasing our tower of cream puffs in a cage of golden sugar. All I can do is watch and try not to let my heart beat out of my chest, because right now, I can't deny my feelings for her.

I've been in love with Jen Newbank for years.

I love that she sticks her tongue out the side of her mouth when she's focusing. I love that she's militant, precise. That she *cares* about things. I love that she's so damn talented, and I wish she could see just how amazing she really is.

She's so attractive that staring at her is like staring into the sun. Blinding.

As I watch her put the finishing touches on it, my smile is tinged with sadness. I'll never be on Jen's level. I just spent the last six months surrounded by ex-cons. I was volunteering my time and doing something worthwhile, sure, but I'm so ashamed of my past. How could someone like Jen ever want someone like me? She might slum it with me when we're in this environment, but what happens when the competition ends?

When the time counts down to zero, Jen steps back from the bench with her hands covered in caramel and her face flushed with excitement. She turns to me with a broad smile on her face, then launches herself at me. I shake off my sadness just in time to catch her as she wraps her legs around my hips. A laugh falls from my lips for a second, just before Jen silences me with a searing kiss.

Heat rips through my core, my cock stiffening in an instant. This is the first time *she's* kissed *me*, the first time she's made the first move—and damn, but it feels incredible. Her fingers are sticky on my neck and she tastes like sugar and raspberry, and it's the most perfect moment of my whole fucking life.

Then a loud bang sounds from the rafters, followed by a yelp and a scream that I recognize—because it came from my sister.

THIRTEEN

NORA

I'M LITERALLY on the edge of my seat watching Jen and Fallon work like they can sense each other's every move. They work perfectly together. It's entrancing, and my heart grows for my brother—especially when I see the way he's looking at Jen. But just as the sound of the buzzer goes off and Jen throws herself into Fallon's arms, the whole bench collapses out from under me, sending me crashing down to the ground. I scream, flailing my arms as I fall back, landing with a hard thud on the wooden planks of the barn's mezzanine.

Simone lands beside me with a groan.

Stunned, I lie back, staring at the big rafters and the corrugated iron roof above.

What the hell just happened?

"Nora!" Fallon yells from below, right before a bunch of faces appear in my field of vision.

Simone props herself up on her elbow and accepts a hand

up. She then reaches down for me, wrapping an arm around my shoulders. "You're okay. Come on, honey, you're good. We both are."

I groan. I'm getting too old for this. I already know I'll be feeling aches and pains from that landing for a week.

"What happened?" Candice frowns, glancing at the bench. We're all sitting on long wooden benches in the mezzanine, and the one I was on was at the very back with Simone. The legs on one end are splayed out to one side, completely snapped off from the seat.

Looking over her shoulder, I see the retreating back of the man who'd been sitting on the end of the wrecked bench. He didn't look at me, didn't speak to me, but when Jen jumped in my brother's arms, he stood up with his fists clenched. He was muttering in what sounded like a foreign language. French, maybe? Italian? I couldn't hear properly. Out of the corner of my eye, I saw him kick the bench, heard a thump, but I didn't realize what had happened until I was on the floor.

Whoever he is, he kicked so hard he *broke the legs off*. Why? I'd gotten the impression he was mostly watching my brother and Jen working, but he could have been with the women at the station next to them—the ones all in denim, who seemed to be burning things left, right, and center.

Was he mad that the ladies ruined their croak-whatever-thing? Or was it when Jen took a running jump and landed in Fallon's arms?

Earlier, when he first sat down on the end of the bench, the hairs on the back of my neck stood up. I dismissed it as paranoia over everything happening with Slim. I see gangbangers every-where these days.

My brother surges past the man just as the bench-kicker disappears down the steps. Fallon's eyes are wild. He's always been overprotective, as if he's trying to atone for the mistakes he made as a teen. He never forgave himself for being a trou-blemaker.

"I'm fine, Fallon." I groan, rubbing my tailbone. I'm *mostly* fine, although I seem to be bruising a lot more easily than I did a few years ago.

He grasps my arms, staring into my eyes before looking at the bench, then back at me. "Are you okay?"

"Yeah, apart from the death grip you have on my biceps."

He loosens his hold, then lets out a long breath. "What happened?"

"Some guy kicked the bench when the timer went off. He was mad about something. Looks like he broke one of the legs." I nod to the broken bits of wood.

Fallon's thick brows tug low over his eyes. "Must have kicked it pretty hard."

Should I tell him that the man did it when Jen kissed him? I'm not sure that's what caused the man's outburst. He could have been angry about anything—another team not finishing, or the time running out, or some issue in his personal life. He'd been rocking back and forth on the bench and muttering a bit. He creeped me the hell out, but I know I'm oversensitive about that kind of thing right now.

So, I just shrug. "Yeah. He left right after it collapsed, so I assume he was embarrassed."

A medic appears and insists on sitting me down to check me and Simone out, which I do with an overdramatic sigh. "I don't need any more reminders that I'm getting older, people. A younger woman would just brush this off."

"Time marches on, sweetheart," Dorothy says, patting my shoulder in commiseration. "You're just a young pup anyway."

"I'll be forty in less than a year!" I grimace. "Honestly, when did that even happen? I'm supposed to be married with two point five kids by now."

Fiona gives me a sympathetic grin. "Doesn't always work out that way, does it?"

Fallon combs his fingers through his hair, watching me, then glancing at the Four Cups crowd. "What's Nora doing here, anyway?"

Candice arches a brow at him, cocking her hip to the side. "Well, we were going to leave her locked up in Jen's jungle for the day, but I took pity on her when I went for today's watering cycle." The sass soaked into every word almost makes me burst out laughing.

I like her.

Fallon's always been a bit uptight when things get stressful. He blames himself for everything. And now, he looks like he's about to blow. "You should have called me. I could have driven her here."

"You're busy with the show, and I'm an adult," I cut in. "I don't need you to babysit me. Candice and the girls invited me out, and I said yes. Do you have a problem with that?"

Fallon sucks in a breath and slowly lets it out. "No, of

course not. I just worry about you. We haven't had a chance to talk."

The last thing I want to do is talk, so I deploy my best weapon: deflection. "How about we talk about all the gray hairs you've got growing in your beard." I flick his chin and—as usual—Fallon isn't fast enough to dodge it. Ha!

In response, Fallon just leans over me and plucks a hair from the crown of my head. I yelp, slapping a hand over my scalp. My brother, with a self-satisfied smirk, dangles a pure white hair in front of my face. "You were saying?"

"Rude!" I snatch the hair and hold it between my fingers, staring.

"Oh, come on," Dorothy says, patting her silvery-white head. "It's not so bad. You young people make a big deal out of the silliest things. I heard gray hair was all the rage these days. Iliana was wearing her grays proudly all week!"

I bunch my lips to the side as the medic straightens in front of me. "She's all good," the medic says to a blond-haired man near the stairs.

"Fallon?" The man arches his brows. "You good to continue filming? The staff will take care of your..." He tilts his head, studying my face. "Sister?"

I nod. "Yeah. Sister."

Fallon gives me a long look. "This isn't over. You and I need to talk."

I force a smile. I'm not sure what else there is to say. Slim found out where I lived and asked me to deliver a message to Fallon. I don't have any other information, but I admit seeing

Slim Miller freaked me out. Last night was the first good night's sleep I've had in weeks.

My breath leaves my lungs in a whoosh when Fallon heads back down the stairs. Candice puts an arm around me and Simone grabs my elbow on the other side, the two of them leading me to a fully functional bench.

Fiona cringes at me. "It's not usually like this, Nora. Heart's Cove is just a sleepy town, I promise."

Simone snorts. "Do you promise that, Fiona? Because last I checked, Heart's Cove is the furthest thing from sleepy."

Fiona chews her lip. "Okay, so yes, dramatic things happen here. But not usually *injury-inducing* things."

"What about Wes's ankle?" Simone asks. "Or Jen's brush with those killer birds? Or Candice's house fire?"

"Is this supposed to be helping?" Fiona plants her hands on her hips and stares at the red-haired woman opposite her. "We should be making her feel *good* about being here. Not fearing for her life!"

My lips twitch. "It's fine. I like it here."

Candice squeezes my shoulders and sits me down next to her, and I realize it's the truth. I *do* like it here. I like the way Candice rang the doorbell this morning and treated me like an old friend. I like that when she invited me to come watch my brother bake with Jen, it didn't seem forced. It felt like she truly wanted me to come along.

For the first time in a long, long time, I almost feel...at home. I hadn't realized how much I needed this.

It's too bad Fallon left Heart's Cove, and from what he told me, he has no plans to move back. Otherwise, we could both make a life here.

FOURTEEN
JEN

"YOUR CARAMEL WAS BROUGHT to the perfect color," Bernard says, inspecting one of the choux he plucked from the croquembouche. "The spun caramel is delicate. Perfect." His eyes flick to mine, and he holds my gaze so long I start to blush, forcing myself not to squirm.

Heather hums in agreement. "The addition of lemon curd was genius. It cuts the sweetness of the *crème pat* absolutely perfectly." She smacks her lips. "I'd take the whole thing home."

I can hardly contain my excitement. Today's challenge felt *good*. Everything went right, and I actually had fun. Even in front of a live audience, with a big, angry timer counting down the time and cameras stuck in my face.

The mezzanine crowd cheers, and I hear Candice whooping loudest of all. Cheeks burning, I can't quite keep the smile off my face. It took a little while to get everyone settled after the bench collapsed, but now the air in the barn is back to being electric.

Fallon shifts his weight, glancing down at me with sparkling eyes. "That was all Jen."

"We figured." Bernard grins. He gives me a wink, and my blush deepens.

"Yeah, all right, all right, no need to rub it in." Fallon puts his arm around my shoulders and tucks me into his side. His movements feel rough, as if he's...making a point.

There's no time to decipher it, because my heart is warm, overflowing. When we bring our croquembouche back to our station, I let out a deep breath and glance up at the man beside me. He was amazing today. Focused, on task, and totally willing to go with all my ideas.

I've never felt that kind of support. When I worked in tech, I was always second-guessed. I saw my ideas being passed over, or worse, repeated by my male colleagues and celebrated. When I quit the job, my boss called me by the wrong name, even though we'd worked together for years. Even though I was the best team member by far.

Being good at things is natural to me. It comes with the perfectionism. But to have someone stand by my side and support me? To have Fallon's quiet strength, his encouragement?

It makes everything sweeter.

When we win the choux pastry round, my whole body is warm and light, and it almost feels like I need to hang on to Fallon to keep me down on earth.

Unfortunately, the Daisy Dukettes come last. They face off

against the Brits and lose in a tight, sudden-death round, which means Sonia and Nikki won't be competing any longer. I'm surprised at the emotion balled in my throat as Nikki wraps me in a tight hug—and even more surprised that I hug her back. Maybe this competition is getting to me, turning me into someone who laughs and hugs and cries.

"Even the great Jennifer Newbank couldn't save us." Sonia pouts. "But I'll be cheering for you to win this thing."

My chest warms. I haven't felt this much support since... well, *ever*. Even Tex uses a meaty hand to slap my back in grudging congratulations. He nearly knocks my teeth out with the smack, but I can tell it comes from a good place.

...I think.

The audience filters out, and I catch Candice's eyes as she winks, promising to talk to me later. Dorothy hangs over the railing and waves. "We knew you could do it!"

"Get down from there," Agnes, the bookstore owner and Dorothy's perpetual rival, hisses. "Do you have a death wish? You could fall over the railing."

Dorothy's eyes widen, glancing over her shoulder. "Are you... Are you *worried* about me?"

"*Pfft*," Agnes snorts. "Hardly. I'd push you over myself if I thought I'd get away with it."

Simone and Fiona start laughing behind them, and I can't help the smile that spreads across my face. Yes, it's probably not the kind of thing normal people laugh about—but are any of us normal? The way I see it, normal is just code for hiding who you really are. We're all freaks on the inside.

For the past year, I've been so busy with the book, with my

feelings about Fallon, with the responsibility of baking every-thing that goes through Four Cups—I'd forgotten how much I loved those women. How much I love this town.

I used to dream about moving to Paris to work in the most prestigious patisseries in the world...but why? Why would I want to do that when I'm happy in Heart's Cove? For the first time in my life, I find myself wondering about all my career aspirations and dreams. Did I only set lofty goals for myself because I thought that's what I *should* be doing? Because living and working in a small town, surrounded by people I love, never seemed like enough?

My lips still feel warm from Fallon's kiss, and a flush sweeps over my face as I meet his eyes. "I lied in the car yesterday. I missed you when you were gone."

His eyes crinkle. "I know."

Before I say anything else, all of us contestants are ushered to the main house for a dinner and wind-down. When we enter our usual lounge room, I let out a long breath. Another chal-lenge survived.

Tex's voice booms in my ear as he claps me on the back again, rattling my teeth once more. "Not bad for a little girl, Jen. Knew you'd be the one to beat."

"Little girl?" I squeak in outrage, sounding very much like a little girl.

"So condescending!" Emma throws in, winking at me. Her mother looks Tex up and down and mutters something that sounds like "Texas longhorn idiot," that makes Emma's face redden as she holds back a laugh.

"How the hell did you have time to make *four* fillings for

those choux? I could barely get the basics done." Reg flops down onto a plush sofa and kicks his legs onto the coffee table.

"She's just *that* good." Fallon hooks his arm around my shoulders, pulling me close to his chest. I let him, falling into the crook of his shoulder as my heart warms.

Emma's eyes flick from me to Fallon and back again. She arches a brow. "I thought Fallon was a fill-in contestant."

"He is." I frown. What's she getting at?

"Looks like you two know each other pretty well, though?" Her eyes flick to Fallon, across his chest. Her cheeks redden, and I recognize the look of a woman admiring a man's body.

Jealousy is a sharp, red-hot spear in my gut, and it takes all my self-control not to let it affect my face. I nod. "We worked together for a couple of years before Fallon left town at the beginning of the year."

Emma tucks a leg under her butt and tilts her head. "Why'd you leave? Seems like a great place to live."

Fallon clears his throat, shifting his body slightly away from me. "Had things to do."

Those words again. The inch of space between us. Will he never tell me where he was? Do I even want to know? Was it another ex-girlfriend? Something he wants to hide?

My brows lower, but now is not an appropriate time to ask Fallon about his six-month sabbatical. He's been so cagey about it, it makes every alarm in my head blare in warning. Would he leave again, even after what happened last night? Even if we did more?

Gus saunters into the room carrying the broom. He makes a big show of glancing up at the ceiling and checking the windows, then lets out a long sigh and wipes his forehead with the back of his hand. "Haven't felt safe in this house all week."

My lips twitch. "The crows weren't that bad, were they?"

A hiss sounds as Gus inhales sharply, clutching his hand to his chest. "You were *there*, Jen. You were attacked!"

Fallon picks up my wrist and shows the room the back of my hand. "She's got the battle scars to prove it."

Tugging my hand away, I let a laugh fall from my lips. "It wasn't that bad."

"Woman, you are crazy," Gus says, glancing out the window again. His knuckles are white around the broomstick, eyes scanning the skies outside.

I surprise myself by laughing.

Tex, who had disappeared for a few moments, opens a side door and walks in with a big bottle of Jack Daniels whiskey in each hand. He lifts them up. "Who else needs a stiff drink after that shitshow? And tomorrow is Sunday, so I'm not going to hear any excuses about resting for the competition."

Surprisingly, Carla is the first person to jump up. The old Latina woman grabs one of the bottles from his hands and cracks it open, beelining for the catering table full of mugs and glasses. "How many?" she asks, counting the number of people in the room.

Before I can protest, a Jack and Coke is thrust in my hands, and—oh, screw it. I haven't had a drink in a long time, and today was really hard. Would it be so bad to sit here and enjoy my fellow competitors' company?

Fallon's body is warm as he tightens his arm around my shoulders, the couch is plush beneath me, and the alcohol burns pleasantly as it slides down my throat. I find myself laughing as Tex and Reg tell us about the first time they made choux pastry —and nearly burned their bakery down.

When Carla tries to top up my glass for the third time, I cover it with my palm. "No more, Carla. *No más.*" I already feel tipsy enough that I'll probably have a headache tomorrow.

"Time for bed," Fallon says, plucking my glass from my hand and heaving me up from the couch. "This one needs her beauty sleep."

Carla clicks her tongue, but takes her seat at the impromptu poker table that Tex set up a few minutes ago. They're using pie weights as chips, and Carla's pile is already much, much larger than everyone else's. I watch her win a round handily, and I turn to smile at Fallon to see if he saw her clean up.

He isn't watching the poker game at all. He's staring at me, and the way he looks at me makes heat flame in the pit of my stomach.

"Let's go to bed," he says quietly, putting a large, warm hand over the small of my back. Saying our goodbyes, we head out the door and toward our guesthouse.

Fallon slips his hand into mine as the cool night air settles over my skin. I inhale the crisp, fresh scent of the outdoors and let a smile slip over my lips. The alcohol left a pleasant buzz in my body, a lightness I haven't felt in a long time.

"That was fun," I announce.

Fallon's hand tightens around mine. "Who are you and what have you done with Jen?"

I whirl toward him and scowl. "I'm not that bad."

"I've never, ever, in all the years I've known you, heard you describe social interaction as 'fun.'"

Biting my lip, I try—and fail—to hide my grin. "You may have a point. Mr. Richter. Maybe I'm finally coming out of my shell. Only took four decades."

Quick as a flash, Fallon nabs me around the waist and hauls me over his impossibly broad shoulder. I yelp, because approaching half a century in age means I prefer to have my feet firmly on the ground, thank you very much, but Fallon just bands his arm across my thighs and squeezes.

Breathless, I try to lift my head and catch myself staring at the way his butt really fills out his jeans. "What are you doing?"

"Having my way with you." He strides down the path toward the guesthouse, and I watch the competition barn pass us on my left.

"Fallon—" He hikes his shoulder and I land with a low *oof*. "Put me down! We're going to the same place! Carrying me doesn't even make sense. Logically—"

Fallon angles toward the barn and ducks around the back, hidden from view from the main house.

"Where are you going now?"

Large hands wrap around my waist and haul me back to the ground. Fallon's body is huge above me, all towering muscle and heated male energy. Hands still on my waist, he slowly walks me backward until my back hits the side of the barn.

"The guesthouse is too far," he says, placing a palm by my head as he crowds me against the wall.

Normally, I'd hate this. I like space and freedom and independence. But there's something about the sin promised in

Fallon's gaze, and the heat of his body pressed up against mine, and the sheer masculinity of his movements that makes me melt from the inside out.

"Too far for what?" I ask, voice breathy.

By way of answer, Fallon just ducks his head and kisses me. With one arm still planted next to my head, his other arm moves to band across my back, tugging me tight to his broad chest. I soften against him, melting into the warmth of his arms. When he feels it, he lets out a low groan that travels straight between my legs.

I've never thought of myself as a sexual person. I've craved intimacy, sure, and I've spent many lonely years pursuing my own passions, wondering if I was missing out by not chasing marriage and kids and a white picket fence. But my near celibacy wasn't always a choice. In my twenties, first dates were usually a disaster. My thirties were swamped with work, and then pastry school and all the grueling hours I spent trying to make it in this industry.

I didn't have time for men—or maybe they just didn't have time for me. I was too driven. I was "intimidating." I balked at the idea of giving up my career, my passions, for the sake of a relationship. Once every few years, I'd go on a date—maybe even sleep with a guy—and always ended up feeling emptier than I did before. They'd use my body, I'd use theirs, and the whole experience would leave me feeling cold.

So I ended up alone, thinking my lack of sexual appetite was innate. I wondered, in the deep recesses of my mind, if something was wrong with me. Maybe I was broken.

But now, I feel starved. My hips rock gently against Fallon, as if some deep instinct has started to awaken. I love the heat of his body, the way he presses me into the wall. I love the way my breasts feel somehow more sensitive, as if I'm craving him to touch them, kiss them. My hands shake as I slide them over his shoulders, tangling my fingers into the thick hair at the nape of his neck.

"Missed this," he groans. "Dreamed of kissing you for a year, Jen. Dreamed of having your arms around my neck like this."

He did?

Pulling back, Fallon's dark eyes look almost black when he meets my gaze. "I'm sorry about Amanda. Truly, Jen."

I shake my head. "It's fine."

"It's not. I invited her to town because I knew she could be the one to give you your recipe book, but I was too much of a coward to tell her that I cared about you. I thought if I ignored it, she'd back off. We broke up years ago, and I thought we were friends, you know? Cordial. I thought she'd give up."

"Stop, Fallon. I pushed you away. I chose the book over you and I didn't even try to talk to Amanda and see how she would react. I just turned my back on you. If you were a coward for not speaking to her, I was a double coward for not even entertaining the possibility."

His thumbs sweep over my cheeks. "Why would you? You've worked so hard to get where you are. You didn't owe me anything. You still don't."

"I didn't give you a chance." And it's one of the biggest regrets of my life. Me, who restarted my career in my thirties, who stepped into the unknown and put my entire life savings into Four Cups, who has jumped from one opportunity to the next—I didn't take a chance on Fallon.

Fallon's lids grow heavy as his eyes study my face. "What about now?" His thumb traces my cheekbone again, sending tiny thrills racing across my skin. "Would you give me a chance?"

I like this, I realize. A lot. I like having him near me, his arms around me. I like when he looks at me like I'm special—like he wouldn't change a thing about me.

"Now..." I say, stretching out the word, "I could be convinced to give you a shot."

His lush lips tip up, hand sliding to tangle at the back of my head. "That's all I ask."

Then Fallon kisses me, and it sets my body on fire. I arch into him, pressing my aching breasts into his chest, squeezing my thighs together as my hips roll of their own accord. Everything is tight, aching, in need of release. When Fallon slides his hand down my sides and back to grip my ass, I gasp against his lips. He touches me like he's dreamed of it, wants to memorize my body. Like he's starved for just a taste of me.

And that feeling is heady. Addictive.

For once, I don't feel awkward. I'm not in my head. My body is in the driver's seat. I move my hands to his waist, clawing his shirt up so I can put my hands on his body, feeling the warm, smooth skin, the writhing slabs of muscle beneath. He groans at my touch, sucking in a breath when I use my nails across his back.

Fallon's kiss turns frenzied. He nips at my bottom lip and

the small bite of pain electrifies me. My nails dig into his back, and then Fallon is palming my ass, groaning as his hands sweep over my hips, my waist, up to my breasts. He tears his mouth away from mine to kiss my breast through my top, biting at my nipple like a man crazed.

I'm no better. I'm losing my damn mind.

My hand slides to his front, the coarse line of hair diving down from his navel directing my touch downward. When I palm his hard cock over his jeans, Fallon bucks against me. He's *big*. I trace the outline of his shaft with my fingers, trembling at the thought of all that length inside me.

"Woman," he growls.

"What?" I lean my head against the barn, stroking him, eyes open but unseeing as my lungs heave with fresh night air.

"You're going to make me embarrass myself." He pulls his head back, eyes frenzied, just in time to see my grin. Like an animal, Fallon growls, then hooks his fingers into the waistband of my pants. I'm wearing loose drawstring pants that are comfortable to bake in. It doesn't take much for him to rip them down my narrow hips, and then his hand is cupping between my legs.

When he feels my heat, he drops his head to my shoulder with a pained groan. "Wanted to touch you for so long." His fingers slide over and back along the gusset of my panties, stoking me like a flame.

"Me too," I pant as I palm him, and I realize it's true. No matter how much I've tried to ignore it, deny it, pretend it's not true, the truth is I've wanted Fallon to take me like this for many, many months. I've wanted the tension between us to snap. I've wanted his hands to brand my body, for his teeth to rake across my skin.

So, when the heel of his hand grinds against my swollen bud, I widen my stance as I lean back against the wall. Fallon takes that as an invitation, and before I can react he rips my panties to my ankles. Then he's dropping to his knees in front of me, freeing one leg from my clothes and hooking my knee around his shoulder.

His hands slide over my thighs until his thumbs brush my center and I buck, whimpering. We're standing out in the open, where anyone could see us. I'm half-naked, and I don't even care. All I want is *more*. I want him to touch and stroke and taste. I want anything he'll give me.

"So pretty," he says, almost to himself. "Perfect."

I've never been perfect at anything. I would know—I've tried my whole life. But for the first time, his words fill me with a new feeling. Maybe, with Fallon, I'm *enough*.

His fingers slide over my slick folds and another groan rumbles through him. The cool air kisses between my legs and I tremble, feeling so exposed—and so cherished.

Then Fallon spreads me with his thumbs, and licks.

Fire spears my core as he runs that broad, flat tongue over every inch of my folds. When it hits my bud, I buck against his mouth, my hand falling to the back of his head. With a low, dangerous chuckle, Fallon spends time at the apex of my thighs, sucking that little bundle of nerves until I'm coming apart at the seams.

"Fallon," I pant. "Don't—I'm—"

Sentences fail me. All I can do is grind myself against his face as he groans with abject pleasure, one hand dropping from my thighs to palm at his own crotch. He presses the heel of his palm against his swollen shaft and the sight of his arousal nearly undoes me.

He *likes* this. He's enjoying the taste of me.

Then, as his tongue makes wicked circles around my bud, his finger probes my entrance. My legs tremble, and Fallon moves his hand from his shaft to my hip so he can pin me against the wall. His fingers and thumb span from my hip bones all the way to the small of my back, and I couldn't move even if I wanted to.

When I bow my back for more, aching to feel that finger inside me, Fallon obliges. For the first time in far, far too long, something other than my own hand penetrates me. And when Fallon groans and sucks my clitoris so hard I see stars, I clench around his finger, wishing it were something bigger.

Head leaning against the wall, back arching, I come like never before. I cry out, clenching my teeth to muffle the sound. My hands fly to his head and my hips grind against him.

"I feel it," he says, laving my center with his tongue. "You're clenching my finger so fucking hard, Jen—"

Another wave of orgasm washes over me, burning through my body and leaving me raw, panting. I finally have to shove Fallon's head away from my thighs when it becomes too much.

Sitting back on his haunches, Fallon looks up at me, lips glistening, with a look of pure male satisfaction. He slips my leg off his shoulder and stands, his hands never once leaving my body as they slide up from my legs to my waist. Then Fallon kisses me. Hard. I taste my orgasm on his lips and my knees go weak.

And that sexual appetite I thought never existed? It comes roaring back as I palm his steel-hard shaft through his pants, and say one word. "More."

THIS FEELS LIKE A DREAM. Ever since I started working at Four Cups nearly three years ago, I've wanted Jen. It only took me two failed dates with other women in the first couple of months after we met—well before we ever kissed or even really talked to each other—to realize that none of them were *her*.

No other woman can compare.

And now, after all that time, after thinking I'd lost her forever through my own cowardice and stupidity, she let me eat her till she came, and now she's begging for more.

I'm going to wake up at any minute. I know this, because it's happened before. I'll wake up with my aching cock grinding against the sheets and have to fuck my own fist to release some of the pressure.

But Jen's touch is soft as she slides her hands over my shoulders. Her lips are searching when she kisses me, little sips, tastes, bites.

It's *real*.

"I want you, Fallon."

The guesthouse is near, but even the short distance seems too far. I glance around quickly to make sure we're still alone, then cage her against the wall again. "I want you too, baby, but I didn't exactly imagine our first time together as me fucking you up against a barn."

Her kiss-bruised lips tilt into a new kind of smile. I've never seen this one before. It's wicked and wanting and so damn hot it makes me ache. My balls are heavy, my cock is swollen, and I feel like I'll die if I don't get inside her.

"What's wrong with a barn?" Jen asks innocently.

My hands clamp around her hips, fingers digging into her flesh as I try to regain some semblance of control. "I've never seen this side of you."

She lets out a huffing laugh. "Neither have I. Maybe you bring it out in me."

I groan. I hope so. Would I be so lucky as to be the man who makes her melt? Who makes her burn?

When her teasing hands slide back down to palm my crotch, I groan and let my lids slide shut. With deft fingers, she unbuttons my fly and slides the zipper down. Then her hand dives under my boxer-briefs and we both let out a slow breath as she wraps her fingers around my shaft. She strokes it, and I buck against her.

"Easy, woman," I growl. "I don't want to come yet."

Another stroke—another buck of my hips. Her fingers barely reach all the way around my shaft and when her eyes drop down to watch what she's doing, I can hardly contain my growl. Jen whimpers in response, and I realize she *likes* this. Reaching another hand into my pants, Jen cups my balls and all I can do is widen my stance and lean my hands against the wall, caging her in. She strokes, fondles, and brings me to a fever pitch.

"Jen," I pant, not knowing what to say.

I'm the luckiest fucking man in the world, because the woman of my dreams has her pants around her ankles, I can still taste her pleasure on my tongue, and she's stroking my cock like she wants to milk every drop of my seed from it.

Rolling my hips, I search for more friction. Using my hand, I claw her shirt up and hold it over her breasts, my gaze riveted on the movement of her fist over my shaft. The head of my cock slides against her stomach, the bead of moisture spreading over her skin. I watch it, fascinated, as my breath grows shorter.

A hand job up against the back of a barn is the hottest fucking thing I've ever done in my life.

Jen lets out the sexiest little moan as she strokes me, both hands working me so well I claw at the barn, my other hand twisted into the fabric of her shirt—

And a branch snaps in the forest behind us.

We both freeze. I press myself against Jen's body, wanting to hide her, protect her. My eyes scan the darkness, watching the gathering shadows beneath the trees, looking for...something.

"What was that?" Jen's hand is on my cock, but she isn't moving. It almost feels like she forgot she was holding me.

Just my luck. The best hand job of my life interrupted.

Throat scratchy, I hum. "Maybe an animal?"

Jen gives me a flat stare. "Sounded pretty loud for an animal." Her hand, I'll note, is still wrapped around my dick.

"The wind?" I say, not wanting to move.

She purses her lips, unimpressed. "Do you feel wind right now, Fallon?"

Damn her and her logical mind.

Disengaging her fingers from my cock—and breaking my heart in the process—Jen places her hands on my shoulders and peers at the forest behind me. I reach down and shove myself back in my pants. Then I reach down to pull her clothes up and turn around to shield her. All I can see are bushes, trees, shadows. The moon is a silver crescent in the sky, and the lights from the main house spill on the lawn. Every shadow looks like the shape of a man, like a monster creeping through the trees.

Ever since this competition started, I've felt like there was someone out there. And then there was Jen's rumpled underwear...

It's got to be the stress. The competition is already getting to us, and Slim has been looking for me. I'm worried and stressed out, that's all. Paranoid. I just spent six months visiting prison every week and it brought up old, forgotten memories from the years I spent inside.

"Let's go to the cabin," I say, hooking my hand around Jen's shoulders.

"You think someone's out here?" Tension lines her face as she scans the forest around us, eyes darting to every patch of creeping blackness.

The night seemed so warm and inviting a few minutes ago. Now a chill seeps into my skin.

"No," I say. "But I was serious about the barn thing."

Jen relaxes, nudging me with her shoulder. "But how am I supposed to get rid of all my uptightness if I don't do things like naughty outdoor sex?"

"That's easy," I say, leading her onto the path and into the trees that will take us to our guesthouse. "Just don't get rid of your uptightness."

She gives me a sideways stare, all sass, the sounds and shadows around us forgotten. "That's not a good solution, Fallon."

"Why would you want to change the way you are? You're perfect."

Her lips drop open, then she shakes her head. "No such thing."

"I beg to differ." I hold her close until we get to the guesthouse, then pull away to unlock the door. "I stared at perfection for a couple years before I worked up the courage to tell you how I felt."

Jen bites her lip, staring at me as if she can't decide whether or not I'm telling the truth. When I push open the door for her to step through, she relents and walks inside. Her eyes dart around the room, landing on her perfectly organized shelves.

She's thinking about the other day, when her clothes were mussed. When she thought someone had been in here.

Then Jen shakes her head and turns to me. "I'm getting paranoid. I need to get a grip." She puts a hand to her head. "Maybe I shouldn't have had all that whiskey."

"If you start blaming the whiskey for what we just did, I'm not going to be a very happy camper."

Her eyes glimmer, a smile tugging at her lips. "Temporary insanity."

"Well, let's work on making it permanent."

She laughs, then jerks her head to the bathroom. "I'm getting ready for bed."

When she comes out again, Jen crosses to the cot where I'm sitting and slides her hand through my hair. I pull her between my spread knees, wrapping my hands around her thighs.

"Bathroom's all yours," she says. "And when you're done, we can see if I'm still insane."

Grinning, I close my eyes as she gently massages my scalp. "God, I hope so."

Chuckling, Jen pulls away and I head to the bathroom. As I brush my teeth, I look at her electric toothbrush and perfectly organized toiletries, and I realize this feels better than anything else I've ever experienced. I like the intimacy of bedtime routines. I like that she teases me in that logical, rational way of hers. I like that we can share a space—and a bed.

If she's insane, then I should be committed, because I wouldn't change a damn thing about her.

But when I exit the bathroom, Jen is in bed, her eyes closed with her lashes fanned over her cheeks. My body still aches for her touch, but my heart softens at the sight of her steady breathing, her slight body curled up on top of the blankets.

Moving quietly, I check the door to make sure it's locked, then slide under the blankets, flipping them up on top of her. She turns into me in her sleep, clutching a fist against my chest as she lets out a little feminine whimper, nuzzling closer to my body.

I stare at the ceiling, fingers sifting through her hair, amazed and grateful for everything that's happened—and wondering when Jen will wake up and realize she's too good for me.

SIXTEEN
JEN

"JEN GOT SCREW-ED," Candice says in a singsong voice when I enter the library above Four Cups the next morning.

Simone glances up from her seat on one of the plush couches, interest sparking in her eyes. "Oh, she *did*. Look at that face!"

"What's wrong with my face?" I slap a palm to my cheek, frowning. "And no, I didn't."

It's not *totally* a lie. Somehow, I fell asleep last night before Fallon and I could take things any further. This morning, he told me he had to go meet with his sister to talk to her. We drove to town together and I made a beeline for my home away from home—the café.

"How was it? Does Fallon have a huge dong? I bet he's hung like a horse." Simone leans her elbows on her knees, rapt eyes glued on me.

"What—no—I don't know! It's not—" I splutter, cupping my

fingers around my cup of chai. "You guys are perverts. Has anyone ever told you that?"

Candice whistles. "Dorothy is going to *love* this."

"Dorothy won't know a damn thing!" I screech.

Simone throws her head back and laughs. "Now I see why everyone was enjoying watching me with Wes. This is a lot more fun when you're on the other side."

"Nothing is happening between me and Fallon," I lie.

"Uh-huh." Candice arches her brows. "Keep telling yourself that."

"Jen, your face is flushed and you have a bounce in your step. You've had at least one orgasm in the last twenty-four hours." Simone leans back and crosses her legs before spreading her palms. "It's science."

"What you just said has nothing to do with science," I deadpan. I let out a huff and shake my head. "We didn't have sex."

Candice sits on the arm of the couch nearest me. "But...?"

"Okay, yes! Fine. We fooled around last night."

Simone squeals. "Let me call Fiona, see if she can come up here. Allie can run the till for a few minutes."

"That's not necessary," I protest.

"Yeah, Fiona?" Simone speaks into her phone. "Jen's here. She hooked up with Fallon yesterday. Okay, yep. See you in a minute." She hangs up. "She's on her way up."

I groan, slouching down as I throw an arm over my face.

Heavy footsteps stomping up the stairs tell me Fiona's on her way up. She bursts through the door. "Tell. Me. *Everything!*"

With much coaxing, I give the girls the broad strokes (literally) of what happened last night. They squeal and giggle and even draw a few smiles from me.

"You guys are going to bang," Simone decrees. "Do it tonight!"

God, I want that.

But I suck in a breath and shake my head. "I don't know."

Candice reads my face. "How come?"

"Well..." Looking at their faces in turn, I voice my biggest fear. "What if he leaves? What if this is just some infatuation, and once we sleep together he decides he doesn't actually like me at all?" *What if I'm not enough for him?*

"He likes you," Fiona says decisively.

I chew my lip.

"Girl, that man is *obsessed* with you." Simone snorts, shaking her head. "The number of times he came in early and stayed late just to be in the same room as you should be a hint."

I frown. "Huh?"

"Oh yeah, I noticed that too," Candice cuts in. "I want all of our employees to be in love with Jen. Free overtime."

Fiona laughs, nodding, while I freeze in my seat.

"Fallon is not in love with me," I say.

"Okay, Jen." Candice pats my knee condescendingly. "Tell yourself whatever you need to get through the day."

"He's not!"

Simone arches her brow at me. "Isn't he? Then why did he come back?"

"He wanted...coffee," I answer lamely.

"Fallon came back from wherever he was because he

wanted *coffee*? As if there isn't a café on every corner of every city?" Fiona snorts. "Right."

"Okay. Well." I chew my lip. "You guys really think he came back for me?"

"The day he got here last week, he marched into Four Cups, looked at the kitchen, and asked where you were." Candice stares me down. "The only reason he was here was to see you. Not for a damn cup of coffee."

"That doesn't make sense," I mumble.

"Here's what's going to happen." Simone leans forward, catching my gaze. "You're going to meet up with him whenever he's done with his sister. You're going to strip naked. You're going to tell him to have his way with you. He's going to screw you till you can't think straight, and *definitely* till you can't walk straight. Then you'll live happily ever after."

Everyone hums in agreement.

She's insane. They all are.

"That is *not* going to happen."

"Sure it will!" Fiona says, clapping her hands. "You just need to break the seal."

"Break...the seal?"

"The tension is killing you both," Candice explains. "Same thing happened with me and Blake. You have to just"—she claps her hands—"get in there and get it done."

"Mm-hmm," Simone says with a nod. "Exactly."

"What if he doesn't even want to have sex with me?"

Simone rolls her eyes. "Girl, he pushed you up against a barn and ate you out. He wants to screw."

Despite myself, excitement curls deep in my stomach. He's

not the only one who wants that. I've been on edge since the start of this competition. Each of his casual touches throughout the days has wound me up tight. And ever since we kissed again? I can hardly think of anything else.

But—"It's a distraction. I need to focus on the competition."

"Jen, sex will *help* with the competition," Candice says with a gleam in her eyes. "It'll work off some nerves. Look at what happened this week! You kissed him last Sunday and immediately started performing better."

"Hmm." I bunch my lips to the side. "You're not wrong."

Simone grins. "Appealing to logic. Why didn't I think of that?"

"I bet if you sleep with Fallon, you'll win the whole damn competition," Fiona says. "It'll center you."

"Either that, or it'll distract me even more," I counter.

"You won the croquembouche round, didn't you?" Candice throws back. "That was after *one* kiss days prior. Imagine how good you'd be after full-on sex!"

Simone nods sagely. "It's science, Jen."

"I'm not convinced you actually know what science is." I try to keep my face stern, but a smile twitches over my lips despite myself.

"But you have to tell us everything," Candice says. "Or else we'll disown you."

I roll my eyes. "No you won't."

"Okay, true," Fiona says. "But we'll be sad."

"Very, very sad," Simone adds. "Devastated."

"You're all perverts, you know that?" I say with a huff, bringing my drink to my lips. "Every one of you."

. . .

WHEN FALLON and Nora get to Four Cups a couple of hours later, the sight of him makes me blush. His face is drawn, but it softens when he meets my gaze.

"Hey," I say.

"Hey, you."

"How was your talk?" I glance at Nora, who's ordering a coffee at the counter.

"It was fine," he says. "Wish she'd never met that asshole, but I've only got myself to blame."

Hmm. What does that mean? "You want to talk about it?"

His eyes search mine, a hand lifting up to tuck a strand of hair behind my ear. "Not really."

"Okay," I whisper. Glancing over my shoulder, I see the girls standing behind the counter, watching the two of us. I roll my eyes as they all give me surreptitious thumbs-ups and try to wave me out the door.

Subtle. Real subtle.

The door to the café opens, revealing Reg and Tex.

"So, this is it, huh?" Tex says, thumbs hooked into his belt loops, eyes scanning the space. "Blondie's domain."

Behind them, Emma and Carla glance around curiously. Tom and David, the Brits, aren't far behind. Within moments, the Four Cups Café is filled with contestants, and I find myself pushing tables together so we can all sit with each other. Fallon, as usual, slings his arm around the back of my chair.

Nora, Candice, Fiona, and Simone come join us, and pretty soon the coffee shop is abuzz with conversation and laughter.

When I lean into Fallon with a smile on my face, I catch him staring down at me.

"What?" I ask.

He keeps staring for a few long moments, as if he's trying to drink in the sight of me. "Nothing," he finally answers. "I just like looking at you."

Warmth snakes through my core, a blush sweeping over my cheeks. His hand moves from the chair to my shoulder, his thumb making slow circles over the nape of my neck. Shivers tumble through my veins at the gentle touch, and I know the girls are right.

It's time for me to break the seal. If I don't have sex with Fallon, I think I'm going to die.

SEVENTEEN
FALLON

AFTER A TENSE MORNING WITH NORA—WHERE we discussed her plans, how to keep her safe, and what to do about Slim—being close to Jen is a balm on my soul. She gives me those secret smiles and subtle touches, and it feels like a gift. She's giving me her attention, and I'm the luckiest man in the world.

So, when she tells me she's going to head back to the compound for an early dinner and a quiet evening to prepare for our challenge tomorrow, I stand up to follow.

As if there's anywhere else I'd rather be.

We took separate cars, so I follow Jen back to the competition grounds in my black Jeep, the windows rolled down so I can feel a breeze on my skin. I reflect on my morning.

When I got to Jen's apartment, Nora greeted me with a smile that looked brighter than it did when she first arrived. She agreed to go for a drive with me, and we ended up winding along a coastal road until we got to a windswept beach. Toes in the sand, Nora told me about Slim's first visit to her house.

"He showed up at eleven o'clock at night," she said, "and only left when I threatened to call the police. Slim said all he wanted was a conversation with you."

We looked out at the crashing waves for a few moments until I broke the silence. "I'm sorry."

"Stop," Nora told me. "You can't keep blaming yourself for what happened twenty-five years ago, Fallon."

"No? Who should I blame?"

"Come on." My sister snorted, eyes on the horizon. "It wasn't even your fault you went to prison. You had nothing to do with the robbery."

"The prosecutor disagreed."

"The prosecutor was an asshole who just wanted a conviction. He took advantage of you, made you plead guilty to something you didn't do."

I chewed my lip, dropping the subject. "What else did Slim say?"

Nora went over the other two times my ex-best-friend came to her house—and the calls she started getting on her phone—and my anger grew. How dare he show up at my sister's house? Threaten her? Scare her?

I left that life behind. The past should've stayed in the past.

Staring at the crashing waves, all I felt was bitterness. "I haven't spoken to Slim in years. Why now?"

Nora just sighed. "I don't know, Fallon."

Slim and I had been best friends, once upon a time. We met in detention after school, and Slim introduced me to a few of his friends. Older boys who had money and confidence and attitude.

I was sick of watching my mother struggle working three jobs. I was sick of living in poverty, of having holes in all my shoes and a stomach cramping with hunger. Sick of seeing my mother close to tears every time she looked at a photo of my father.

Slim Miller was cool, carefree, and he made me forget how hard things were at home.

By the time I was seventeen, I was hooked on the feeling of independence. I wanted an easy way out of the struggle I knew. We wanted to form a brotherhood, didn't care about laws or morals, just wanted to make money and be free.

I was young and angry at the hard knocks I'd gotten in life. The lifestyle Slim was offering seemed like my only way out.

My mother wasn't happy. When I barely scraped by to get my high school diploma, she gave me an ultimatum: get a job, or get out from under her roof.

It was an easy decision. I didn't even pack my clothes—they were rags anyway. I just walked out of the house with a chip on my shoulder and anger in my heart. I had a future, and it wasn't going to be working myself to the bone the way my mother had.

The tattoo spanning the width of my back was proof that I'd found a new family. Forever.

I was such a fucking dumb kid.

Nora nudged my shoulder with hers. "Hey. We all make mistakes, Fallon. You've more than made up for yours."

Even thinking about it now, as I lean my elbow on the window opening and feel the cool forest air whip around me, shame threatens to overwhelm me. I've spent two decades trying to distance myself from that life, but somehow, everything always comes full circle.

Nora told me she was thinking of staying in Heart's Cove. She'd bought a new SIM card for her phone, started looking for an apartment. "Reno was good, but I have no ties there anymore. I work from home; why not do it here?"

Why not, indeed.

When the farmhouse comes into view, I slow down and park a little way away from Jen. I watch her exit her car, the afternoon sun gleaming on her blond hair, her face turned up to catch the rays. She inhales deeply, then exhales as she turns to look my way.

Truly, that woman is beautiful.

I open my door and watch her walk with her precise, controlled gait to approach my car. She tilts her head to stare into my eyes, then nods to a nature trail. "You want to go for a walk with me?"

"Yeah," I answer, because it's the truth. There's nothing else I'd rather do.

Being around Jen makes me forget about my shame. I forget that I'm an ex-con. I forget about the past that has one hand gripped around my ankle, preventing me from walking away. When I'm with Jen, my head is quiet. My heart is full.

We walk on the pine needle-strewn path, wind rustling through the trees as squirrels and birds go about their business.

After a few moments, Jen takes a deep breath. "I think we should have sex."

My cock is immediately rock hard. Stumbling over my own feet, I choke on a cough, then quickly recover. "What?"

"I said, I think we should have sex." Her face is pointed straight ahead, her fists clenched.

"Um." I clear my throat, trying to ignore the tightness in my jeans. "I mean, I'm all for it, but I just—where is this coming from?"

"Well, I thought about it." She tucks a strand of hair behind her ear, and I see the tip of it is bright red. "I...enjoyed...what we did the other night. And it might help us figure out...where we stand. Plus, we did really well in the croquembouche challenge and the bite-sized challenges this week, and that was after just a kiss. Sex might help us win."

I don't know whether to laugh or feel insulted. For some reason, my shaft grows harder. "You want to have sex with me because you think it'll help us perform well in a baking competition?"

"Well, no." She bites her lip. "I mean—yes. I don't know."

"Usually, women have sex with me because they think I'm attractive."

"What women?" Her head whips toward me.

Surprise makes my brows arch. She seems almost...jealous. And that pleases me. Like the cat getting the cream, I let my lips curl into a satisfied smirk. "Don't worry, Jen. Right now, there's nobody that interests me but you."

"Right now," she repeats. Then, under her breath, she says, "This was a mistake."

Oh, no it wasn't.

Catching her hand, I tug on her arm until she whirls

around and crashes into my chest. She fits so perfectly it makes my heart sing. I band my arm around her back and palm that beautiful ass of hers, pulling her tight so she can feel the effect she has on me. "'Mistake' is not the word I'd use to describe us."

Her eyes darken. Unable to resist, I duck my head and take her lips between my own. Jen's answering moan is like sustenance to me, and I swallow it down like a man starved. With one hand palming her ass, I use the other to angle her head so I can deepen the kiss. My cock is so hard it hurts, already beading at the tip and moistening my underwear.

At this point, I've craved Jen for so long that if she wants to use me to win this competition, I'll take whatever I can get. If she thinks sex is her ticket to the grand prize, I'm more than happy to oblige.

Especially when she softens in my arms like that, clinging to my shoulders like her legs can no longer support her weight.

"Fallon," Jen whispers, her hands shoved into my hair.

I nip her earlobe, inhaling the scent of her hair. "What?"

With great effort, Jen pulls away from me. She puts a hand to her forehead and lets out a huff. "I haven't done this in a while."

My hand squeezes her ass as I smile down at her. "So far, you're doing great."

Her cheeks are tinged a pretty shade of pink, lips kiss-bruised and shining. Taking my hand from her ass, I move to rub my thumb over her lower lip. I groan when she opens her mouth and lets her tongue dart out to lick the tip.

I want this woman forever. Even if I don't deserve her. Even if she's in a different league. I want her to be mine until the day I die.

But if she just wants to use me until the end of the competition, that'll have to be enough. Grabbing her around the waist, I lift her up so she wraps her legs around my hips.

"What are you doing?" She clings to me, nails digging into my shoulders.

I grin, loving the little points of pain her fingers give me. "I know a place near here."

She blinks. "I can walk, you know."

"When I'm done with you, woman, I'm not sure you'll be able to."

A sharp intake of breath. A squeeze of her legs around my hips. Then I'm carrying her down the path, angling down an overgrown animal trail. I've lived in Heart's Cove for years, and I know every inch of the surrounding land. When the trees open up to a sun-drenched clearing, Jen sucks in a breath. I let her slide down my front and turn in my arms as she takes in the tall grass, the patches of flowers, the fresh scent of the clean forest air.

Then she arches a brow at me. "You won't do me up against a barn, but you'll do me here?"

"The barn can be round two," I growl, crowding my body into hers.

Jen backs up, lips twitching as her eyes flash. Her hands move to my biceps, and I love the soft, gentle touch of her skin against mine. Then I'm picking her up again and laying her down in the center of the clearing. Draping my body over hers, I look down at her eyes and try to memorize this moment.

Finally, *finally*, I'll get to have Jen—at least until the end of the competition.

EIGHTEEN
JEN

FALLON'S LOOKING at me in a way that makes my heart thump. Am I making a mistake? I'm listening to my crackpot friends and sleeping with a man who's been the object of my affection for more than a year. He already left once without looking back—what if he does it again?

What if he *is* a distraction, and sleeping with him turns out to be a mistake? I could lose this whole competition.

But when his lips descend on mine, all thoughts flee from my mind. I lift my knee so he's cradled between my hips, loving the weight of him against me. He ducks his head and puts his mouth on my breast over my clothes, and I can't help but arch my back into it. He nips at my stiffening peaks, sucking me through the material until I'm whimpering.

"I love the sounds you make," he says, lips moving over the damp fabric. "Love that you make them for me." His mouth moves to my ear, hot breath sending shivers over my skin.

"Want you to be moaning for me, Jen. I want you to scream my name when you come."

When his hand moves down to cup me over my jeans, I whimper. "Fallon."

"Good." He gives me a squeeze, sending a jolt of pleasure through me. I gasp, eyes flying open to find him staring at me with that inscrutable expression. His lips curl. "You're so pretty when you're turned on."

Shifting his weight, he leans on his elbow and keeps his eyes on mine. His other hand works the button of my jeans open, slipping underneath my panties. His hand is big and hot and it covers me completely. My mouth drops open, drawing Fallon's gaze to my lips.

His fingers start a slow torture, sliding from my bud down to where I'm wettest, pulling a groan from his throat. "Wet for me already," Fallon rasps. He dips his finger inside me and makes another harsh male noise. "Can't wait to have my cock in there."

His words are doing almost as much for me as his hand is. The grass is soft beneath me, the sky blue above. I smell nothing but fresh, clean air, Fallon, and my own arousal. I want him so badly everything aches. My heart thumps when I think of that big, beautiful cock sliding in and out of me—just like his finger is doing right now. He fits another digit inside me, using his thumb to tease my bud.

This is happening too fast. No—too slow. I can't think. Can't process this.

My hips roll toward him of their own volition, causing Fallon to smile. "You are so fucking hot when you start losing control, Jen."

"I'm not losing control." I gasp when he pumps his fingers into me, pleasure arcing between my thighs.

"No?" Fallon grins, eyes still on mine. "I must not be doing my job, then."

His hand slides out from my panties and I feel so unbearably empty without his fingers inside me. Hooking his hands into my waistband, Fallon rips my pants and underwear off my legs in one swift movement. Then he's between my legs, his lips trailing kisses from one hip to the other as I writhe beneath him. Those dextrous fingers tease my folds again, circling my clitoris before diving back inside me—just as Fallon puts his lips on my bud.

When he sucks the bundle of nerves and flicks his tongue over it, his fingers delving deep inside me, an orgasm crashes into me. My back bows as my lips fall open with a cry, Fallon's name on my tongue. My fingers dig into the dirt at my sides, nails embedded in the earth. He growls in satisfaction, not stopping his ministrations until I push his head away, dazed and limp.

Fallon kneels between my legs, his eyes on my center. He licks his lips, tasting me again with a satisfied groan. "You taste so good I could do that every day and never get sick of it."

"Sounds good to me," I say on a sigh.

Fallon's lips curl, and then he's reaching into his pocket. From his wallet, he pulls out a condom, eyes flicking to mine as if to ask if I still want this.

A thousand thoughts fill my head—about vulnerability, distractions, winning, succeeding—but I can't quite catch the threads to think logically. All I know is whips of pleasure are still lashing my body, and Fallon's eyes are promising more.

So after what he just did to me? *Hell yes,* I still want this.

When I nod, reaching for his belt, Fallon closes his eyes with a groan. Then he's helping me, pushing his pants down to mid-thigh so his pulsing erection can spring free.

My heart bangs against my ribs when I'm reminded of his size. I suck in a breath, smelling fresh grass and pine and Fallon. Sitting up, I wrap my hand around his shaft and pump, watching with fascination as moisture beads at the tip.

"Jen." Fallon's watching me through half-lidded eyes, lips parted and still glistening from my orgasm. He uses one of his broad hands to push my chest back down so I'm nestled in the soft grass. "Spread open for me, kitten."

Blushing, I let my knees fall open completely. Fallon groans, watching me with such fierce possession that I might come just from him looking at me. Eyes still on me, he rips the condom packet open and rolls the latex over his erection, holding the condom at the base for a moment, as if he's trying to stop himself from spilling already.

Gaze flicking up to mine, Fallon just shakes his head. "You're so fucking perfect, Jen." His hand smooths over my thigh with such gentle reverence that—for what feels like the first time in my life—I actually believe him.

Then he's using those strong hands to tug me forward and position me where he wants me. The head of his cock is nudging against my opening, and my heart is in my throat.

This is happening. After everything, after all the heartache and rejection and hard decisions, Fallon and I somehow ended up together here.

I wonder if it was inevitable. We've circled around each other for so long, gotten to know each other's quirks and moods through work, shared blazing kisses and lots of hurt. But he came back—and it wasn't because he wanted coffee from Four Cups.

When Fallon pushes my shirt up so he can sweep his broad palm over my stomach, memorizing my curves and taking in the sight of my half-clothed body, a single, clear thought clangs through me:

We belong together.

Then, Fallon's eyes dip between my legs, and he enters me with a slow, unyielding thrust. Gasping at the stretch, I arch my back, body locking up until Fallon ducks his head down to my breast, nudging my bra aside so he can lave my nipple with his tongue. His hand dives between us so he can tease my bud, and pleasure starts to mount inside me. My body goes soft, hips rolling of their own accord, hands clawing at his hair, his shoulders, his shirt.

When I try to pull his shirt off, Fallon growls, thrusting inside me hard. I moan, eyes rolling back. Fallon uses my distraction to pin my wrists above my head, his huge body covering mine as he drives inside me to the hilt. I meet him thrust for thrust, breathless.

I've wasted my entire life thinking sex wasn't for me. I've settled for so much less than I could have—and this is proof. Pleasure gushes through my veins, and all I can do is say

Fallon's name over and over and over. He growls with pleasure at the sound of it.

"Told you you'd be screaming my name." He thrusts hard as if to underscore the point.

"Arrogant jackass," I pant, back arching.

Shifting both my wrists to one hand, Fallon uses the other to lift my knee for better access. I'm totally under his control, at his mercy.

And I love it.

The grip I usually keep on myself slips, and my mind is completely, gloriously quiet. There's no worry that I'm doing anything wrong. No thought about consequences. No analyzing the situation and wondering if I'll regret it.

All I feel is Fallon's hard shaft driving inside me, his hands branding me, his beard rasping against my skin when he angles his head to kiss the side of my neck.

"So tight and wet," he pants. "You feel better than I imagined," he says, his voice a low growl. "So much fucking better, and I was imagining heaven."

He imagined what I'd feel like. That thought alone nearly sends me over the edge.

"So do you," I manage.

His eyes flash, hips slowing to a maddening, teasing rhythm. "You fantasized about me?"

I can't lie. "Ever since we kissed."

A triumphant look flashes in his eyes. He releases my wrists, moving his hand to my cheek. When Fallon kisses me this time, I wrap my arms and legs around his hips, needing every part of me to be touching every part of him. Arching my hips up to meet his, I let my head fall back as pleasure mounts.

And when Fallon changes the angle so he's grinding against my clitoris, I don't stand a chance. The best orgasm of my life rocks through me, making my back bow. I scream so loud birds flap out of trees around us. Fallon's answering growl of satisfaction makes another wave of pleasure wash over me.

"You were made for me, Jen," he says, eyes intent.

Boneless, all I can do is nod.

"You understand?" He thrusts inside me, his shaft getting impossibly bigger, harder.

"Yes," I pant, because that's exactly how I feel. I've never felt like this before. So connected to someone else. So thoroughly sated.

"You're my woman," he growls.

"I'm your woman," I repeat, and the words sound like a vow.

Fallon's eyes darken when I speak—then, with a yell, he throws his head back and pulses inside me.

For the first time in my life, I wish there was no barrier between us. I wish I could feel him inside me, skin to skin.

And when he drapes his body over mine, cock still pulsing inside me as his heart thumps against mine, I close my eyes and come back down to earth.

Fallon shifts his weight, keeping himself inside me as he props his head on his elbow. His eyes gleam with humor when he says, "Now, Ms. Newbank. In your opinion, was that good enough to win the competition?"

I grin. "I don't know. We might have to do it again just to be sure."

The sun warms my skin as Fallon smiles down at me, and for a perfect, beautiful moment, I feel utterly happy.

NINETEEN
JEN

MY ENTIRE BUTT is covered in grass stains and my shirt is ruined. As I check the shower temperature and discard my clothing, I can't quite bring myself to care. That light, airy feeling in my bones is keeping me floating above the surface of the earth, and my mind is blissfully quiet. I soap myself up and wash the green streaks from my skin. Blades of grass fall from my hair and I smile at the sight of them rushing toward the drain.

That was not at all what I expected, but it was amazing. I've never felt so sexy, so desired. I've never had my mind go so beautifully blank while I had sex. I wasn't worried about how I looked or what noises I was making. I wasn't worried that Fallon wasn't enjoying himself.

It made me realize that all my other sexual experiences were pale imitations of the real thing.

And I get to do it again and again—at least for the next two weeks.

When I exit the bathroom, I find Fallon already in bed. He turns onto his side and grins at me, jerking his head to the space beside him. Already, sleeping with him feels natural. I can hardly remember what it felt like to go to bed alone.

THE TWO OF US DO, in fact, end up winning the next elimination challenge. It's a chocolate challenge, and the few hours we spend on set are full of laughter and ease. I end up tempering chocolate and enduring endless teasing from him— but loving every second of it. I haven't had that much fun baking in a long, long time. Not since before I started working on the book.

Fallon's jaw is set with determination as he places a chocolate dome over a delicate caramel confection, and he catches me staring with a twinkle in his eyes. "Can't get enough, can you?"

I purse my lips. "Just making sure you're doing it right."

Fallon leans in close to my ear and says, "Liar."

The rest of the challenge is a blur. All I can think about is making the best chocolate dessert I can, then getting alone with Fallon as soon as possible.

Tori and Hank, the mother-son duo from New York City, get eliminated, and again I feel sad for them. I realize I'm making friends here—and for the first time in my life, it's easy.

When we get back to the cabin that night, Fallon wraps his arms around me and kisses me tenderly. "Maybe there's something to your sex-our-way-to-victory strategy."

"I told you the logic was sound," I inform him.

"We should keep testing the theory." He yanks me by the waistband of my pants, hands already clawing at my clothes. It only takes a few moments for Fallon to get me naked, on my back, and with his tongue between my legs. He wasn't kidding when he said he'd be happy to do that every day. But when I try to grab his shirt, he again pushes my hands away, moving to kneel between my legs.

"I want to feel your skin against mine," I say as he spreads my knees open and fits himself between them.

"My shirt stays on," Fallon says in a voice that brooks no argument. Before I can ask him about it, though, he's inside me and all thought flees from my head.

"Okay," I manage to gasp.

Fallon just gives me that heart-stopping grin and pistons into me again.

Shirt stays on. Got it.

From there, we fall into a hectic routine. Sex in the morning when we wake, showers, and full days of filming. If we don't come in first place, we're at least in the middle of the pack. I don't have to do any more sudden-death challenges, thank goodness. Most evenings, Fallon takes my hand and puts out a plate of nuts and seeds "for our crow overlords." I'm pretty sure he just does it to see me roll my eyes and break down laughing, because he always searches my face with a gleam in his eyes until I start giggling.

I'm no longer jumpy around birds. Every time I see a black shape in the sky or on a roof eave, I just smile—then I wonder if that was Fallon's plan all along.

Fallon makes good on his promise to pleasure me with his mouth every single day, always pushing my hands away when I try to undress him, then distracting me with mind-bending orgasms.

The rest of Week Three brings us three bite-sized challenges and one more elimination challenge. We do bite-sized challenges that involve macarons, gingerbread construction, and ice-cream churning. I'm in a daze of baking and happiness, my own little bubble with Fallon. The only time he seems annoyed is when Bernard Franco compliments my skills, which happens after nearly every challenge.

I'd ask him about it, but he usually just shakes his head and clears the annoyance from his expression before I get the chance.

For the elimination challenge, we make a three-tiered wedding cake and are rewarded with first place. I glance up at the rafters to see Simone hanging over the rail, yelling, "Aren't you glad you had all that practice?"

They all laugh triumphantly when I crack a grin. Yes, I had practice baking all their wedding cakes—and they'll never know how much I enjoyed it, even if I did complain at the time.

Tom and David are eliminated when they underbake their cakes and fail to complete all the decorations they'd planned. With just Fallon and me, Carla and Emma, and Tex and Reg left, the six of us will compete next week for the title—and the hundred-thousand-dollar prize. I can hardly believe it.

Okay, that's a lie. I *can* believe it. I planned for it. Like I said —I like to win.

· · ·

ON SATURDAY NIGHT, I find myself in the main farmhouse with all the competitors—those who have already been eliminated as well as those who haven't. It's a big group, and I normally would feel uncomfortable in this type of situation, but I find I'm enjoying myself. We have a few drinks with everyone, then head back to our cabin.

That night, most of the way through the competition—and most of the way through our time together—I end up pushing Fallon to his back and kneeling between his legs. When I have my first taste of him, Fallon looks at me like I'm the most precious being in the world. He cups the back of my head, pushing my hair out of the way so he can watch while I pleasure him.

Kissing him like this, I feel powerful and confident and so damn sexy. It's a heady feeling, one I'm not used to. But he tastes so good, and I'm already lost in him. I could do this daily too, I realize—and not just for another two weeks. I'd be with Fallon forever if he wanted me.

When Fallon throbs against my tongue and calls out my name, I feel so connected to him that I wonder how the hell it took so long for us to get here. Grabbing me by the armpits, Fallon pulls me up and wraps me in trembling arms, holding me tight to his body like he never wants to let me go.

The feeling is mutual.

THAT SUNDAY, the two of us head to town to meet up with our family and friends. I can't help placing my hand on Fallon's thigh as he drives, my head leaning back on the headrest as a smile tugs at my lips.

"Almost there," Fallon says with a grin. "Next week you get your hundred grand."

"Fifty," I correct. "We get fifty each."

Fallon clears his throat. "Mm," he hums.

I stare at the greenery outside the window, loving this part of the world in the summer. Maybe I should spend more time outside the kitchen when the competition is over. My time with Fallon in the clearing opened up a whole new world of possibilities for outdoor activities...

When we get to the Four Cups Café, I see a motorcycle out front. Trina and her boyfriend, Mac, must be back from their trip along Route 66. We stop out front and Fallon tells me he's going to go find his sister.

Slipping out of the car, I turn to say goodbye to him when a high-pitched scream pierces my eardrums.

"There she is!" Candice squeals from the café doorway. "In the flesh."

Instead of the *Heart's Cove Hotties* T-shirt the staff usually wears, she's got on the same tee her mother had been wearing a few weeks ago—one with a huge image of my face. Above it are the bedazzled words, *Heart's Cove's Hottest Baker.*

Behind Candice, Simone, Fiona, Trina, all the kids—Clancy, Allie, and Trina's two, Toby and Katie—crowd in. They're all wearing shirts with my face on them.

"Um..."

When I glance through the car at Fallon, the tension around his eyes has melted. He's grinning again. "Enjoy, Jen."

"I might call you sooner rather than later."

He chuckles. "I look forward to it."

Closing the door, I turn back to the crowd and am surprised to find my own lips tugging. Maybe all my time making friends and baking over the last three weeks has loosened something tight in my chest.

Candice throws herself into my arms for a tight hug. "We're so proud of you, honey. You're going to kill it next week. They just released the first bite-sized challenge online! We've watched it twice already."

Simone shoulders her way closer. "Forget the competition. Tell us about Fallon!"

My face goes bright red, and Simone just squeals in excitement.

Glancing at Trina, I jerk my head. "How was your trip?"

"Magical." Her eyes gleam. "It's good to be home, though."

As the girls drag me inside, I have to say I feel the same way. The competition is fun and intense, but being back in the café reminds me why I'm trying to win. Because I love these people, and I love this place, and I've worked hard to make something special here.

Now, the only thing that's missing is Fallon by my side.

TWENTY
TRINA

THE FOUR CUPS Café is pandemonium, as usual. Once I fight my way to Jen and manage to give her a quick squeeze on the elbow—she doesn't like hugs—I make my way back to the table near the back. My kids are happy to be here, busy with their grandmother, and I sink into a chair next to Iliana.

"Didn't think I'd see you here when I rode up this morning." I smile, sipping my coffee. My eyes drift to the other side of the café, where Mac is leaning against the counter looking good enough to eat. He's smiling at something Fiona's husband, Grant, is saying, the two of them looking far too sexy to be standing in a quirky café.

"And I didn't think I'd see you riding on the back of a motorcycle," Iliana quips, brow arched. She jerks her head to my man. "He's pretty easy on the eyes."

A flush rises up my neck. I nod. "Tell me about it."

"Naughty Trina, hooking up with her daughter's teacher." Iliana clicks her tongue. "You've certainly changed."

"Oh, shush." I hide a laugh behind my mug, then go on the offensive. "What about you? Why are you popping up in this small town after globetrotting for so long?"

Iliana's face grows shuttered as her eyes slide to the side. Then, as if nothing happened, she just squares her shoulders and paints a smile on her face. "It was time to come home."

She's hiding something, but I'm not sure what. Before I can ask her about it, my daughter, Katie, jumps off her chair. She sprints to Mac and thrusts a piece of paper in his hands. "I made this for you!"

Mac takes the paper, crouching down next to Katie. I love that he does that. He never speaks to my kids from his full height. Whenever he has to talk to them, he'll sit or kneel or crouch so they're eye-to-eye. He looks at the drawing Katie gave him as his eyes crinkle. "It's beautiful, Katie."

"That's you." Katie points. "You're on your motorcycle with Mommy. And that's me and Toby waving with Nana. Can I ride your motorcycle, Mr. Blair—um, I mean, Mac?"

Mac glances at me, a smile tugging his lips. "Not for a few years, kiddo. Your mom might kill me if I did."

"She wouldn't do that. She loves you!"

I choke on my coffee. It's true, but I didn't think Katie would realize it!

"All the more reason to keep her happy." Mac smiles, and Katie launches herself into his arms for a hug. I can't believe I was worried about my kids accepting Mac into the family. They already can't live without him.

When we were on our two-week vacation together, Mac told me he wanted to move in together. He said he'd wait as long as it took, but he wanted to be a family.

Seeing Katie hugging him makes my heart swell so much I can hardly breathe. Maybe I won't have to wait so long, after all.

"Trust Trina to land on her feet," Iliana says, snorting. She pops a brow. "Divorce looks good on you."

"It isn't the divorce that looks good on me," I answer. "It's Mac."

"Damn right," Mac says from behind me, his sinful hands sliding over my shoulders.

Flushing, I tilt my head when Mac bends down to kiss my neck.

Iliana gives me a smile that looks tinged with...sadness.

Before I can ask her about it, the café door opens, and another wave of cheers and hellos rings out. Fallon walks in with a woman that looks a lot like him, eyes immediately searching and landing on Jen.

I watch Jen blush and bite her lip, and my brows inch up.

So they finally decided to give in to temptation. About time.

The woman with him walks over to our table. "Hi, Iliana." She glances at me. "Hey. I'm Nora, Fallon's sister."

I smile. "Nice to meet you."

Iliana pulls a chair out for her, then points to me and Mac. "That's Trina and Mac." She waggles her finger between us. "They're in love. It's gross."

Nora laughs. "Between them and my brother and Jen, I can't get away from it."

My mother straightens up from the kids' table and saunters

over to the new arrivals. "Fallon Richter! Get over here and give an old woman a hug."

Fallon's lips curl, and he does as my mother says. She squeezes his arms and stares into his face. "You going to stick around this time?"

He rears back. "What's that supposed to mean?"

"No more leaving without a word. Got it?"

"Mom, give the man a break," I interject. "He doesn't need to stay in Heart's Cove."

"Why the hell not?" Lottie plants her hands on her hips, leveling me with a stare. "Why would he give up the affection of a woman like Jen—for what? What could possibly be better?"

I know Fallon and Jen have a tangled history, so I just shrug and let my mother natter on.

Fallon cuts in smoothly, putting his arm around her shoulders to quiet her down. "What I want to know," he says, "is why Jen is the only one who gets her face on a T-shirt. What am I? Chopped liver?"

"We were worried it would cause too much involuntary female fainting if your face was all over the place," Lottie says, smooth as anything. "Wearing your face on a shirt would be a public health risk."

Fallon's lips twitch. His eyes land on his sister, and Nora just waves him away. Then, like a magnet, I watch him drift toward Jen. He slides his hand over her lower back and leans in to say something in her ear, which makes her blush all the way to the tips of her ears.

"They're cute together," Iliana says with a sigh. "Can no one be a miserable spinster with me?"

Nora lifts her palm. "I volunteer as tribute."

Iliana grins. "Thank goodness. I can't stand this much lovey-dovey energy."

Mac squeezes my shoulders while I tilt my head.

"You used to love all things lovey-dovey," I tell her. "What happened?"

Iliana shrugs. "Life happened."

A banging starts, and the hum of conversation dies. My sister Candice is holding a pot and a wooden spoon, whacking the two together as she climbs up on top of a table. "Attention, attention!"

"Aunt Candice, why are you standing on a table?" Katie squeals, immediately trying to climb up with her. Mac leaves my side and nabs my daughter around the waist, throwing her over his shoulder as she squeals, delighted.

Candice clears her throat. "Next week, our very own Jen Newbank and Fallon Richter will compete for the title in the *Boss Baker* competition."

Cheers sound in the café.

Candice continues: "I'd like to announce an official event on the day of the final competition. We'll start here and head over to the live filming together. There will be T-shirts and signs to be decorated for the finale. I want every single one of you over there cheering them on!"

I can't help but grin. Jen probably hates this—but when I glance over at her, she's just tucked up against Fallon's side, listening to him saying something else in her ear.

"Home court advantage, huh," a booming voice from the door calls out. "Y'all are playing dirty."

A man with a cowboy hat and a huge belt buckle is standing next to another equally large cowboy-looking man.

"You scared, Tex?" Jen calls out, and my jaw nearly drops.

Jen does not banter with people. She doesn't tease. It takes her about a decade to warm up to new arrivals—yet here she is, laughing at the sight of the two of them.

Tex snorts. "Only thing I'm scared of is how all these people will react when we beat your ass."

A low hum courses through the café—until Jen juts out her chin. "Bring it, Tex." Her smile is bright, and Fallon squeezes her shoulders with a grin of his own.

Iliana leans across the table. "Jen seems different. More confident."

I look at the baker as she moves to greet the two other competitors, and I nod. "She's finally growing into herself."

"Took long enough," Iliana says, and all I can do is hum in agreement.

Took me a while, too, but it feels damn good to be comfortable in my own skin again.

WHEN I LEAVE Four Cups and head back toward the hotel, I let out a sigh. It feels strange to be here. Candice moved here years ago with her husband before he died, and it seems like the whole family has been drawn to the place like magnets.

Even me, perpetually looking forward to my next trip, has been dragged back to this small town.

I have a reason, though. A secret that will come out sooner rather than later—and I'm so not prepared for the consequences.

Veering off course, I cross the street and enter the bookstore. Agnes is a grumpy old lady, but I have a bit of a soft spot for her. I don't think she's actually all that negative. I think she's a realist.

But Agnes isn't behind the counter. Instead, her grandson Rudy is sitting behind the till, head bent over a book. He's sitting on a stool with his knees spread wide, one hand wrapped around the seat in between his legs. A chunk of unruly blond hair falls over his brow.

I don't know if it's the light, or my vulnerable state, or the fact that everyone in this town seems to be in love, but I stop in my tracks and stare.

Rudy looks *good*.

But he's young, isn't he? I'll be forty in six weeks, and I'm sure Rudy is in his early-to-mid thirties. What's that stupid rule again—half your age plus seven? Does that apply to women?

I shake my head. Why am I even thinking about that? I can't date anyone right now!

Then Rudy lifts his gaze to mine, his blue eyes so piercing they strike me mute. Smiling genially, he slides off his stool. "Hi. Iliana, right? We met at Thanksgiving a few years ago."

"I remember," I mumble. "You were dating my sister."

Candice and Rudy had a flirtation going on. I encouraged her to tap that because, well, look at the guy!

But Rudy just laughs. "I wouldn't go that far. We had one date and one kiss. Schoolyard stuff." He tilts his head as he holds my gaze, his eyes dropping to my lips.

Heat lashes across my middle, and when our eyes meet again his expression has changed. The air between us grows charged.

I clear my throat and turn to one of the stacks of books to hide the flush in my cheeks. "You can call me Lily, by the way. Most people do."

"Lily," he says slowly, and a thrill pierces my stomach. "Cute nickname." Did his voice just get lower? Why does that make my secret place clench?

Don't think about your secret place.

"Trina couldn't say Iliana, so she'd call me Lily when she was a toddler. It stuck." Nice and neutral topic—childhood nicknames. Growing up. Totally non-sexual and won't make me want to jump over that counter and throw myself at Rudy.

I glance at him and immediately regret it. Those blue eyes are intent on mine, pinning me to the spot. He moves slowly, leaning against the counter. His shirt drags across his chest, palm moving up to scrub the stubble lining his strong jaw.

I fucking *love* stubble.

We stare at each other for a few long moments until I drag my eyes back to the table full of books in front of me.

"Can I help you find something?"

Well, I came in here to see what kind of smutty romances Agnes had, but maybe I would be better off downloading an eBook. The thought of buying a stack of sex-filled stories—of having Rudy's broad hands all over the books while he rings them up—is too much for me.

"How about a book that will make me forget about the world around me?" And all the problems I'm dragging around like an overstuffed suitcase.

Rudy's full lips twitch and he moves from behind the counter. "You don't work part-time in your grandmother's bookstore from the time you're thirteen to thirty-four without a few good recs. Follow me. I've got a few books I think you'll like."

He's thirty-four. That's only six years younger than me. That isn't too scandalous...is it?

As soon as the thought pops into my head, I mentally smack myself across the face.

Repeat after me: Now. Is. Not. The. Time.

Men do not exist for me right now. Not for a long, long time. Maybe ever.

Sleeping with Agnes's grandson would be an epically bad idea. Even by my standards.

I still end up buying every book he thrusts into my arms, though. And I do promise to come back and tell him what I think of them.

TWENTY-TWO

FALLON

WITH ONLY A FEW days remaining in the competition, dread knots in my stomach. Once this is over, I'm not sure Jen will want to continue. Didn't she say the whole reason we were sleeping together was to win the title?

What happens after?

She'll realize she's way too good for me, and I'll be left on my own again.

But after a day in town watching Jen bloom around all the people who love her most, I can't help but wrap my arms around her and press my lips to hers. As evening falls all around the guesthouse, we drift toward each other, clothes falling away from our bodies.

Jen doesn't tug at my shirt, but I wonder if I should remove it. She might ask me about the tattoo, though, and I'm not ready to tell her about my greatest shame. I only have a week left in this little bubble. I don't want to ruin it with stories of prison.

I'm not ready to see the look on her face when she realizes I'm not the man she thought I was. So, instead, I lay her down on her back and I eat the best dessert of all.

Only when she's done writhing and calling my name do I move between her legs and give in to the pulsing of my cock. Elbows near her shoulders, I cup her head and kiss her as we make love slowly, intensely, as if nothing else exists. She's gorgeous and undone underneath me, and for a few more perfect days, I can pretend that she's mine alone.

When I feel her contracting around me, I can hardly hold back, but I force myself to watch, to memorize every moment of this. It might be one of my last orgasms with her—I want to be able to remember it.

She falls asleep tucked up against me, her hand curled into my shirt. Just before her breath evens out, Jen mumbles, "I always knew we belonged together."

My chest clenches. I'm not sure she'll think that when she finds out about my past.

It takes a long time for me to fall asleep and when I do, I dream of her.

THE FINAL ELIMINATION challenge between our team, Tex and Reg, and Carla and Emma is a pie-baking extraordinaire. We need to make six pies—three fruit pies and three custard pies—and decorate them with as much detail as possible.

Jen has her game face on, and she's never looked better. Hair pulled back in a tight bun, white chef's jacket on, and hands clenched behind her back, she looks ready for anything.

I'm so damn proud to be by her side.

In the rafters, all of Heart's Cove is here—with bells on. I spy my sister with a blinding smile on her face right beside Dorothy, Margaret, Lottie, and Agnes. The Four Cups girls are all there, along with Trina and Iliana—and all their men.

I can't believe I walked away from this place. The years I spent in Heart's Cove were the best of my life...but was I just running from my past? I can't stay here knowing Slim is looking for me—knowing I'm bringing that shit on all these good people's doorsteps.

My attention turns to Jen. When the judges walk in with Carrie, Jen slips her hand in mine and gives me a squeeze. My heart grows as I hold her hand, feeling more connected than I ever have. I owe this to her. She deserves to win, to prove to everyone—and herself—that she's the best.

So, when the timer starts, I'm ready.

"Cold butter this time," I say, producing a block from the fridge.

Jen grins. "You're a quick study."

"I've got a good teacher."

We work so well together, I never want this day to end. Jen makes an apple filling and places it near the edge of the barn near a window to cool slightly. Then she moves on to a mixed berry filling while I mix pie dough ingredients.

A flap of wings makes us glance at the window. A large black crow is perched on the edge of the bowl of apple-pie filling, pecking at the spiced fruit. Jen screams, rushing the bird. The bird hops but doesn't fly away. It just stays near the bowl, dragging it closer to the edge of the window with its talons.

When the whole bowl topples out the window, Jen stumbles to a stop and gapes. Then turns to glare at me. "Appeasing our overlords, huh." Her head cants. "Making peace with the birds. Isn't that what you said?"

I cringe, hands still working the butter through the bowl of flour in front of me.

"Getting them on our side." Jen walks up to our station, glancing back at the window. "You said the crows would be our best allies."

Clearing my throat, I pause what I'm doing. "I may have misjudged the consequences of my actions."

Story of my life.

Jen surprises me by snorting, then bursting out laughing. She covers her mouth with the back of her hand and shakes her head at me. "I wasted fifteen minutes on that filling." Eyes glimmering, she gives me a cheeky grin. "You're lucky you have other skills."

If I was worried that Jen was the type to hold a grudge, the apple-pie filling proves otherwise. She just gets back to work peeling and chopping more apples, working at double speed. My shoulders drop, and I allow myself a smile.

The competition means everything to Jen, but still, she's not angry. Just like when she saw me for the first time in the guesthouse—she had every right to be angry at me for leaving Heart's Cove at the start of the year, but she seemed to forget about it as soon as we started working together. She forgave me for the croissants within an hour of saving us from elimination.

Maybe I could tell Jen about my past, and she wouldn't react as badly as I think. Maybe... Maybe there's a chance this could work between us. If I told her about my time in prison, would Jen just shrug and move on the same way she did just now? Would she shoot me a little grin and accept me for who I am, dark past and all?

Or would my hidden secrets be one step too far? Maybe I'm burning through Jen's good graces.

Turning back to the pie dough, I trade out with Jen so she can add the water and start forming the dough to chill it.

Hours tick by, and the two of us work like magic together. I've never felt as good in the kitchen as I do with Jen by my side. She gives clear, direct instructions, but still trusts my skills. I watch her shape and carve pie dough into beautiful leaf shapes to put on top of our pumpkin pie, then she uses scraps to make more sculptural floral arrangements out of pie dough to use for later decoration. The apple pie is covered with a fine, delicate lattice.

As I watch her crimp the sides of a glossy, delicious-looking cherry pie, my heart thunders.

At one point, Jen glances at the clock and gets this impish look on her face. Working quickly, she makes mini pies, which she bakes, unmolds, and uses as decorations on top of larger pies. It's ridiculous, but it looks incredible.

I've been in love with Jen for so long it shouldn't surprise me to feel this way. But as the timer counts down and I watch her work miracles, completely in her element, I wonder if I ever stood a chance against her.

From the moment I saw her stomping around the Four Cups Café with her kitchen scale tucked under her arm, I should have known I'd fall for her—and fall hard.

I need to go all-in.

Tonight, when we're alone, I'll tell her about my past. I'll tell her I was in prison, that I'm an ex-con, that my own mother kicked me out when I was a teen, and even after all these years, I'm not sure she'd want to reconcile. I'll tell her I got out of prison after three years, at age twenty-one, and started working in kitchens because it was the only job I could get. I'll tell her that this year, I spent six months volunteering to teach incarcerated men how to cook so they might have opportunities when they get out. I did it in the hopes that if I faced my past, I could move on from it once and for all.

It didn't work, but I tried.

I'll lay it all out on the table. I'll show her my tattoo, and I'll tell her why she deserves so much better than me—but that I'm not ready to let her go.

Tonight, I'll tell Jen that I'm desperately, hopelessly in love with her.

TWENTY-THREE
JEN

AS I STAND before the judges, a sense of calm descends over me. Fallon's steady presence warms my side, the sound of a knife slicing through crisp, flaky pie dough the only noise disturbing the silence in the room.

For the first time in my life, I feel completely, utterly satisfied. Today was a rush. Fallon and I worked perfectly together, entering a state of flow that I've only ever experienced on my own.

I'm...proud of myself. Truly. To my core.

Never have I ever done something that I've been utterly happy with. I've always nitpicked at my own work. *This pastry is gummy. I slightly overbaked that cake. I could have balanced the sweetness in that recipe better. I shouldn't have said that. Did I act weird when I met that person?*

Why? Why have I done that to myself?

My hand slips into Fallon's, and when he gives it a squeeze I know at some point over the last four weeks, I've changed.

Last year, when Fallon kissed me right before Amanda showed up in town, I felt starved for his lips on mine. I felt elated that he looked at me like a woman, a sexual being. And when it all fell apart, it was devastating. When Fallon left Heart's Cove, it felt like he was leaving *me*. Like there was this void inside me that would never be filled.

Now, I still feel a gnawing need for him, but it's not coming from a place of insecurity. I'm not clinging to him because he's the first man to pay attention to me in years. I don't feel like I need to choose between him and my career—between him and *me*.

I am enough. He doesn't complete me; he centers me.

Whatever happens in the next hour—whether we win or not—doesn't matter. I'm proud of myself either way.

A barrier collapses in my mind, and for the first time in my life, I allow myself to be happy. I allow myself to look beyond my own imperfections and just *be*.

I don't need to be perfect to have the love of a good man. I don't need to win this competition to be worthy of my own book, my own bakery, my own name.

"The pie dough is absolutely incredible," Bernard says, his tongue darting out to catch a crumb on his lip. "Flaky and light, yet still holds its shape. Perfection."

It's not the first time Bernard has complimented me, but it's the first time I've heard his compliment and accepted it. That pie dough *is* incredible, *thankyouverymuch*.

I smile. "Thank you."

"And these mini pies? I mean, how *cute.*" Heather grins, slicing the palm-sized pie in half and shaking her head at the perfectly defined layers of custard and whipped cream. "Jen, Fallon, you've outdone yourselves."

Fallon's hand slips out of mine as he moves his arm around my shoulders. I glance up at him, grinning from ear-to-ear, feeling like my heart will beat right out of my chest. "You're amazing, Jen," he whispers. "I'm so damn proud of you."

"I'm proud of me too," I whisper back, loving the way his eyes crinkle, dark eyes twinkling.

I'm high on life, about to float right into the sky from how light I feel—

A door opens, and my parents walk into the barn. Reality brings me crashing right back down.

I pull away from Fallon, wide-eyed.

"Surprise!" Carrie beams. "We thought you could use some extra support today."

Support. Right.

A mask falls over my face as I turn to my parents. My mother is wearing a silk blouse and perfectly tailored pants. Her hair is dyed a dark-chocolate color, twisted neatly at the nape of her neck. My father is in a three-piece suit, his silver hair combed back from his forehead. They walk with the same confident gait I recognize so well, something like haughty pride glimmering in their eyes.

"Jennifer," my mother says, grasping my arms to give me an air kiss on each cheek.

"Mom." I force a smile. "Dad. I wasn't expecting you."

My mother gives me an assessing look, glances at Fallon for

a fraction of a second, then turns back to me. "We were delighted to be invited out for the finale. Your father and I are very keen to see how you rank."

How I rank. Of course. Do they really think that's the same as being here to support me?

"How wonderful!" Carrie laughs, clapping her hands, and the whole barn follows.

Once the greetings are over, I notice the production crew has also led Nora out to stand beside Fallon. Is she the only family of his they could find?

Fallon and I are led back to our station while our family members are directed to a few chairs on the side of the barn. We watch Tex and Reg bring their pies to the front and receive glowing reviews. More perfect pastry, but slightly simplistic decoration. Their custard pies look better than ours, though. Tex's and Reg's wives are led out with their children, and tearful greetings are exchanged. Emma and Carla had a harder time, with two of their pies having soggy bottom crusts, but apparently delicious fillings.

"Your chocolate and Mexican chili pie is incredible," Heather says. "I'm going to need that recipe."

Carla preens, and I can't quite hide my smile. Then, the third family reunion happens. Carla's husband is a short mustachioed man with tears in his eyes. He walks out of that same door and practically runs to his wife and daughter. A section of the mezzanine erupts in cheers, and Emma cries out at the sight of what looks like dozens of family members cheering and chanting for Emma and Carla.

That is support.

My eyes dart to my parents, and I feel like I'm twelve years old again, getting yelled at for a B+ on a test. My mother is sitting with her back ramrod straight, eyes on the front of the room, a dour expression on her face. My father glances at me, inclining his head in an almost regal way.

It makes me feel small.

My nerves come back with a vengeance. If I don't win, will I need to endure snide comments from them? I'm exhausted at the thought of it. I've lived my life dragging around impossible expectations that colored the way I see everything. I've held myself to an unreachable standard. I've kept myself apart from friends and acquaintances because I didn't feel good enough.

This past month, in the safety of this competition bubble, I've learned that I *can* make friends. A weight has been lifted off my shoulders. I can laugh and engage in small talk. I can *hug* people and not hate it. I can laugh without worry.

...but will it last?

Fallon must sense the stress mounting in me, because he puts his hand on my lower back and gives me a sly wink. My tension eases.

When the judges break to deliberate, I let out a long breath. With a squeal, I hear my girlfriends jump up from their chairs above.

"You got this, Jen!" Candice shouts. "We love you!"

She points to her T-shirt and this time, when I look at the blown-up image of my face, I just laugh. Then my eyes flick to my mother, who has a brow arched in disdain and her lips pursed.

My smile fades.

I know I shouldn't care. I'm a grown woman. I have a business of my own. By any metric, I'm undeniably successful. Why does it bother me that my mother doesn't approve of my friends?

Seeing that expression on my mother's face is like picking at an old scab that's never quite healed.

Shifting my gaze to Fallon, I realize why.

My parents' love was conditional. When I did well, they showed affection. When I was less than perfect, they'd be cold, removed. They withheld affection when I was anything less than what they expected. That's how I learned my worth as a child—and I carried those wounds for over forty years.

My one and only boyfriend cared about me only when I was ticking his boxes. As soon as I wasn't what *he* wanted, fitting into *his* perfect life, he pulled back. He withdrew his affection, too.

But with Fallon, it's different. When we messed up the croissants, he didn't think less of me. When I tried to nitpick any of our bite-sized challenges, he'd pull me back from the edge. He'd remind me of everything that went well, or kiss me until I forgot what I was talking about. For the whole month, I've felt nothing but unwavering support from him. How we did in challenges never changed how he treated me.

His affection is *un*conditional—and I realize I've never felt that before. From Candice and the girls, sure—but never from a parent. Never from a lover.

Never from *myself*—until that brief moment when we stood in front of the judges.

I've been such an *asshole* to myself!

Emotion clogs my throat, and I find myself turning to

Fallon. I need to tell him how I feel—that he's cracked my mind and heart right open. I need to scream this epiphany to the rafters. By standing beside me throughout this whole experience, he showed me what it means to have someone to lean on.

He showed me love...

And I love him back.

I open my mouth to say the words that come rushing to the fore—but the judges appear with Carrie as a hum of excitement rushes through the barn. They're about to announce the winners.

TWENTY-FOUR
FALLON

"IT WAS A VERY DIFFICULT DECISION, but ultimately there was one team that shone throughout the competition," Bernard says, his eyes moving to each contestant in turn.

Did they linger on Jen?

My heart thunders. My palms grow damp. I close my eyes as I inhale through my nose, needing to regain control over my rioting body.

I need to win this for Jen. I want to be the man who stood beside her and was able to give her the money to pursue her dreams. She needs to see how incredible she is.

"Congratulations, Fallon and Jen, you are the winners of the *Boss Baker!*" Bernard's face splits into a smile as he turns to us. Carrie advances with the trophy.

Jen stands frozen, eyes wide, so I move to intercept it.

I turn to Jen and present the trophy to her, loving how reverently she accepts it—but most of all, loving the emotion swirling in her eyes when she meets my gaze.

"We did it, Fallon," she whispers, hands curling around the trophy.

The emotion in her voice hits me like a hammer to the side of the head. Too many words come flying to the surface, and I'm struck dumb.

—*I love you.*

—*I've been in love with you for years.*

—*You're the most incredible woman I've ever met and the past month has been the happiest of my life.*

—*You deserve this.*

—*I never want to leave your side.*

—*I don't deserve you.*

My lungs constrict and my vision goes blurry from the tears in my eyes, and soon we're swarmed by contestants and judges and family members. Jen's parents stand off to the side, noses in the air, as if *they* just won the trophy and deserved every bit of it.

Jen is laughing, tears streaming down her face as she wipes her nose with her sleeve. Her eyes find mine again, hand reaching toward me. She squeezes my fingers, then lifts our joint hands in the air, trophy held aloft in the other. The mezzanine goes nuts.

I laugh—and then I can't resist the temptation of Jen's lips. Tugging her to my chest, I bury my hands in her hair and kiss her so hard it'll probably need to be edited out of the show. Shouts and hollers sound from above, and I recognize Simone's voice shouting, "Get a room! This is a family show."

Jen smiles against my lips, eyes alight. When she pulls away, my chest constricts. She's so damn beautiful I can hardly stand to look.

But we're swept up in the celebrations, interviewed on camera, and finally someone calls, "That's a wrap!"

The audience is allowed down from the mezzanine, and Jen and I are swept up in more hugs and congratulations. I keep close to Jen, ready to throw her over my shoulder in case this becomes too much. I know she hates crowds—I still remember how she looked in Four Cups that day, when she was on the verge of a panic attack from all the people.

Jen is radiant, though. A change has come over her, and for the first time ever, I watch *her* seek out hugs from her friends. She's beaming, surrounded by people, looking totally in her element.

A tap on the shoulder draws my attention to a small, reedy man in a black button-down. His weaselly face is pinched as he lifts his chin up to look down on me. "I suppose you think you deserve the win, *hmm?*" He's got an accent I can't place—French, maybe?

Frowning as his words sink in, I turn to face him fully. "Excuse me?"

"I've seen the way you bake. You're no match for Jennifer." He rolls the *r*, making her name sound like *Gennifeuur*.

Definitely French.

"Do I know you?"

He purses his lips. There's something about him that makes my skin itch. A gleam in his eyes. The way he's standing. I want to figure him out, but before I can ask anything else, a hand grips my elbow.

Jen appears at my side. "Fallon, Lottie wants a picture with — Oh! Guillaume!" Her brows jump at the sight of the man beside me. "What are you doing here?"

"I came to congratulate you, of course." A smarmy smile tugs Guillaume's lips. "The restaurant hasn't been the same without you."

Jen's face melts into a smile. "No, I suppose it hasn't—but I'm sure you manage! You should stop by Four Cups some time, see what I've been working on." Jen turns to me, her arm hooking through mine. "Guillaume was my boss before we opened Four Cups. He gave me my start after I completed pastry school."

"I could tell Jennifer was a raw talent," Guillaume says, nose stuck in the air. "Ready to be honed."

A chill skitters up my spine. The way this guy is staring at Jen makes me uneasy—but am I just being overprotective? Am I just worried about what happens once we come down from this high?

"Sorry, Guillaume, I'm going to have to steal Fallon. We need to report for photo duty. I'll come find you later!"

"I look forward to it." He gives her that smarmy smile again, and I can't help putting an arm around Jen's shoulders. I want her close to me if that guy's going to stick around.

Jen doesn't seem to notice. She's still holding the trophy, talking to our fellow competitors, meeting their families, posing for pictures. When she's dragged away by an adorable little girl who we learn is Carla's granddaughter, I slink out the side door for some fresh air.

We won. We *won*.

Jen will be able to start her bakery or expand Four Cups, or do whatever that brilliant head of hers dreams up. I'll stick around Heart's Cove, because, really, what was I thinking? I could never stay away.

Tonight, when the party's over, I'll tell her about my past. I'll confess my feelings, and I'll hope she feels the same way.

Sucking in a long breath, I release it slowly. Things are looking up.

Not wanting to leave Jen alone for too long, I turn back to enter the barn, only to run into Jen's father. I pull back to let him walk by, but he steps into my path.

"Fallon Richter, is it?" he asks, bright blue eyes on mine.

I clear my throat. "Yes. You're Mr. Newbank."

"Indeed. A word, please?" He gestures outside with a smooth, practiced movement, as if he's used to being obeyed.

With one last glance at Jen, I nod to her father and follow him to the side of the barn. We walk a few paces, and I try to keep a straight face when we stop near the place where I had my first real taste of Jen, up against the side of this barn.

Mr. Newbank clears his throat. "You and Jennifer have gotten close."

It's not a question, so I say nothing.

Studying me, the man narrows his eyes. He glances out at the forest, eyes taking on a faraway look. Finally, after a long pause, he speaks. "Our Jennifer is special," he starts.

"She is." *Understatement of the century.*

"Her mother and I can be...protective."

I frown. Protective? Judging by what Jen says, they call her twice a year and call it a day. Doesn't exactly sound like a close familial relationship to me.

"When we were approached about attending the finale, the showrunners mentioned your name. We saw the first bite-sized challenge online, and were surprised to see the two of you so close. The producers made it sound like my daughter and you were...involved." He pauses. "You can understand our surprise, seeing as Jen never mentioned you."

Even though I know Jen isn't close with her parents, the barb still stings. What is he getting at?

Mr. Newbank turns to face me once more, his face hard. Unyielding. "My wife and I took the liberty of doing some cursory checks on your background."

"Excuse me?" My brows lower. Is this guy for real?

"Mr. Richter, you must know that with your"—he cants his head—"*history*, we would understandably be worried about your involvement with our daughter."

"Your daughter is a grown woman capable of making her own choices."

"Of course. One question, though. Does she know about the felony charge? Does she know what you've been doing for six months? How *involved* you are in the prison community?"

Heat blasts through me as aggression explodes inside me. I *will* tell her. I'll tell her tonight, when we have time! I'll explain everything that happened, and Jen will be able to decide for herself if she wants to keep pursuing whatever exists between us.

Plus, what I've been doing for six months has been *good*. I was a felon with no prospects, and I know how dehumanizing that felt. Teaching people real-world skills so they can start their lives over once they get out of prison is not a *bad* thing. But Jen's father doesn't seem to agree.

Plus, the truth is I haven't told her. I've kissed her and claimed her and accepted her love—and I've kept that part of myself separate.

Jen's father must see it on my face, because he rocks back on his heels. "I didn't think so. Do us a favor and back away from Jen, Fallon. You're not the man for her."

With one last loaded look, Mr. Newbank walks away from me. I stand tall until he's out of sight, then lean back against the barn and drop my head into my hands.

I'm insulted that they ran a background check on me. Horrified at what they saw. Ashamed of my past. Angry that they dared to tell me how to live my life—and are trying to stop Jen from living hers.

But most of all, I feel bleak, bottomless despair.

Because he's right. I'm not the type of man that could ever be worthy of Jen. Even if she listened to my past and accepted it, the fact is, she deserves better than me.

TWENTY-FIVE
JEN

THE SOUND of my name makes me turn to see Amanda Bailey walking toward me. She's wearing stilettos, her hair is blown out, face impeccably made up, and she's beaming at me.

My chest seizes. Did she see me kiss Fallon? Would she care?

"You. Are. *Amazing!*" She makes to hug me, then pauses and awkwardly squeezes my shoulders instead.

I appreciate it, even though a hug would have been fine. I'm getting used to them, but I still feel like I'll need a week of seclusion to recover from all this socializing and physical contact.

Rubbing the back of my neck, I clear my throat. "Amanda. Nice to see you. I wasn't expecting you."

"I knew you could do it." She smiles at me, her red lipstick looking sophisticated and sexy on her full lips. Eyes darting behind me, she arches a brow. "I wasn't expecting to see you and Fallon together, though."

"About that…"

When Fallon quit his job at Four Cups and decided to leave town, she seemed to accept that they weren't getting back together. But will she still feel that way now?

She laughs and waves a hand. "Girl, go for it."

Hope blooms in my chest. "Really? I thought you might have feelings for him…"

She tilts her head from side to side as she hums. "I mean, kind of. Yes. Okay, sure. When he first emailed me, I thought maybe there was a reconciliation in the cards for us." Shrugging, she spreads her palms. "But we're two completely different people now. I'm over it—and I *know* Fallon is too."

A breath slips through my lips. What a relief.

"I just wish you two had told me about this"—she waggles her fingers at me—"before Fallon left town. Would have saved everyone a lot of time."

"I thought I had to choose between Fallon and the book," I answer honestly, then bite my lip. "I thought maybe you just gave me the book deal because you wanted to get back with Fallon and it gave you a reason to be here."

Amanda gives me a strange look, then shakes her head. "Jen, no. You got the book deal because you're good. Because you deserved it."

My heart hammers. "Oh."

"You should have told me you were interested in Fallon, Jen," Amanda says, giving me a sad smile.

I huff. "I didn't want to jeopardize the book deal. But now I'm wondering if I wasn't just scared of my feelings for him."

Amanda gives me a kind smile. "Well, either way, I'm happy for you." She points a finger at me. "But I'd better get recognition in every award acceptance speech you ever make. Don't forget who signed you up for this competition in the first place."

Grinning, I incline my head. "I won't. Thanks, Amanda—for everything."

She smiles, then excuses herself to go talk to Heather Brennan. I watch her go, feeling lighter than I did before. Amanda gave me the book deal because I'm good. Plain and simple. Not only that, but she doesn't care if Fallon and I are together—which means there really is no reason for me not to jump into his arms and tell him how I feel.

But as I scan the room, I don't see him anywhere. Dorothy appears at my elbow and sweeps me into another conversation, and soon there's no time to think about my feelings for Fallon.

When the impromptu afterparty on set starts to wind down, Candice announces that all are welcome to come to Four Cups to continue the festivities.

Eyes landing on me, Candice arches her brow. "Bring the trophy," she commands.

I cringe. "Um, the NDAs? I don't think I'm allowed to announce the win yet."

Candice releases a long sigh. "Fine. Bring yourself and Fallon, and I *guess* that'll be enough." She winks, heading for her car.

Scanning the room for the big, bearded, dark-haired man who made this all possible, I find myself wandering out the barn doors to the fresh air outside. Dusk has fallen, the sweet scent of summer lingering in the air. The grass under my feet is soft as I wander toward the guesthouse.

I find Fallon sitting on the front steps of our guesthouse, flicking seeds at a trio of crows near the base of a tree. Planting my hands on my hips, I tilt my head. "You're just encouraging their misbehavior now."

Fallon throws another handful of seeds, then meets my gaze. His face looks...sad.

I pause. "Are you okay?"

Fallon lets out a long sigh and tosses the rest of his crow food, then stretches up to his full height. "I'm good. Just needed a bit of quiet."

"I get that." Closing the distance between us, I make to give Fallon a hug—then pause when he turns his back.

He opens the guesthouse door, not meeting my eyes as he heads across the room to take his suitcase from the closet.

He's packing already? We don't need to be out until tomorrow morning.

My footsteps echo on the wooden floorboards, the trophy dangling from my fingertips. "Candice invited us all back to Four Cups for an afterparty. You want to drive over together?"

Fallon pauses his movements, an old, worn tee clasped in his hands. "You go ahead. I'll meet you there."

"It looks like you're getting ready to leave."

He shoves the tee into his suitcase. "Just packing my stuff, Jen."

I place the trophy on top of the dresser and cross my arms. "What happened? Aren't you happy? We should be celebrating."

Fallon turns to face me, his expression unreadable. He gulps. Then, as if he's sick of holding back, walks over to me with three long steps. His palms sweep over my cheeks, thumbs brushing my skin. "I'm so proud of you, Jen. You deserve this win."

"*We* deserve this win. It's as much mine as it is yours."

"We both know that's not true."

My brows lower. "I don't know what's going on, but I don't like it. And I'm not leaving until you tell me what's up."

Fallon's eyes flick from my eyes to my lips. A breath slides from his mouth as his eyelids slide shut, and dread curls in the pit of my stomach.

"Fallon?"

"I'll meet you at Four Cups. Okay?"

"You promise?" My voice sounds small.

"I promise." Hands still on my cheeks, Fallon leans down to press his lips to mine. This kiss isn't as hot as some of our others, but it makes my pulse thump. It feels...significant. When he pulls away, Fallon's eyes are dark. "You deserve this, Jen."

"So do you." I tilt my head up for one last kiss, then let out a sigh and head for the door.

I'm nearly at the door when I hear Fallon say, "Hey." I turn to see Fallon holding up my trophy. "You forgot this."

Grinning, I reach for it, the metal cool against my skin. "Unfortunately, this baby will have to stay hidden for now, but you better believe it's going on display as soon as the show airs. We need a photo with it to frame for Four Cups."

Sadness flashes across Fallon's eyes, but he quickly hides it. He smiles. "I'm sure Lottie got at least one useable one."

Nodding, I squeeze his arm and linger. Something makes me hesitate. I don't want to leave. But, not having an excuse to stay, I make him promise he'll be at Four Cups soon, and I leave the guesthouse behind.

I TAKE my car into town, parking down the street from Four Cups. When I exit the vehicle, I can already hear loud music and intermingling voices. There must be dozens of people at the café.

Strangely, the thought doesn't fill me with fear like it used to. My steps are light as I make my way toward the café, and I find myself smiling when I enter. I'm no longer worried about all the people, the questions, the conversations.

They're here for me, and there's no pressure.

A cheer sounds when I walk through the door, splitting my face into a smile.

"Coming through!" Simone elbows her way through the crush to reach me, eyes twinkling. "VIP in the house!" She hooks her arm through mine and drags me deeper into the café. I say hellos to all my neighbors and friends on the way past, then let Simone drag me toward a wall, where a new shelf has been erected.

Simone thrusts her arm to the shelf, where there's already a candid photo of me and Fallon in the kitchen from a couple of years ago. "Grant put the shelf up this morning," Simone says with a wink. "We knew you'd come home with the trophy, and this is where it's going to go."

I smile. They put this shelf up before I'd even completed

the challenge. Every single person in this room *believed* in me. My heart is so full it's about to burst.

How could I have not realized that I had support all along? Why did I put so much pressure on myself? Why did I avoid affection and help from all these people that believe in me down to their core?

Beaming, I give Simone a hug, pulling away to see a shocked expression on her face.

"Who are you and what have you done with Jen?" She turns to Fiona, who walks up to us at that moment. "Jen just hugged me unprompted. I think she needs to get her head checked."

"I'll call 9-1-1," Fiona answers, dead serious, reaching for her phone.

"*Har-har*, guys." I roll my eyes, but crack a smile. I'm swept up in more conversations and congratulations, and I bask it in.

The only thing that could possibly make this moment better is if Fallon's muscled arm was slung across my shoulders. I glance at the door, wondering when he'll show up. He needs to be here to celebrate just as much as I do.

Instead of Fallon at the door, I see my mother and father walking in with none other than Bernard Franco. Bernard is deep in conversation with my mother, who looks oddly triumphant.

My father waves me over. "Jennifer," he booms. "Come."

Trundling over to them, I pick up a glass of champagne on the way and down it in one gulp. When I reach them, my father looks me up and down. "We were just discussing your performance with Mr. Franco."

"Oh?" I give Bernard a tight smile.

"We're so proud of you, Jennifer," Mother says, her brown hair tied in a neat French twist. She looks every bit as refined and uptight as I remember her.

A memory pops into my head. I remember being young—a toddler—and running to the door when my mother got home from work. I'd been eating something chocolatey, and it was smeared all over my hands and face. When I gave my mother a hug and a kiss, she looked at the brown smears on her clothes and pulled away from me with disgust.

The nanny was fired that evening, and chocolate was banned from the house.

I was a *toddler*.

Staring at my parents, I wonder how many of those moments were burned into my subconscious. How many years have I spent trying to be good enough for them? How much joy did I give up because they didn't approve?

Now that they look at me with real pride—or just plain satisfaction—in their gazes, it feels...empty.

I want Fallon's warmth. I want his breath on my neck as he squeezes me tight. I want his generous laugh and twinkling eyes.

It would mean more to me than the trophy. More than this empty, haughty pride.

"We were just talking to Mr. Franco about your next steps," my father says, drawing my attention to him.

I frown. "Next steps?"

"Well, officially, the prize is cash," Bernard says. "Unofficially, I'd like to tell you how impressed I was by your work." He takes a step closer to me, his eyes burning with intensity.

I resist the urge to take a step back, my eyes darting to the door. Where the hell is Fallon?

"Jen, I was hoping you and I could talk." Bernard takes my hand, squeezing it meaningfully.

"Talk?"

"Maybe outside?" He nods to the door. "Alone?"

"What do you want to talk about?"

"Jennifer, darling, don't be rude." My mother's lips pinch, her lipstick gathering in the creases.

I nod, gesturing to the exit.

Bernard keeps a hold on my hand as he drags me outside, then turns to face me. His bright eyes are intent, and he's standing too close. I take half a step back. "Your parents are remarkable people," he starts.

"That's a common opinion," I answer noncommittally.

"And they have a remarkable daughter." He closes the distance between us.

If I back up any more, I'll be up against the wall. Instead, I just clear my throat and glance to the door. "What did you want to talk about?"

Bernard lets out a breath. "Jen, I've watched you flourish in this competition, and I wanted to tell you how impressed I was with your work. You have real, raw talent."

The same words Guillaume used earlier—as if raw talent is something to be plucked from the ground by one of them.

"Thank you." I nod, fists clenched. He's standing too close.

"I know you've felt something between us."

My eyes snap to him. "What?"

"We've shared moments, Jen."

"Moments?" What the hell is he talking about?

"Dinners when we spoke about your recipes. The whole room fell away and it was just you and me talking pastry." He reaches for my hand again as my heart thumps in my ears.

Discussing my recipes with Bernard at dinner? I vaguely remember doing that, but I was more focused on the heat of Fallon's thigh against mine.

"And you can't tell me you weren't giving me looks every time I came to your station during filming."

"Looks?" I shake my head. "I wasn't giving you looks."

He laughs like I'm joking. Not the way Fallon does it, where it's like he's so full of affection that it tumbles out in a laugh. With Bernard, it seems like he's observing some bumbling, naïve child who does something cute. I'm so *sick* of people looking at me like that! I'm forty-fucking-seven years old! When will it end?

"Jen, there's something between us. I know you feel it. I want you to come to Paris with me. I'm opening a new restaurant, and you will be my head pastry chef. I have a residence in Saint-Germain and a vacation home on the Mediterranean. You'll have free access to both."

Um, *what?*

"You want me to work for you?" I feel like I've lost my mind. What the hell is happening?

"I want you to work *with* me. And live with me. *Be* with me."

Okay. Working in Paris under a celebrated pastry chef—*très* cool. Having him proposition me as if this is a done deal? Insinuating that we'd be together more than professionally? *Not fucking cool.*

"Listen, Bernard," I start, palms up.

"I won't take no for an answer." He takes another step closer to me, pushing me up against the wall. "I've been looking for someone whose talent matches mine. You're nearly my equal in every way, Jen. You're perfect for me."

Nearly his equal? What the hell kind of compliment is that supposed to be?

Staring into this man's—this stranger's—eyes, I see nothing but an odd sort of light shining in his irises. He doesn't know me. Doesn't *see* me. All he wants is some doll he can insert into his perfect life. He's presenting it to me like he's doing me a favor. It's a done deal, and he's just telling me about it.

Curious about how he'll respond, I ask, "What if I wanted to stop baking?"

"Don't be ridiculous." He snorts. "Why would you throw away an opportunity like this? You'll be the face of a prestigious restaurant with my name on it!"

Calm settles over me. Bernard doesn't want *me*. He doesn't even know me. He's built up this image in his head of who I am —a pastry chef that he can shape and mold into the woman he wants.

The same way my first boyfriend wanted me to be the mother of his children instead of my own person. The same way my parents wanted me to be a mini version of them.

For the first time in my life, I square my shoulders, and it doesn't make me sick to say no to a great opportunity. A year ago, I would have jumped at the chance to work in Paris. I thought it was my dream.

But dreams change.

I sidestep away from Bernard and shake my head. "I'm sorry, Bernard, that's not what I want."

His face twists. "You'd throw away this opportunity for what? For that criminal?"

I freeze as his words clang through me. "What are you talking about?"

"Darling," my mother's voice says behind me, "there's something we need to tell you."

"And there's something *I* need to tell you!" Dorothy pops her head out of the café, a leopard-print scarf tied over her head. Chunky turquoise earrings dangle from her ears as she spreads her arms wide, a tumbler of alcohol sloshing in one hand. Her other finger points at me. "You. Are. Incredible!"

Agnes, looking very sophisticated in a new outfit Trina must have picked out for her, appears at her side and puts her hand around Dorothy's bicep to drag the drunk older woman back inside. "Get a grip, Dorothy. I knew whiskey was a bad idea."

"Whiskey is *never* a bad idea." She pauses, throwing me a serious look. "Unless you're already sad, in which case whiskey is a *very* bad idea."

"Excuse me," my mother interjects, her brows pinched. "We are *busy*."

Agnes glares, not in the least bothered that in heels, my mother is nearly six feet tall and Agnes is about four foot nine. She just snorts and shakes her head. "You're worse than Dorothy, and that's saying a lot."

"You know, Agnes, if you weren't so horrible, you'd be okay." Dorothy gives Agnes a pat on the head, then dances her way back inside.

The door closes behind them and my mother lets out an exasperated sigh.

I press my lips together to stop from smiling, then remember what Bernard said earlier. Looking my mother square in the eyes, I cross my arms. "What's this about a criminal?"

TWENTY-SIX
FALLON

ACID COATS my throat as I watch Bernard fucking Franco take another step toward Jen. My hand grips the car door, but I hold myself back. Jen's mother appears, with that awful, pinched expression on her pretentious face.

I should go over there. With my low-class upbringing and my criminal record, I should barge right in and claim Jen's lips in front of everyone.

But Jen looks at Bernard and she doesn't push him away. She lets him take her hand—lets him *touch her*, and says nothing.

Watching Jen and Bernard together is like watching a precious jewel fall through the grates of a storm drain only to get swept away. She showed me just how happy I could be, but I can never have her.

Mr. Newbank's words echo in my head. *You're not the man for her.*

All the fight leaves my body when the truth of those words rings through me like a bell.

Because someone who *is* the type of man who should be with Jen? Bernard Franco. He's worldly and successful and educated. I've heard him bragging about his house in the south of France, about his dozens of restaurants and his cachet in the pastry world.

He is Jen's equal. Not some ex-con kitchen grub like me.

Coming to this afterparty was a mistake. I should have just thrown my packed bags in the back of my Jeep and left town again. I've done it once, and it didn't stick—but second time's the charm. This time, I'll leave and I'll stay gone—but as I turn the key in the ignition, my phone rings.

Nora's name lights up the screen and I swipe to answer. "Yeah?"

"Well, good evening to you too, Grumpy."

"What do you want, Nora?"

"Wow, what bee got in your bonnet?" There's a rustling sound behind her.

"Nora," I growl, "I'm not in the mood."

"Did Jen come to her senses and break up with you?"

Stunned, I say nothing. Even my own damn sister knows Jen is too good for me.

Nora inhales. "Oh, Fallon, I didn't mean it." The rustling stops. "Shit. Fallon, I thought she was in love with you. I was expecting wedding bells. I was just teasing you. I'm so sorry."

"Why are you calling, Nora? I thought you'd be at the Four Cups party."

"I came home instead to pack up my things. Have to be out

of here by the morning so Jen can have her apartment back." She inhales. "But, Fallon...I've decided to stay."

I frown, eyes darting back down the street, where Jen is now surrounded by both her parents and Bernard. They're crowding her up against the wall. "You're staying at Jen's place?"

"No. I'm staying in Heart's Cove."

I tear my eyes away from Jen. "You..."

"I like it here," my sister says quietly. "I have friends for the first time in years. I feel like I might actually have a future."

"This place has that effect on people," I answer neutrally. Once upon a time, I felt that way too. It was right around the time Jen was coming in early to work in the café by herself. Around the time I noticed she drank masala chai and had an unhealthy obsession with kitchen scales.

I'd come to work for an extra unpaid hour just to be next to her, and she never even gave me a second glance.

Thinking about it now, I should have known. I've wasted more than three years of my life on that woman.

"Fallon," my sister continues, "I was hoping you could come with me to Reno to pack up the rest of my stuff. Your Jeep is bigger, and plus...I'm worried Slim will be there, and...I know it's a lot to ask, but..."

"Of course," I answer. "We can leave first thing tomorrow morning. I'll talk to him and make sure he leaves you alone. Leaves *all* of us alone."

She exhales. "Thank you."

We say our goodbyes and hang up, and by the time I glance down the street again, Jen has disappeared.

Not wanting to put on a false smile to celebrate with

everyone in town, I turn my car around and head back to the guesthouse.

I'll be gone before Jen returns.

TWENTY-SEVEN

JEN

KNOWING I'll encounter lots of protests if I tell anyone I'm leaving the party, I end up slipping out the back door of the Four Cups Café to make my way back to my car.

I need to talk to Fallon.

My parents and Bernard told me a lot of things about him, and I'm not sure how many of them are true. Things about the past six months, and his frequent visits to prison. Things about the years he spent in prison himself...and even possible gang affiliations?

He's never said a word of that to me, and I want to know why.

"Uh-uh!" a voice says behind me. "Where do you think you're going, missy?" I turn in the back alley to see Candice standing by the back door, hands on hips with a sassy arch of her eyebrow. "You think you can sneak out on us?" My oldest friend strides toward me, then stumbles when she sees my face. "Hold on. What's wrong? Who do I need to kill?"

I snort. "No one."

She lifts a finger. "No one...*yet*."

"I'm just tired, Candice. Thought I'd turn in early."

"Girl, I've known you for decades. Do not lie to me."

My shoulders drop. "Fine. My parents tried to convince me to move to France with Bernard to be his... I don't even know! His concubine? His employee? His mistress?"

Candice rears back. "What? What about Fallon?"

I let out a sharp huff. "Well. That's a whole other thing."

"What's a whole other thing?" Simone saunters out from the café, joining Candice and me in the alley.

I swallow a groan. "I just need to talk to Fallon."

"Where is the big guy, anyway?" Simone asks, frowning. "The nerve of him missing a party we threw in his honor!"

"Fallon's not coming?" Fiona drifts through the door.

This time, I can't hold back my groan. So much for leaving without anyone noticing.

Candice curls her fingers around my elbow and drags me closer. "Now, Jen. You haven't told us a single detail about you and Fallon. We've been patient for weeks, but it's time to fess up. Where is he? Why didn't you come together?"

"I..." I look at each of them in turn as my throat locks up. "I'm not sure. He was packing up his things when I last saw him."

Fiona tilts her head, dark brows tugging together. "He was packing? Like, to leave? Right after you guys won?"

My pulse speeds up. I *knew* that was weird!

"Hold on." Candice throws up her hands. "First of all, you guys *have* been sleeping together, yeah?"

I nod. "Yeah."

"And what's this about your parents trying to sell you to one of the judges like chattel?"

"*What?*" Fiona and Simone yell in unison.

"They cornered me. Bernard kept talking about us having a 'connection.' Wanted me to move to France to live with him."

"Creepy." Simone frowns, glancing over her shoulder. "I'm going to get Wes to kick him out."

"You're not actually going to France though... Are you?" Fiona stares at me.

I actually laugh. The last thing I want to do is go to France with someone who thinks we have a *connection* when the only thing we have is a contract to appear on the same television show. Bernard doesn't actually know *me*. He just sees what he wants to see—same as my parents.

I'm the lump of clay they can mold into whatever they want. Never mind that I'm an actual human with thoughts and feelings and desires.

"I'm not going anywhere," I finally say. I pause, slightly afraid to say the next words out loud. "I might take some time off, though."

Candice's brows arch. "Time off work? Time off baking?"

"I'll train someone to take my place," I put in quickly. "I won't leave any of you in the lurch. I'll find someone. The young woman who was supposed to compete with me, Mary-Ann, she said she needed a job."

Candice flicks her wrist to wave the comment away. "I don't

care about that. As long as I've known you, you've never taken a vacation. Always focused on success and career and growth." She shakes her head. "I get exhausted just thinking about it. I'm fully supportive of time off. You should take a month off. Two months! Six!"

I blink. "You wouldn't be mad?" I look at each of them in turn.

Fiona just frowns.

"Mad? At you? For taking a vacation?" Simone snorts. "I'll be mad if you *don't* take a vacation. Then I won't have to worry about you going into manic baking frenzies at three o'clock in the morning."

"You've been worried about me?" I stare at Simone.

"Oh, Jen." Fiona squeezes my arm. "Obviously we worry about you. We love you."

Tears well in my eyes, and for the second time today, I realize people love me—*unconditionally.* These three women don't care about me because I'm the resident baker. They don't care about me because I'm a business partner, or because I can go work in their fancy restaurant and become their talented arm candy.

They care about me because I'm *me.*

"I need to go find Fallon," I blurt. I need to tell him how I feel, and how much he means to me.

"Go." Candice waves me off. "We'll hold down the fort."

I turn to leave, then pause. "Dorothy's drinking whiskey. Don't let her near anything flammable."

Fiona immediately starts for the door, and Simone cackles, hot on her heels.

"Good luck," Candice says, and the three of them disappear into the café.

I MAKE it back to the farmhouse in record time, and exhale when I see Fallon's black Jeep parked in the lot. He's still here. Falling out of the car, I hurry down the beaten dirt path to the little guesthouse that's been my home for the past month.

I've learned a lot about myself during this competition—and none of it had to do with my baking skills. I've learned that my drive to achieve success might have stemmed from a place of insecurity. I've always wanted to prove that I was worthy. If I was successful in my career, maybe I'd deserve love and affection. All those years when I was a child, wanting to get good grades so my parents would give me attention and affection— those feelings never went away. I've been carrying baggage around for *decades* without realizing it.

Until Fallon.

He showed me what it meant to be supported. He stood by my side, a quiet, strong presence that was always there to ground me.

I can't let him leave again. Not when I feel like I'll burst if I don't touch him, kiss him, love him.

When I step inside the guesthouse, Fallon is zipping up the last of his bags—like he's about to leave. I freeze, not wanting to understand, not wanting to believe what I'm seeing.

"Fallon?"

He straightens up, turning ever so slowly to face me. "Jen. I thought you were at the party."

"I was. I came looking for you."

He snorts. "Why's that? I thought you'd moved on to better things."

Rearing back as if slapped, I frown. "What's that supposed to mean?"

"I saw you with Bernard." He spits the name.

The floor creaks as I shift my weight, cocking my hips to the side. "Right. And what did you see?"

"I saw you with a man who would be a much better match than I could ever be." He spreads his arms. "You got what you wanted, Jen. We won. You said if we had sex, it would help us focus on the competition, and it did. It's over now."

"So that's it?" I'm barely able to force the words out. "That's all this past month meant to you?" A weird mix of confusion and hurt coagulates in my throat.

I don't even know this man.

"You have no idea what this month meant to me," Fallon says, turning back to his bags.

"No, you're right. And while we're discussing things I don't know, how about you tell me where you were the past six months? Visiting prison three times a week? Going to see your old gang members?" He freezes, and I snort. "That's right, I found out about that. Why didn't you tell me? Who even *are* you?"

"Jen."

"You know what, I'm getting *real* sick of men trying to use me for what they need. Bernard wanted to use me to be the shiny new jewel in his stupid pastry king crown. You wanted to use me for... Shit, I don't know. Sex? To win the cash prize? To get back at me for rejecting you?" Is it so much to ask that a man actually want *me*? "Is that why you came back after six months incommunicado?"

"No." His voice is low, vehement.

"Right. And I'm supposed to just believe that? You haven't told me *anything* about you. I worked with you for three years and I didn't even know you had a sister!"

I'm shaking. The words are coming out of me so fast I can hardly breathe. The past month meant something to me, but Fallon just wants to pack up and leave again.

How fucking stupid can I be?

There's no such thing as unconditional love and support. He never felt the way I do.

"Why didn't you tell me anything about yourself, Fallon? Was the past month all fake to you?"

Fallon whirls on me, his eyes wild. *"Fake?"*

"You heard me. We've known each other for years, and you act like you care about me, but here you are packing up and leaving at the first chance. I find out through my *parents*, of all people, that you were in prison for three years when you were younger!" I throw my hands out to the side. "I was so *stupid* to think you cared about me for me. So fucking naïve—and I still haven't learned my lesson, because I thought I was in love with you, but I don't know a damn thing about you. I've never even seen you without a shirt on!"

"You want to see me shirtless?" Fallon seethes. "Fine." Grabbing the neck of his shirt near his nape, Fallon rips his shirt off in one smooth motion.

The first thing I notice is that Fallon's body is absolutely droolworthy. I'm mourning the past month, when I could have kissed every hard inch of his chest, traced the lines of his muscular stomach with my tongue. I could have rubbed my lips against his coarse chest hair and run my tongue over the flat discs of his nipples. I could have kissed his stomach and spread my hands over his skin, and woken up wrapped up in the scent and heat of him.

The second thing I notice is Fallon looks furious, staring me down with fire in his gaze. "This is what you wanted to see?"

"Uh...yes?" I frown. What is he getting at?

Fallon spins around, arms spreading wide. His muscles pop and writhe under his skin, and he looks like a work of art. Across his back, a massive tattoo stretches over his shoulder blades and wraps around his ribs. Two snakes twist around an anatomically accurate black heart. Each snake scale is shaded to perfection, the heart dripping black blood from each severed artery.

It's...beautiful. Unexpected and kind of dark, but beautiful. I knew he had a tattoo, but I never expected it would look like that.

"Look at it, Jen," Fallon says, his voice losing its edge. "This is who I am."

I frown. "You're...tattooed?" I'm not seeing the issue. Personally, I have no interest in getting inked, but I don't have a problem with them. Fallon's is *hot*.

"I got this tattoo when I was eighteen. My dumb friends and I wanted to join a 'brotherhood,' as we called it." Shirt still grasped in his clenched fist, he turns to face me. "A gang." He snorts. "We weren't the smartest kids on the block."

"I think it's kind of beautiful," I tell him honestly.

"No, you don't."

My own shirt rasps against my skin as I cross my arms, anger flaring in my chest. I'm getting *real* sick of people telling me how I should feel and act. "Yes, I do."

"Jen, I didn't tell you about my past because I knew you'd think I was an ex-con loser—because that's what I am. Right now you're high on winning, achieving every goal you set for yourself—as usual—so you can't see what's right in front of you. You can do better."

"Better than what?" I ask. "Better than you?"

"Don't play dumb, Jen. It isn't like you."

"It's an honest question, Fallon. Do you honestly think that a tattoo would turn me off so much that I'd want to end things between us?"

His eyes flare. "How about the knowledge that I went to prison for three years for aiding and abetting a robbery? From eighteen to twenty-one years old, I was locked up. How about the fact that the robbery was committed with a deadly weapon? Does that change what you think of me?"

My parents told me of his conviction earlier, but it still stuns me. I guess I was expecting him to have some sort of explanation.

Thoughts whirl in my head, but I can't quite seem to make words. I still feel the same way about Fallon. I still love him. I still want him to stay. I believe that people can change, and just because he made mistakes in his youth, it doesn't change that I know him to be a good man.

But why wouldn't he *tell* me?

Fallon must see the look on my face, because he shakes his

head and pulls his shirt back on. "I'm going to make this easy on you, Jen. Move on. I know I will."

Then, with one bag grasped in each of his strong hands, Fallon walks past me without looking back. In the silence of the night, I hear his engine turn over, then fade in the distance. My eyes shift to the dresser, where my trophy gleams silver in the moonlight.

I may have won the prize, but I lost the only man I've ever wanted.

THE ONLY HOTEL in town is owned by the two biggest gossips I've ever met, so I end up sleeping in my car. Bleary-eyed, I pick up Nora at six o'clock in the morning, and we start to journey to Reno, Nevada.

The drive takes just over seven hours, the first three of which pass in complete silence. Nora has her own demons to battle as we head back to the home she's leaving behind, and my thoughts never stray far from Jen.

I saw the look on her face when I told her about my criminal conviction. I know she was judging me, seeing the real me for the first time.

I'm a felon. An ex-con. That's a fact that will never change.

When my sister and I stop for lunch after barely saying a dozen words to each other for hours, she stares at me from across the restaurant booth.

"What?" I bite out.

"You're surlier than usual. What's up? Aren't you all cashed-up with an extra fifty grand and a dream woman by your side?"

I just snort. "Something like that. You sure you want to move to Heart's Cove?"

Nora squares her shoulders. "Yes. I can't believe you ever left."

"Small towns can get stifling."

She frowns, searching my face. "Are you nervous about going back to Reno? Is that what this moodiness is about?"

Reno is where I got arrested. I might feel a bit apprehensive about going there, but I spent six months in Carson City this year, going to the Nevada State Prison three times a week to provide cooking lessons to the inmates. I'm not worried about being in Nevada.

I feel like shit because the woman I'm in love with will always be too good for me—and now she knows it too.

"Things don't always work out for people like me, Nora," I finally answer.

My sister stares at me for a beat, as if I've just spoken in a foreign language. "People like you?" She tilts her head. "What does that mean?"

"Criminals, Nora." How hard is it to understand?

My sister starts laughing, then stops when she realizes I'm not. "Wait, you're serious?"

"I went to *prison*."

"Yeah, because that piece of shit Slim used *your* knife to rob a convenience store. You weren't even there!"

"I still have a criminal record, don't I?"

"Because the prosecutor knew you were a dumb, broke eighteen-year-old, and he pressured you to plead guilty!" Nora cries, throwing her arms out to the side. "Are you seriously blaming yourself for your time in prison?"

"You've seen the tattoo on my back," I hiss. "You know I wasn't an angel. I deserved to be in prison. It's who I am."

"You're unbelievable." My sister crosses her arms, jaw clenched. "You were in a gang for what, four milliseconds?" She scoffs. "Please. It wasn't even a real gang! It was just a bunch of dumb kids smoking too much weed. The only gang you're in is the Heart's Cove Hotties—and that gang includes mostly elderly ladies who think it's funny to urinate in each other's gardens."

"I see you've delved into the Dorothy-Agnes feud," I note with a pop of the brow.

At that moment, the waitress comes to our table with our drinks. "A Diet Coke for the pretty lady," she sing-songs. "And a water for the handsome gentleman." Winking at me, the waitress doesn't seem to notice the tension emanating from the two of us.

When she walks away, that fake customer-service smile still plastered on her face, my sister leans forward. "Fallon, you are *not* in the same league as Slim fucking Miller."

Setting my jaw, I stare my sister down. "In the eyes of the law, I am. We were convicted of the same crime."

"Yeah, and he served fifteen years while you served three. You think the judge didn't know you had nothing to do with the robbery? He gave you the minimum possible sentence! And Slim's been in and out of prison every few years since then." She snorts, shaking her head. "Come on, Fallon. You can't be serious."

"You're my sister, so of course you see me differently than the rest of the world." I stare out the window, not wanting to see the incredulous look on my sister's face. I can feel the frustration emanating from her on the other side of the booth.

"What about Jen?" Nora asks quietly.

Tension seizes my muscles. "What about her?"

"She didn't seem to mind when she was launching herself into your arms at every opportunity."

"That was before she knew about my criminal record."

Nora's quiet for a few moments. "You told her?"

"Her parents did. I confirmed what they found." Shifting my gaze back to Nora, I give her a shrug. "She made it pretty fucking clear that she didn't approve."

"But you told her you weren't even at the convenience store when Slim robbed it, right? You told her you pled guilty to something you didn't do?"

"It was my knife."

"Which Slim *stole* from you! The only reason the prosecutor was able to put pressure on you was because it was Dad's knife and everyone knew you always carried it on you." Nora blows out a breath, lifting her eyes to the ceiling. She lowers her gaze back to me. "You know, for a smart guy, you're pretty fucking dumb sometimes."

"I don't want to talk about this anymore."

The sunny waitress floats back to the table with our food, which Nora and I eat in tense silence.

My sister is *wrong*. I have a criminal record. I did time in prison. Hell, I'm *still* connected to the prison system! Why else would I be teaching cooking classes to ex-cons? That's not exactly in the same league as publishing a recipe book and winning every competition I ever enter.

Jen deserves better, and I deserve everything I got.

WE MAKE it to Reno by dinnertime. I slow the Jeep down as we enter the city limits, and Nora directs me to her apartment even though I know every inch of this city. When we pull up outside, I let out a breath and follow her up the steps to her second-floor apartment.

Nora flicks on the lights. "Well, I'd better get started. I don't have much, but it'll still take me a while to pack up. You can either help or go hunt for our dinner." She glances at me with her brow arched. "Since you're still in a terrible mood, I vote you leave me alone and go get us some takeout."

"Ever the diplomat."

Nora grins, then waves me out the front door.

Instead of going to get takeout, I sit behind the wheel of my car and grit my teeth.

There's somewhere I need to go. I drive through the familiar streets, noting all the things that have changed—and all the things that haven't. When I get to my old neighborhood, my heart starts to thump.

According to Nora, Slim is still living in his parents' old house, which he inherited when they passed away. Driving onto his street, I look at the overgrown lawns and rundown houses in need of a lick of paint. Or a bulldozer. Tightness squeezes my throat and chest as I pull up outside Harvey "Slim" Miller's house.

I never thought I'd come back here. Never thought I'd face this man again—but he was harassing my sister, and that shit needs to stop.

So, stepping out of the Jeep, my leaden steps take me up the weed-infested path to the front door. Loud music thumps from within the walls of the house, with stained lace curtains hiding whatever's happening inside.

I ring the doorbell and wait, then finally pound my fist against the door.

Pulse hammering, I stand on the stoop and listen to the heavy footsteps approach the other side of the door. For the first time since I got out, I'm going to lay my eyes on the man who put me behind bars for three years.

TWENTY-NINE

JEN

ALL MY PLANTS survived the month, which is good, but Fallon left this morning, which is...less good.

Terrible. It's terrible. I feel like shit.

This morning I woke up in my apartment, feeling like a stranger in my own home. I would stuff my face with leftover pie, but when I checked the barn refrigerators, they were all gone. So I can't even pig out and eat my feelings.

Fallon is gone.

Fallon is a *felon*. What? Since when?

The day was spent wandering around my house, setting things right, checking my plants, and staring off into the distance wondering what the hell just happened. I also turn off my phone when my parents start incessantly calling. They told me they'd stay in town until I made a decision about Bernard, but then they ignored me when I said I'd already decided—and the answer was no.

I'm guessing the decision they're waiting on is for me to change my mind. They'll wait a long time.

As I cook up a couple of eggs for dinner, I stare at the pan, still reeling from Fallon's revelation.

Replaying our interaction makes me cringe. I reacted badly. I should have gone to him, assured him that I didn't care. But it felt like I was dealing with a wounded animal likely to lash out. Being neutral seemed like the better strategy. The more reasonable option.

God, why am I so bad at this? Did I miss the lessons in school that would've taught me to act like a normal, empathetic human being?

I don't care that Fallon went to prison. I've known him for over three years, and I've gotten to know who he is *now*. My parents told me he went to prison from age eighteen to age twenty-one. He got out of prison twenty-five years ago!

People change. Fallon isn't a criminal or even remotely violent in any way. I've seen him catch and release a huge, furry spider, for crying out loud. He nearly tamed a whole murder of murderous crows!

The smoke alarm starts blaring. I jump at the sound, splashing some oil from the pan onto the open flame of my gas stove. The whole pan goes up in flames, and I scream.

Shitshitshit what do I do?

Deep breath. Oil fire. Need to smother it.

I turn the burner off and scramble to find a lid that will fit my pan. I open the cabinet where I keep all my pots and pans neatly organized and curse when I see the jumbled mess inside. Did Nora not see the organization system I had?

Tearing drawers and cabinet doors off their hinges as the fire in the pan burns hotter, I finally remember I bought a fire blanket years ago and stuffed it in the back of my pantry. Rushing to grab it, I pull the tab and unfurl the blanket, then throw it over the incinerated eggs.

I slump down in my chair and lean my head against the wall. My lids slide shut, and the irrational desire to start sobbing wells up inside me. All I smell is smoke.

Why do I feel like crying? I've worked in kitchens for years. So I burned some eggs—who cares?

But a voice in my head tells me it isn't the fire that makes me want to cry. It's the fact that the one man who actually saw me for me is gone.

Rubbing the heels of my palms against my eyes, my mind flits to my conversation with Bernard.

Did I give him signs that I was interested?

I remember a cast dinner together a couple of weeks into the competition, when he complimented me on my chocolate cake recipe. I admit, I preened. I struggled with that particular recipe for weeks, toying with the leavening agents and flavor balance until I got a reliable, easy, but delicious recipe.

It's the type of recipe that seems deceptively simple, but is incredibly delicious and requires a bit of finesse. To have a world-renowned pastry chef compliment me for it made my chest warm with pride.

And there was Fallon's finger, making maddening shapes on my shoulder all the while. His thigh pressed up against mine. His big, broad body so close, my head spun.

Is it possible Bernard mistook my attraction to Fallon for attraction to *him*?

Groaning, I drop my head in my hands.

No wonder I haven't had a boyfriend. They're too much damn work. The male brain is an organ I don't think I'll ever figure out.

Pounding on the door draws me out of my eddying thoughts. I drag myself to the door and check the peephole, then brace myself for a hurricane before opening.

"She lives!" Simone exclaims, then sniffs. "Is something burning?"

"I had an accident in the kitchen," I explain.

Simone immediately puts the back of her hand to my forehead. "No fever. You sure you're okay?"

I roll my eyes. "I've burned things before, Simone." I open the door wider to let everyone in.

"We brought reinforcements," Fiona says, jerking her thumb to Candice and Trina behind me. "But first, you need to tell us everything about last night. You never came back after you went out looking for Fallon."

Trina lifts a bag. "We were thinking we could get you all dressed up and looking like a million bucks, then go to the Grove." The Cedar Grove is a bar just outside the town limits. Mac's father, Hamish, owns the joint.

Candice wiggles her eyebrows. "You could invite Fallon."

"We're not done celebrating your win!" Simone bustles into my apartment, then stops, gaping at all the greenery. She glances at Candice. "You weren't exaggerating."

Letting them all inside, I scratch my head. "Fallon left with Nora this morning."

Silence crashes down on us.

Fiona's the first to speak. "He left?"

"We, um, kind of had a disagreement last night," I say.

All eyes are on me. I squirm.

"What happened, Jen?" Simone prompts.

With a deep breath, I let everything out. I start by telling them about Bernard again, going over our conversation from beginning to end, and am rewarded with more outraged gasps. Fiona assures me that I didn't lead anyone on—he was the one who pushed himself on me. Then I tell them about my parents revealing that Fallon went to prison for robbery, and that a deadly weapon was used in the crime.

Everyone blinks as they stare at me.

Candice glances at Fiona. "Did we know that?"

Fiona chews her lip. "We hired Fallon because he'd worked for Wes's parents." Wes's parents used to own the café space when they were alive. "I gave him the paperwork, but I'd have to check if it asks about criminal records. He never mentioned it."

"Either way," Simone interjects, "Fallon was a model employee. You said this happened when he was eighteen? I mean, shit, I should have been arrested for a hundred things when I was a dumb teenager."

"Yeah, but did you rob a convenience store at knifepoint?" Candice asks quietly.

Simone pinches her lips.

"There's got to be an explanation," Trina says, her bag of clothes and makeup forgotten. She's the resident style icon, and

I'm secretly glad I won't be getting a makeover today. All I want to do is crawl under a mountain of blankets and go to sleep for a hundred years.

"If there is, I haven't heard it." I slump onto a sofa and kick my legs up.

Fiona heads to the kitchen, and I hear her rummaging around—probably for tea. She's a tea fiend. I almost call out to tell her that I only have chai, but the words stay stuck in my throat.

A couple of years ago, Fallon started making me tea fairly regularly. It was before the kiss, before the messiness, before everything. I'm not sure I have it in me to drink the spiced tea now—it'll only remind me of Fallon.

"Well," Candice says with a long sigh, "let's talk about something happier. What are you going to do with your prize money? And when can we display your trophy?"

"When the last episode airs in three months."

"And will you be opening your own bakery, or what?" Simone smiles at me. "We know you've got big things planned."

I stare at my hands for a moment, because the truth is, right now I just feel tired. The thought of opening a bakery just seems redundant when I could keep working at Four Cups. All the reasons I wanted to win seem so...small.

"I haven't decided yet," I finally answer. "I think I might just take it easy for a bit."

The girls exchange loaded looks. That's not the type of thing I usually say.

Candice pats my knee. "Okay, honey."

Conversation moves on, and before I know it there's food

and tea and water being presented to me. The girls make sure I'm fed and comfortable, then leave with stern orders to get a good night's sleep.

When they're gathering their things to leave, I still have remnants of feelings that I don't deserve their care and affection. What have I ever done to get friends like these?

Candice must see something in my expression, because she walks up to me and squeezes my arm.

"Why are you being so nice to me?" I blurt.

Candice tilts her head. "You've been my best friend for decades, Jen."

"Yeah, but...why?"

Her eyes are steady on mine. "Well, you're loyal and caring. You're reliable and funnier than you realize. Supportive. You're great! Even if you are a logical little weirdo."

I frown at the last sentence.

My friend just grins. "I'm just telling you I love you—exactly the way you are. I'm fully supportive of you taking some time off, of figuring out what you want to do. If you don't want to start your own bakery, then don't. Hire someone to help out at Four Cups. Take a breather. You deserve it."

"Once Fallon comes back and begs you to take him back, you should take two weeks or so to hole up in some secluded resort somewhere so you can sex each other to within an inch of your lives," Simone suggests.

I just roll my eyes. "I think you mean *if* Fallon comes back. Big *if*." As in, this time he's probably gone for good.

Didn't I always know this would happen?

"He'll come back," Fiona says, slinging her purse over her

shoulder. "You should have seen his face when he walked into Four Cups and asked for you after six months away. Looked like a man starved."

They say their goodbyes and leave me to myself, but their words rattle around my brain. Everyone seems so sure that Fallon will come back and want to see me...but what if he doesn't?

THIRTY
FALLON

SLIM LOOKS *OLD*. His face is haggard, blotched with red, with yellowing eyes. When he grins at the sight of me, I see his browned teeth, a few of which are missing. He's still skinny as hell, though.

It's shocking, really. Would I look like this if I had spent my entire adult life in and out of prison?

"The great Fallon Richter finally decided to grace me with his presence!" He guffaws, opening the door wider. "Come in. Drink?"

"I'm good," I answer, but Slim still heads for the fridge to grab a beer.

I catch a can against my chest when he tosses it, then nod in thanks. His kitchen is filthy. After working in professional kitchens for years—and spending the last few years alongside perma-clean Jennifer Newbank—this space makes my skin crawl.

There are old, crusted bowls and plates piled high in the sink. The same lace curtains as out front, gone brown with age, hang limp in the kitchen window. There's brown sludge in the corner between the counter and the backsplash, and worn, ripped linoleum over the floor.

My apartment in Heart's Cove was nothing like this place. Maybe I'm not like Slim at all. We came from the same place... but we've grown into very different men.

Slim belches, then cracks his own beer open. "Long time no see, brother."

The word *brother* rankles, but I hide it behind a sip of beer. "My sister told me you were looking for me. I don't appreciate you harassing her."

Slim leans against the kitchen counter, his wrinkled, stained shirt riding up at the front. He nods. "Straight to business. You haven't changed a bit."

Suddenly, I feel worn out. I'm on edge in this space, worried about Slim and his cronies talking to my family, and my heart hurts from missing Jen. With a sigh, I put my beer down and spread my arms. "What do you want, Slim?"

"I invite you into my home, I give you a drink, and this is how you speak to me? Come on, man. I want to catch up!"

"I've got shit to do." I cross my arms.

Slim holds my gaze for a moment, then laughs. "All right, all right." He gestures to a rickety table and chairs. "Have a seat."

He throws himself onto a wobbly chair with missing braces between the legs, and I sit much more gingerly on the seat across from him, half-expecting it to collapse. Slim slurps his beer and burps behind his fist again, and it takes every ounce of patience not to get up and walk right out.

But I need to know why he was haranguing my sister—and I need to make sure he's not going to do it again.

Finally, Slim speaks. "I have a business proposition for you."

"Not interested." I make to stand, but Slim puts his hand out.

He waits until I've lowered myself back down onto my seat before speaking. "I heard from a few boys on the inside that you were visiting the Nevada State Prison earlier this year. Giving them some cooking lessons and shit."

I'm not quite sure what the "and shit" portion of that sentence means, but I still nod. "Yeah. So? You got a problem with that?"

Slim throws his hands up and laughs again. "Nah, man. I think it's good. Giving back and all that." He leans forward. "But you know you could be making a killing doing that, right?"

"I could be making a killing teaching convicts how to cook?" I blink. "I'm not following."

Slim snorts. "Brother. Not for the cooking lessons. For the supplies you'd bring with you to the classes." He stares into my eyes, his meaning clear.

Slim wants me to be a drug mule to bring gear into the prison.

In that moment, faced with the idiot who caused me to go to prison, I feel a moment of clarity. Slim has wasted his life. His body is a broken husk, and his house is a contamination zone that has *Biohazard* stamped onto every filthy inch. The man in front of me is stuck in a cycle of crime—a cycle that I escaped.

I'm nothing like him.

We were convicted of the same crime. I, apparently, aided and abetted *his* robbery. When we were eighteen, our criminal record was almost identical—but we aren't the same men now. Maybe we never were the same, even as teens.

I pled guilty, but I never felt like it was right. The prosecutor was a bull of a man with big, meaty fists he loved to lean against the steel table in the interrogation room. He knew the knife was mine—had irrefutable proof. He had photos of me with the knife, and witness testimonies that proved the knife had been my father's before it was passed down to me.

In Nevada, someone who aids and abets a crime can be charged with the same offense as the principal. Robbery carries a sentence of two to fifteen years. Use a deadly weapon like a knife? Tack on another one to twenty.

The prosecutor told me he'd ask for the maximum for me unless I pled out.

I was afraid of spending my entire life in prison, and I let the prosecutor intimidate me. I pled guilty to a robbery that happened when I was at home in bed. The only thing I did wrong was befriend Slim and let myself be influenced by the appeal of a gang. I was a kid. I was fatherless. I was *hurting*.

For the first time in my life, what Nora was saying earlier today sinks in. My criminal record doesn't define me. I moved on, made something of myself—something humble, sure. But I've lived an honest life.

Have I been punishing myself for decades for something that wasn't my fault? Have I been holding myself up to an impossible standard?

Taking a deep breath, I look Slim in the eyes. "I won't bring anything to the prison for you. If I decide to give more cooking classes to inmates, it'll be so they can make an honest living when they get out. Not to give addicts their fix."

Slim's smile fades. His chair creaks as he leans back, the linoleum groaning underfoot.

I stand, turning for the door, then pause. This guy sent people to Heart's Cove to look for me. They creeped through the woods, watched me with Jen, went through her stuff. I played it off at the time, but I know someone messed with her clothes when we were in the guesthouse. If that happens again, I won't hesitate to go on the offensive.

"One more thing." I face him. "If you ever send anyone to my home again, I'll make sure they know they're not welcome. Stay away from my sister. Stay away from my woman. Stay out of my life, Slim. I'm not your fucking brother."

Slim's brows arch for a moment, then lower over narrowed eyes. "Understood." I make it to the front door before Slim calls out again, standing at the other end of the hallway. "I'll admit I asked Nora to contact you, Fallon. But I never sent anyone after your woman. Shit, I didn't even know you had one." He holds my gaze until I open the door and walk out.

My mind is spinning so much that I don't even realize I've driven all the way back to Nora's place. I park outside, then realize I never picked up any dinner. Sighing, I lean against the headrest and close my eyes, replaying my conversation with Slim from beginning to end.

I'm nothing like him. I'm not sure I ever was.

A weight lifts off my shoulders, and for the first time in decades I feel like I can breathe.

One thing bothers me, though. If Slim didn't send anyone to Heart's Cove, then who was creeping around our guesthouse?

I jump when someone knocks on the car window. Nora opens the passenger door, then makes an exaggerated show of looking around the car. "Where's dinner?"

I grimace. "Didn't know what you wanted to eat."

She frowns. "So you came back? Ever heard of a phone?"

"Shut up, Snotface."

Her smile lights her face. "And he's back! Did you do some soul-searching in the two hours you were gone?"

I nod. "Yeah. I realized you were right. I shouldn't punish myself for my criminal record."

Nora rolls her eyes. "What a revelation," she says sarcastically, then climbs into the car. "Come on. I know a good Thai place not far from here."

When her door slams shut, I turn the key in the ignition and let my lips slide into a smile. If I can forgive myself for my mistakes, is it possible that Jen would understand, too? That she would see me as more than my criminal record? Is it possible that her father is *wrong* about me...and maybe I *am* worthy of a woman like her?

Nora tells me of her plans to pick up some boxes tomorrow. She says she's rented a trailer that we can hitch to the jeep for the drive back, and I'm to pick it up in the morning.

"How long do you think it'll take to pack up your apartment? Have you spoken to your landlord?"

"All sorted. My lease ends in a month anyway, and he was

giving me stink so I just said to keep the last month's rent and not bother me. Couple hundred bucks is worth it to start over." She hums, then arches a brow. "If you stop driving around aimlessly and actually help me pack, I think we could be on the road by the end of the week."

Less than a week. I can do a week. It'll feel like an eternity, but I can do it. By next Sunday evening I could have Jen in my arms, begging her to forgive me for taking off.

I nod. "Sure. But there's something I need to do tomorrow first. Need a few hours to head to Truckee."

Nora's eyes glimmer at the sound of the city just on the other side of the Nevada-California border. My little sister gives me a proud nod. "That, I'll allow."

THIRTY-ONE
FALLON

THE SUN IS ALREADY PROMISING a scorching day by
the time I enter the retirement village located in Truckee, California. Small, single-story houses line the street, all with acces-
sible ramps and handrails as far as the eye can see.

I scan the house numbers, my stomach clenching when I
find my destination. It's the first time I've been here.

Glancing at the time, I suck in a long breath. It's just after
nine o'clock in the morning, which means my mother will definitely be awake. She's always been an early riser.

So, before I can chicken out, I exit my car and make my way
up the gently sloping path to the front door. The seconds that
pass between my ringing the doorbell and the door actually
opening are excruciating—but within moments, my mother's
shocked face appears on the other side of the threshold.

My mother is seventy-two, but she looks ten years younger.
Her waist-length hair is mostly white now, although streaked

with black, and knotted in her customary single, thick braid. She's wearing an old sweatshirt with my high school's name on it, furry slippers, and tan shorts.

Her mouth opens, then closes. She gapes.

Oh, God. This was a bad idea. I haven't seen my mother in person in nearly a decade. Ever since I got out of prison, our relationship has been hanging on by a thread. If I'm honest, once she gave me that ultimatum and I walked out of her house, I was too ashamed to ask for forgiveness.

Which means it's been *decades* since we saw eye to eye.

What if I misread the situation? What if coming here was a mistake? She could be totally done with me, not wanting a relationship at all. She could slam the door in my face and tell me to leave her property.

I scrub the back of my neck. "Hey, Ma. Hope this isn't a bad time."

A high-pitched keening sound comes from my mother, then she launches herself at me. Her arms wrap around my neck as she drags me down, peppering my face with kisses. Her fingers clutch my neck, my hair, her slight body trembling.

She smells like she always has: that scent of laundry detergent, fragrance-free lotion, and Mom. A thousand memories assail me as soon as I inhale, my vision going blurry with moisture.

"Mom—"

"My baby is here." She smacks a kiss onto my cheek then pulls back, her eyes roaming over my face, my body. "You've been working out." She squeezes my shoulders. "So strong. Last time I saw you, you looked so tired and drawn. You've put on muscle."

That was ten years ago. I gulp. "Can I come in?"

"Of course. Yes, yes. Come in." She leads the way inside, closing the door behind me. There's a bench next to the door. My eyes land on a shoehorn with a handle long enough to reach my hip. My mother follows my gaze and snorts. "I'm an old woman now, Fallon. I can't even bend down to put my own shoes on."

"You look great, Ma."

She just waves me into the kitchen, heading for the gurgling coffee machine.

My brows jump. "You never used to drink coffee."

"An ex-manfriend got me hooked on it."

"Manfriend?" Why haven't I heard about this?

My mother throws me a glance over her shoulder that says, *Don't even start with me, boy.* My lips twitch. She pours a couple of cups of coffee and sits down at the small, round break-fast table across from me. Reaching her hand across the table, she squeezes my fingers.

For the second time in two days, I'm sitting across from a skeleton from my past. This time, though, I want to be here.

"What a start to the day," she says on a sigh. "I'm so happy to see you, Fallon."

All my fears evaporate. I've avoided my mother for years. I thought she was disappointed in me, ashamed of my past—but there's none of that in her gaze now.

My revelation last night at Slim's house comes rushing back to me. Have I been punishing myself for my mistakes all these years? Did I push my mother away not because *she* was ashamed of *me,* but because *I* was ashamed of *myself?*

Bright eyes study my face before my mother leans back and brings her cup to her lips. "So, who is she?"

I cough into my fist. "What?"

"You look well-rested, your shoulders are back, and those shadows in your eyes aren't as dark. You met a woman, fell in love, and she made you realize that you're worth something."

My eyes hold my mother's for a beat, then I huff out a laugh. "Well...yeah. But that's not why I'm here."

"Oh?"

"I'm here to apologize, Ma. I was a shitty son and I turned my back on you. I should have called you more, visited. I was only a couple of hours away in Heart's Cove for the past few years, but I never even came to visit."

My mother gives me a sad smile. She reaches across the table to squeeze my hand again. "You're here now, Fallon. That's all that matters."

"I've been so stupid. I've pushed so many people away because of how I felt about myself."

Her grin turns wry. "Well, I guess that means the apple doesn't fall far from the tree."

"Huh?" I tilt my head. My hand plays with the bottom of my mug, mind still reeling that I'm actually here and that my mother seems happy to see me.

"I had a falling out with my parents too, you know. I was a second-generation kid from an immigrant family with very conservative parents, and I married for love." Her lips curl, eyes faraway. "They didn't approve of my American husband, didn't approve of my children having American names, didn't approve of a lot of things I did."

"I don't remember your parents at all."

"You only met them once when you were about eighteen months old," she tells me with a shake of her head. "I had a huge fight with my parents about how I was raising you and who I was married to, so I vowed to do it without their help. Even after your father died, I never reached out again." She sips her coffee, arching a brow. "So I guess you've got one over me. You're a bigger person than I was."

"I didn't know any of that."

"I was embarrassed and angry. I thought I could do everything by myself, but evidently that didn't work out." My mother snorts. "Look what happened with you. Maybe if we'd had a support system, things would have turned out differently."

My chest clenches. "Ma, you had nothing to do with me going to prison."

"Didn't I? What if I'd been around more? If I had asked for help, I could have gotten you into counseling when your father died. I could have been at home instead of working myself to the bone. I could have saved you from ever meeting those boys."

The pain in my mother's face cracks my heart right open. I never knew she blamed herself for all that. Frowning, I swallow past a lump in my throat and say, "Is that why you didn't push it when I told you not to come visit me?"

"I've been blaming myself for what happened to you for decades, Fallon. I'm the one who gave you your father's knife."

"That fucking knife." I snort and stare at the ceiling, then clamp my mouth shut, waiting for my mother to scold me for swearing.

But she just huffs. "That fucking knife is right."

A surprised laugh falls from my lips, and pretty soon the two of us are laughing in earnest. When I quiet down, I shake my head. "Ma, you can't blame yourself for what I did. I just realized yesterday that maybe I shouldn't blame myself as much as I have been either. It happened, I did my time, and it's in the past."

Her eyes glimmer. "Hmm. So, no more deflection. Who is she?"

Another laugh escapes my lips, and it's like a balm on my soul. I haven't laughed with my mother in years—maybe not since I was a kid. But we're here, sharing a coffee, and there's no rancor.

What if I had done this two decades ago? I've wasted so many years stuck in my own head, in my own pain. I could have had a good life with my family all around me, but I chose to walk alone.

Just like my mother did.

Maybe it's time for me to stand up and break that cycle. To actually forgive myself for my past and rise above it. I can't bear the thought of losing Jen because I'm too bullheaded to get over my issues.

I clear my throat. "Her name is Jennifer. Jen. She's a genius, Ma. You'd love her. Her brain is like this intricate machine that looks at the world in ways I've never even considered." I grin. "She likes your masala chai recipe."

"Uh-uh, Fallon." My mom slurps her coffee. "She likes *your* recipe."

My chest puffs, lips tugging. "Yeah. I guess she does."

"So, why isn't she here with you?"

My thumb runs over the grain of the wood table. "Well, that's the thing. I think I might have messed up, but I'm not really sure how to fix it."

My mother lifts a finger, gets up to grab the coffee carafe to top us up, then sits back down. She nods. "Tell me everything."

THIRTY-TWO

JEN

A FAMILIAR KEY slides into the guesthouse door, and I place my bag inside, shoulders dropping with a sigh. When I told the girls I was taking a week to myself, they were very encouraging.

When I told them I'd be staying at the Heart's Cove Manor Retreat, I got a lot of funny looks—but I like this place! I have good memories, the guesthouse is comfortable, and it's far enough that it feels like a vacation without being too far to be inconvenient.

Plus, I can still grab breakfast from Four Cups in the morning.

I'm a creature of habit. I'm not Iliana; I don't need to go jet-setting all over the world to feel like I'm getting a holiday. And maybe I feel like I need some closure...or an action plan in case Fallon comes back.

I've been able to avoid my parents for the past few days, and my hope is that they'll give up and leave Heart's Cove and let me live in peace. Hopefully by the time Fallon comes back, they'll be out of my hair.

The cot is gone. I sit on the edge of the bed and lie back to stare at the ceiling, blowing out a breath.

I spent a couple of days in Four Cups, prepping enough baked goods for the week I'll be here. I bribed Candice to take care of my plants until early next week, and I visited the library and Agnes's bookstore to stock up.

Turning my head to glance at my bags, I lift myself up onto my elbows. Might as well get started.

I've got research to do.

The first book I pull out of the bag is a thick hardback with a grizzled man's face on the front. *Life After Incarceration* is emblazoned in bold, yellow letters, and I run my fingers over the text. It's as good a place to start as any.

Curling up under the blankets, I read late into the night, using sticky tabs to keep track of insightful passages that I want to return to. I fall asleep for a few hours when dawn starts lightening the sky, then head to Four Cups for a croissant and some tea.

It's not as good as Fallon's tea, but it'll do.

Then I'm right back at the guesthouse, dragging a chair to the front porch to sun my legs while I power through book after book on prison, the legal system, the psychological effects of incarceration, and how to care for someone once they get out of prison.

It's been more than two decades since Fallon got out, but he still bears the scars. I intend to mend them for him.

A crow hops into view, its head tilting as if in question. *Where's my food?*

"Well, lucky for you, crow, I came prepared." Reaching down, I pull out a bag of bird seed. This is probably a bad idea—I can just imagine flocks of birds harassing tourists for food—but it makes me think of Fallon. For once in my life, I want to do something that might not be entirely logical.

So, I feed the birds. Sue me.

ON THE THIRD day of my sabbatical, I get an email notification that my payment from the competition has been disbursed. Confused when I see the amount, I call Gus.

"Hey, champ," he says. "Still basking in your win?"

"Uh, about that," I say. "The email I just got says the full hundred grand was disbursed to me. Why wasn't that split between me and Fallon?"

"He didn't tell you?" Gus asks.

I frown. "Tell me what?"

"He insisted on a clause that gave the prize money to you before signing the contract. Everyone thought it was awfully romantic, and it was one of the reasons I was rooting for the two of you."

I blink, throat tight. I remember his noncommittal response when I mentioned we'd get fifty grand each. Fallon never agreed with that. This whole time, he planned on giving me the prize?

Emotion swirls inside me. My eyes grow moist as my breaths turn sharp. Fallon never entered the competition just for the money.

He did it entirely for me.

"I'm not sure what to say," I finally manage.

"I think you could start by thanking him," Gus replies on a laugh. "Is he there with you? I'm assuming the two of you are still celebrating your win."

"Uh..." I stare at the familiar walls of the guesthouse. "No. He's not here."

"Well, when he gets home, I'm sure the two of you can discuss it. I have to go now, but I'll talk to you later."

We hang up, and I sit on the bed, dazed. There's a book sitting on my thighs, my cell phone still gripped in my hands.

Fallon participated in the *Boss Baker* competition for *me*. Entirely for me. Signed off on his prize money because he thought I deserved it more.

I don't know whether to be upset or flattered. All I know is I want to see him. Kiss him. Talk to him—and tell him that he's not a loser or an ex-con or a felon who doesn't deserve good things. He's Fallon, and he's perfect.

But when my fingers hover over his phone number, I can't quite bring myself to tap the screen. What would I say? How can you have a conversation like that over the phone?

Looking at my stack of books, I blow out a breath. I'll finish my research, come up with an action plan, *then* I'll call him—once I know how to approach things the right way.

ANOTHER FEW DAYS PASS, and on Sunday I end up heading into Heart's Cove to visit with the girls. I spend the afternoon in the library above the Four Cups Café, laughing with my friends and feeling more at home in this town than I ever have. When the sun starts to set, I push myself to my feet and say goodbye to the girls.

"Are you heading back?" Candice asks, glancing up from her phone.

I nod. "I'm tired."

Her fingers fly over her screen. "Okay. Drive safe!"

"Next time you take a vacation, Jen, promise me you'll take an *actual* vacation. Like, outside of the town limits." Iliana arches a brow. "I can recommend some places for you to visit."

Pausing at the door as I hike my purse over my shoulder, I glance at my friend's sister and give her a smile. "That sounds good, Lily. I'd like that."

And it's the truth. Because I know there *will* be a next time. I'll be taking more vacations from now on.

The drive back to the Heart's Cove Manor Retreat is full of elongating shadows and pastel skies I spy through the gaps in the trees. Tonight, I'll finish the last book in my collection and come up with an action plan. Then I'll call Fallon and tell him to get his butt back here.

But when I pull into the parking lot, my heart jumps. There's a familiar Jeep parked in one of the spaces.

Fallon's Jeep.

He came back? I creep closer, glancing in the jeep to see one of his sweatshirts balled up in the back seat. *He came back!*

Is that who Candice was texting so frantically earlier?

Fallon's here!

I suck in a breath, ready to sprint inside the main farmhouse, then I freeze. I haven't formulated a plan yet. Shit! I need to make him understand that I don't care about his past. I like him for who he is *now*.

Gus's words come back to me. I could start by thanking him —and not just for the prize money, because I fully intend on splitting it. No, I can thank him for being there for me for the past month. For putting me in contact with Amanda and making my recipe book a reality. For being a steady presence at my side during many a baking meltdown.

When I hurry along the path, I'm surprised to see lights on inside the barn. One of the big doors is cracked open, and I drift closer. The familiar kitchen islands are still set up, with refrigerators lining the back wall. I inhale the scent of the room, memories of the past month flooding my head. I fell head over heels with Fallon in this room.

Maybe we can take cooking classes together here. Maybe we can *teach* cooking classes together here.

The shape of a man is bent over a refrigerator on the far wall, his body silhouetted in the light.

"Fallon?" I call out, easing my way inside the door. "What are you doing?"

The man straightens, and it's not Fallon at all. He turns, and the first thing I notice is that he's shirtless. The second thing I notice is smears of something on his chest...blood?

No.

Pie. The man has cherry pie all over his chest and mouth, like a toddler, a chunk clutched in his hand.

Then I register his face.

"Guillaume?"

"*Ma chérie*," he croons, stumbling closer to me. "Finally you came to me."

Cherry pie is smeared all over his lips, his chin, dripping onto his bare chest, as if he stuffed his face right into the pie.

What the fuck?

"What are you doing here?" I'm frozen on the spot, heart racing.

My old boss takes another step toward me. "I've been waiting for you to realize we belong together. I know you love me."

Uh...

Oh, *hell* no. Another one? Two in one week? Is there something in the water? Why are these men now obsessed with me, thinking I feel the same way? I haven't had a real boyfriend for two decades, but all of a sudden these men are coming out of the woodwork trying to get with me? What the hell is going on?

Is it the money? The trophy?

And the one man that I actually want lied about his past! Or at the very least, lied by omission....and then he left!

My limbs are shaking. Guillaume takes another step closer, and I throw a hand up. "Stop right there."

"I've watched you this past month, Jennifer. Watched you with that big, bumbling oaf. You deserve better. He's finally gone, and you're here with me. You're just as beautiful as I remembered in our kitchen. I know you've missed the long nights we spent together, cooking and cleaning until the sun came up."

"Actually, no," I answer. "I don't miss those nights at all."

He chuckles. "You're so sweet when you lie to me."

"I'm not lying. Come one step closer and I'll call the police. You shouldn't even be here. Whose pie is that? Did you steal someone's food from a cooking class?"

"You deserved to win. This is your pie. I've hidden it here all week, but I couldn't resist finally eating it."

I stare at the smears of cherry all over his body. "I can see that."

He comes closer, and my eyes are drawn to a strip of pink near his waist. I inhale sharply, eyes bugging. "Are you... Are you wearing my undies?"

That day I thought someone had messed with my stuff...that was *Guillaume? He's wearing my underwear?*

Breath fills my lungs, horror floods my system, and I scream.

THIRTY-THREE
FALLON

I'VE GOT two gifts to give to Jen, which will hopefully help mend whatever went wrong between us. The first gift is contained in a basket dangling from my fingers, and the second is housed safely in my pocket. My mother insisted I take it when I left her house, and now it sits like a weight against my leg.

I've just finished knocking on the guesthouse door and am waiting with bated breath to hear Jen's footsteps when I hear...a scream? What was that? An alarm or a whistle of some kind?

Then I hear the crows.

It starts with just one bird cawing, soon to be joined by too many to count. The racket gets so loud I step out from under the porch, only to see dozens of birds flapping near the barn.

What the...?

Frowning, I put the basket down near the door and step away from the cabin. Glancing up, I see the black birds going wild in the sky. One flies above the trees toward me, alighting on a branch. It caws loudly before flapping its wings to circle overhead.

"What the hell is wrong with you?" I yell at the bird, half expecting it to answer.

Glancing over my shoulder at the dark guesthouse, I exhale and walk onto the path. These fucking birds. Jen was right; I never should have fed them. I just wanted to make Jen laugh, and look what I've done. I've created a monster—a deafening murder of crows that goes ballistic on a quiet Sunday evening.

But...I've never seen the birds like this before, and over the past month, I've spent a lot of time feeding them.

And I *did* hear a scream—or was it another bird? An animal?

My feet take me down the path, through the trees, and into the clearing. Glancing up at the sky, I watch the birds flapping and cawing like I've never seen before.

What the hell is going on?

Then I see movement. Through the windows of the darkened farmhouse, I see a man—

And Jen. She's rushing for the door, her face panicked.

Adrenaline dumps into my veins, and before I know it, I'm sprinting. I rush around the side of the barn and tear the door open so hard, one of the hinges snaps clean off.

Jen stumbles out, eyes wild. "He's wearing my undies!" she cries.

Protective instinct roars inside me. There's a man in the room stumbling after Jen, and he needs to fucking go *down*.

I rush him, so full of fury that I'm ready to rip his head off with my bare hands. Pop it off like a champagne cork. Right before I tackle him to the ground, I register his face.

Guillaume, then man who accosted me the day of the finale. What the hell is he doing here? Why is he covered in pie? Why isn't he wearing a shirt?

The sight of Jen's undies sticking out from his pants blankets my vision in red. I wrap him in a bear hug and slam him on the ground, a primal yell tearing out of my throat. I reach for something—anything—and manage to find a metal bowl.

The clang of the bowl hitting Guillaume's head rings out in the space, but does little to stop him squirming.

He snaps his teeth at me, and I just manage to avoid them by jerking my head back. Flipping him over, I grab his wrists and try to subdue him, but he bucks like a man crazed.

"The cops are on the way!" Jen yells, phone in hand. She rushes around the room, producing some kitchen twine. With shaking hands, she wraps his wrists as I do my best to hold the man down. He's speaking gibberish, yelling things as his body writhes.

It's not until his wrists and ankles are bound that he quiets down, panting, trussed up like a pig with his face down on the floor. Jen slaps a hand to her forehead, eyes wild.

The sound of sirens in the distance makes her shoulders relax. She turns to me and wraps her arms around my waist so tight I can feel her heart thumping against me.

Then she pulls away. "I'll go direct the cops." She points a finger at my face. "Don't you dare go anywhere in the meantime. I need to talk to you." She heads for the door, then whirls back to face me. Planting her hands on my cheeks, she drags me down and kisses me so hard our teeth click. Then she's running out the door and toward the parking lot.

Dazed, I turn back to the creep on the floor. He's struggling against his bonds, the rough twine already slicing his wrists. I feel no sympathy as my eyes move to the pink material poking from under his pants.

It wasn't Slim's cronies sneaking around us at all. It was this fucking guy.

The cops burst through the door and instinctively, I stiffen. But they rush to the man on the ground, handcuff him, and drag him away.

Then Jen and I are giving statements to the police about what just happened. It takes forever. I get a lot of weird looks when I mention the crows alerting me something was wrong, but what can I say? That's what happened.

I'm still keyed up by the time the police leave. Jen watches them walk away, her arms hugging her middle. When I make a move to go to her, three familiar faces rush toward us from the parking lot.

"Jennifer!" Mrs. Newbank cries. "Oh, you're okay!"

Mr. Newbank whirls on me. "This is your fault. I *told* you to stay away from my daughter."

"You *what?*" Jen straightens, jaw slack. "You told Fallon to stay away from me? What the fuck, Dad?"

"Don't speak to your father that way," her mother chides. She steps aside, and who walks out from behind her?

Bernard. Fucking. Franco.

A growl rumbles through my chest before I can stop myself.

Jen glances at me, her chin held high, shoulders pushed

back. She turns to her parents and Bernard. "Mom, Dad, Bernard. Thank you for stopping by. As you can see, I'm safe and Fallon is safe, so your concern isn't necessary. I'm tired, though, so I'll call you tomorrow if you want details about what happened."

"Who was that guy?" Mr. Newbank demands, ignoring Jen's speech. "Is he from Fallon's gang?"

"I'm not in a fucking gang," I spit.

Jen's father just snorts. "Right. That's not what your criminal record says."

"Dad, that's enough." Jen puts up a hand. "You can't speak to Fallon like that."

He puffs his chest. "Jen—"

"Dad. Stop." Jen's voice is hard as steel. She turns to Bernard. "If you're here to invite me to Paris, save your breath. I'm not going with you. We didn't have a connection. I'm never going to date you."

Bernard scoffs, eyes darting to me. "Is this because of Fallon? Jen, you can do so much better."

I cringe, waiting for Jen to deflect. But she faces Bernard with a snarl on her lips. "There is no one—*no one*—better than Fallon. Goodnight to you all." She starts to turn, then pauses. "Feel free to leave Heart's Cove at your earliest convenience. I'll talk to you when whoever's birthday is up next. Or the holidays. Or never. I don't care."

Her mother splutters as her father protests. Bernard gapes like he just got slapped.

Jen ignores them all. She faces me and extends a hand. "Fallon, take my hand and take me home."

This woman. My heart cracks right there in my chest, and I cross the distance between us. In a familiar movement, my arm slides around her shoulder, and everything feels right again. We walk far enough that the trees hide us from our audience and Jen pauses, wrapping both her arms around my middle. When she turns to snuggle into my chest, I let out a breath.

This is perfection. Having Jen in my arms makes something click inside me, like the last piece of a jigsaw slotting into place. With her head nestled under my chin, I pull her close and wrap my arms around her. We stand like that for a few long moments, inhaling each other, letting the tension of the last couple of hours seep out of our bodies.

Then Jen pulls away and frowns at me. "You left."

I tuck a strand of hair behind her ear. "I'm sorry."

She bunches her lips to the side. "I suppose you *did* come back. And you sort of saved me from my creepy, stalker ex-boss. And you've been kind of amazing for the past month." She glances at the sky. "And did those crows sense something was wrong? I've never seen them react like that."

"Maybe they're loyal because we fed them for a month."

Jen's brows tug together. "I'll have to look up if that's even possible. But if it is, then I should definitely be thanking you."

My lips twitch. "So the crows tip the scales in my favor?" I can just imagine the pros and cons list Jen is making in her mind, trying to figure out if she's happy I'm here or not.

She slides her gaze back to mine. "Only if you promise to stay the night."

"That, I can do," I answer. "Plus, I brought you something. I left it by the guesthouse door."

She straightens, dropping her arms from my waist. "You did?"

I can't resist catching her hand in mine as we turn down the familiar beaten dirt path. "I did."

We walk in silence until the guesthouse comes into view, then I pull away from her to grab the basket. I present it to her and watch as she pulls away the tea towel I laid over the contents.

Tilting her head, Jen picks up one of the croissants in the basket and inspects it. Her eyes flick to mine. "Croissants?"

"I felt the need to redeem myself."

Her eyes glimmer as her lips curl. "You made these?" Jen's smile widens. "You learned how to make croissants for me," she says, almost to herself. Then she gets that focused look on her face as she rips the baked good open. "Good layers," she says, inspecting. "Crisp on the outside, tender inside." She pops a piece in her mouth and chews, nodding. "You used good butter."

My lips twitch. "I did."

"It's good, Fallon," she says, finally lifting her eyes to mine. "Really good."

"Spent all week trying to get them right. My mom and sister think I'm crazy."

Jen's smile is like the first ray of sunlight after a never-ending storm. She places the pieces of her croissant back in the basket, then straightens and reaches for the door. "I spent all week thinking of you too," she announces.

On the other side of the door, I find the guesthouse scattered with books. Each of them has color-coded tags throughout, dozens per tome. There's a thick notebook and pen on the night-stand. Jen makes a beeline for the journal, flipping it open to read the first page.

My eyes land on the title of the nearest book: *Psychology of a Prisoner*. Heart thundering, I grab it and flip it over to read the back, then open one of the tabs Jen must have put in it. It lands on a page that details the difficulty of starting your life over after a prison term.

Throat tight, I realize what Jen's been doing. She hasn't been judging me for my past; she's been trying to *understand* it. She never turned her back on me when she learned I'd been to prison. In Jen's typical rational way, she just set to work untangling the complicated strands of my past in a way that made sense to her.

Emotion clogs my throat. How could I ever think that she would look at me differently after learning about my incarceration? My past could never stand between us. When she asked me about my conviction, her reaction was one of shock, but not judgment. I thought she was pushing me away, but she was just trying to figure out how this puzzle piece fit into the whole.

"So," Jen says, consulting her notes, "I've read a dozen books so far, but I think it would help if I understood the intricacies of your case. Three years seems pretty short for robbery with a deadly weapon, based on everything I've read about Nevada law. My best guess, without going through your case notes, is that you pled guilty, but you weren't directly involved. You were so young, you know? Facing that kind of prison time must have been terrifying." She clicks her tongue, still scanning her notes.

My heart warms, lips unable to stop twitching. "You've been reading about Nevada law?"

Jen frowns, eyes still on the notebook. "Yeah. I'm trying to figure out your headspace so I can convince you to stay here and be with me. But I need to understand what you've been through, at least on some level. My next step was to try to find the details of your case to confirm my hypothesis about the guilty plea and the light sentence, but I figured I'd ask you first since that seemed kind of...invasive." She bites her lip, flipping to a new page to scan her neat handwriting. "Hold on, I know I wrote something about long-term effects of incarceration. I had a whole plan for how we would talk about this."

I. Fucking. Love. Her.

Reaching over to toss her notebook away, I band an arm around Jen's back and tug her close. "You don't need your notes to talk to me. I'll tell you everything you want to know, Jen. Ask me anything, and I'll do my best to answer."

Her brows climb. "Now you want to talk about it? You've had a change of heart."

"I've had a revelation," I answer.

"Oh yeah?"

I nod. "Yep."

"What's that?"

"That I love you," I say. "I'm crazy about you. Can't live without you—and the only way for me to do that is move on from my past." I cup her cheek, thumb brushing the slight hollows under her eyes. "I also realized that I don't need to be defined by my past. It's time for me to move on. If you'll let me, I'd like to grow into the type of man who's worthy of you."

Jen's eyes fill with tears as she places her palm over my hand, tilting her face into the touch. "Fallon, you don't need to grow into anything. You're already the perfect man for me."

"Jen," I say through a tight throat, "I've acted like a fool, but that'll change. No more running. No more pushing you away. No more hiding all my scars. I want to be better."

"What could be better than you?" Her hands drift to my chest, sliding up to wrap around my neck. "I love you just the way you are, Fallon. Wouldn't change a thing." She brushes her lips against mine, then pulls away, a serious expression on her face. "But I draw the line at the crows. They might have saved me today, but I won't have flocks of birds following us around everywhere."

Grinning, I lean my forehead against hers. "Deal."

Then I kiss the woman of my dreams, lay her down on the bed, and love her till we fall asleep in each other's arms.

For the first time since I was a child, my heart beats easy, and I'm at peace.

EPILOGUE
JEN

IT TURNS out Fallon had nothing to do with the robbery that landed him in jail. He wasn't even there. Some deadbeat used Fallon's father's knife, the knife got tied to Fallon, and he got bullied into accepting a guilty plea.

Fallon's been beating himself up about it for *decades*.

I'd give him stink about it, but I'd be the pot to his kettle. I've been beating *myself* up for decades because I've never lived up to some impossible standard that was embedded in my brain when I was too young to know any better. Just like him, I never questioned the story I told myself about, well, *myself*. I thought I was a winner. I thought I was successful. I thought my success was what made me worthy of love.

But the magical thing about Fallon is he's made me understand that what makes me worthy of love is that I'm *me*. He loves me just the way I am, quirks and houseplants and all. And

I love him for him, weird hang-ups about misspent youth and all.

Slowly, we're working through it.

We stay in the guesthouse for another three days, mostly in bed with a few food and shower breaks in between bouts of crazy-hot sex. I turn my phone off when Candice starts blowing it up on the second day, knowing the girls will give me a mountain of shit for shutting them out.

I don't care.

My man is here, he's in my bed, and I can have a couple of days to enjoy that fact.

I find out that Fallon texted Candice when he arrived in town to ask where I was, since I wasn't home when he stopped by. That's who she was texting furiously when I left the library the evening of my confrontation with Guillaume.

Since Fallon already gave up his apartment in town, he moves in with me. I make him promise not to touch my plants. He jokes about buying a bird feeder to add to the balcony garden, then laughs at the look on my face.

Then his arms are around me, and we end up christening my bed...and the couch...and the kitchen counter...and the bathroom...

The police keep Guillaume in custody and end up pressing charges against him when they found a tent in the forest not far from our guesthouse. He'd stolen a bunch of my underwear and had lots of photos of me. He'll be assessed for psychological problems and hopefully kept in custody for a long time. There's a restraining order against him as well, so if he ever comes near me again, he'll be straight back in jail or a psychological facility. To be honest, I don't even care. I hope he gets the help he needs.

Fallon is with me, and I know he'll keep me safe. There's nothing that can bring me down from the high I'm on—not even a creepy ex-boss.

My parents ended up leaving Heart's Cove in a huff the day after the confrontation. I couldn't give a shit, and it's the best feeling in the world. They get put on a strict information diet. In our first phone call after the incident, they criticize the fact that I refused Bernard Franco and threaten to cut me out of their will. I'm just...done. Now that I've seen what it's like to be supported unconditionally, the way my parents use emotional manipulation and threats leaves me feeling oily and unclean.

I'll call them on their birthdays, but I won't work myself to the bone trying to make them love me.

I've already got people in my life who love me even when I mess up. Judging by how hard Fallon laughs when it happens, sometimes I think he loves me *because* I mess up.

Bernard never speaks to me again. He's probably prancing around Paris with another baker who fits his requirements for arm candy. Good riddance.

I decide not to open another bakery for now. Maybe I will down the line, but the girls are right. I need more vacations. More time off. Less pressure.

Plus, Four Cups is a rocking coffee house with a kick-ass kitchen. I can bake to my heart's content back there, and I know I'll be surrounded by people who love me. By the time Fallon and I are moved into my apartment, I get a call from Mary-Ann, the chocolate expert who was supposed to compete alongside me. She agrees to come work with me at Four Cups, and I feel excited that I might be able to hand off the reins to someone else.

In the meantime, Fallon and I pick up shifts at Four Cups. We talk about future plans—no new bakery, but maybe something else? I feel like the whole world has cracked open to offer up opportunities to me. If I don't need to be the *best* at what I do, it means I can do anything! I can pursue a passion project or just sit on the beach and drink cocktails for a month.

Fallon still stubbornly refuses to split the winnings with me. I confront him about it one day a few weeks later, when we're in the Four Cups kitchen, baking late into the night like old times.

"You only refused to split the winnings because you didn't feel like you deserved the money," I tell him, wrapping a tray of baked goods in plastic.

He grunts. "Yeah. Exactly."

I turn to face him and cross my arms. "So what about your big revelation? The fact that you're not defined by your past, that you deserve good things too?"

"That's different."

"How?"

He puts a clean bowl away and turns to face me, crossing his big beefy arms as he leans against the counter. "It just is."

"Fallon, you told me a couple of days ago that you'd like to get a degree in counseling so you can work with ex-cons. You talk about giving more classes to people who have been incarcerated. Those things are much easier to accomplish when you have money!"

"I have money," he stubbornly replies. "And I'll use my own money for those things."

"There's fifty grand of your own money sitting in my account! If you'd just let me transfer it over, you could enroll in community college tomorrow and maybe even start your own cooking school for ex-cons."

He bunches his lips to the side as if he's considering it, but then he shrugs. "It's not my money. It's yours. I like those ideas, but I'll find some other way of accomplishing it."

I huff, crossing my arms. "Explain to me why you don't want any part of this cash prize. If your argument is compelling, you know I'll agree." I point at my head. "You're the one who said I had a big, fat brain."

His eyes sparkle. "I'm starting to regret that."

"No, you're not."

Lips twitching, he takes a step toward me. "Okay, I'm not. How about this: We spend the money on something together. A down payment for a house, or a round-the-world trip..." Fallon reaches me, hands sliding over my hips. "Or a wedding."

"I'm not spending a hundred grand on a wedding." I arch a brow.

He tugs me closer, lips curled into a full, satisfied smile. "But you're not opposed to the wedding itself?"

"Is this how you're proposing to me, Fallon? In the kitchen of the Four Cups Café when we're covered in sweat and oil and flour?"

I mean, seriously! I know I'm not romantic, but this is the second time a guy has just assumed I'll marry him. Fallon and I haven't even been together for a full month since the end of the competition!

Fallon's hands hook behind my back, fingers interlacing right above my ass. "Yep." He backs me up against the counter. "I've known you for years, and most of our time spent together was right here. Plus, you'd hate a big, elaborate proposal. Photos and people and hugs and crying?" He shakes his head. "You've gotten more comfortable around people lately, but you're still an introvert."

Hmm. He has a point.

"What about my big honking diamond ring?" I challenge. "Don't I get one of those?"

Reaching into his pocket, Fallon pulls out a little velvet box and flips it open to reveal a vintage Art Deco ring. Tiny diamonds are studded in fine looping patterns around the center stone which glitters under the lights of the kitchen. It's delicate and unique and really freaking cool.

"My mother gave it to me when I told her about you," Fallon says, eyes soft. "I've been carrying it around for weeks."

Okay, that's a little romantic. I take back what I said earlier.

Fallon pops the ring out of the box and positions it near my finger. His eyes meet mine, the question clear.

Throat tight, all I can do is nod. When the ring slides over the third finger on my left hand, I let out a breath, watch the stone glitter for a few moments, then throw my arms around Fallon and kiss the daylights out of him.

I'm not going to be an old, perfectionist spinster. I'm not a robot who hates sex.

I've got a whole world of possibilities open in front of me

and an unbreakable support system at my back. But most importantly, the man of my dreams will be at my side for whatever comes next.

Fallon nuzzles his nose against mine, then pulls back. "Would you really encourage me to keep working with ex-cons? That wouldn't make you uncomfortable?"

"Fallon." I sigh. "No. It would make me *proud.*"

His face splits into a smile, then he dips his lips to kiss me.

With my arms wrapped around the man of my dreams, a big honking diamond ring glimmering on my finger, and a world of possibilities opened up in front of me, I'm happier than I've ever been.

This isn't midlife. I'm just getting started.

LILY

THINGS ARE DIRE.

Jen is all loved-up, Candice and Trina are the same, and my mother keeps dropping hints about me finding a man of my own.

And I'm still carrying this secret inside me that will change everyone's opinion of me. The secret that's about to change my life forever.

There's one thing I know for sure: I should stay far, far away from Rudy with his sparkling blue eyes and his muscular arms and his sexy stubble and that smile that burns the panties right off my body.

Somehow, though, my traitorous feet take me right back to the bookstore when I see him through the window. I've finished all the books he recommended, and I *did* promise to tell him what I thought.

I'm just keeping my word, is all. Being polite.

I'm not walking through this door and hoping he'll give me that heated look and drop his voice when he says my name again.

Nope.

Just normal, a platonic conversation between two consenting bookworms. I promise.

Lily is back in town...and she has two very big secrets. Does she dare tell handsome, successful Rudy the truth, or should she enjoy theire budding romance while it lasts?

Check out Book Six: DIRTY LITTLE MIDLIFE SECRET!

BONUS EPILOGUE

JEN

STANDING ON A CHAIR, I keep my eyes on the spider crawling across my floor. It skitters back and forth along the edge of the room, pausing as if to taste my fear in the air.

"Fallon?" I call out, keeping my eyes on the critter.

I hear a mumble right before the bedroom door opens and Fallon steps out. The sight of him draws my eyes away from the spider.

He's got pajama pants sitting low on his hips to reveal carved lower abs. I follow the line of black hair up to his navel and by some miracle, stop myself from drooling. His chest is bare, with a sprinkling of hair across his pecs. A muscular bicep flexes as he lifts a hand to run his fingers across his scalp, eyes bleary and half-asleep.

When he sees me from his spot just outside the bedroom, he stops and frowns. "Why are you standing on a chair, Jen?"

I point. "Spider."

331

But when I glance at the spot where the spider used to be, all I see is bare floor. I freeze, eyes scanning the room.

"Where?" Fallon yawns, walking right beside the last known whereabouts of the eight-legged creature. As if he doesn't even *care.* He steps into my tiny kitchen and pours himself a cup of coffee from the pot I made for him, then stands in the doorway to the kitchen and leans a big boulder shoulder against the frame. His eyebrows climb as he meets my gaze, slurping his drink.

The chair I'm standing on shakes as my legs start trembling. I make a slow circle, scanning the baseboards, then the walls, then the ceiling.

"I can't see it." Clutching the back of the chair, I glance behind me. "Damn those buggers move fast. This is your fault."

Fallon's lips twitch. "The spider is my fault?"

"No." I huff. "If you weren't so damn good-looking, I'd have kept my eyes on it. But you had to walk out with your muscles and your skin and your bare feet looking all sexy and sleepy, and I got distracted." I flick my eyes back to his. "Your fault."

Fallon grins, cup still in hand, and starts making a slow circuit of the room. He pauses to glance under the couch, then stretches up to his full height to slurp his coffee. I glance at the table next to me and consider climbing up higher. This chair seems awfully close to the ground.

Steps silent as he walks, Fallon does a slow circuit and inspects the apartment. He circles closer, closer, closer, until he's standing right next to my chair.

"Maybe it went outside," he says, placing his cup on the table.

I put my hands on my hips. "How? The windows and doors are closed."

"How big was it?"

My lip feels soft when I sink my teeth into it. "It was a daddy-long-legs," I admit.

Fallon meets my gaze, brow arching high, eyes full of mirth. "A harmless daddy-long-legs got you jumping up on a chair?"

I let out a harsh breath, not wanting to dignify that with a response. Fallon seems to have a similar idea, because before I know what's happening, he's got his arms around my thighs and he's throwing me over his shoulder. I yelp, clinging to his back while he marches back toward the bedroom.

"Fallon! I'm an old woman! You can't manhandle me like this."

"I'll manhandle you like this until my body gives out," he replies, kicking the bedroom door open before tossing me on the bed.

I bounce once and land sprawled across the sheets, flushed and breathless. Hooking his thumbs into his pajama pants, Fallon pushes the bottoms to the floor and steps out of them.

Squealing when he pulls at the tie of my robe, I splutter out a panting, "The spider!"

"Give me thirty seconds and you won't be thinking about any spiders, Jen," Fallon says as he pulls my pajama shorts down my legs and tosses them over his shoulder. When his big, broad hands skate down my thighs, thumbs spreading me wide, I still give a halfhearted protest.

But then his fingers do something magical to my center,

diving deep inside me as my back arches right off the bed. I gasp, knees falling open, and Fallon gives me a growl in return.

Then he's kneeling between my legs, and he's right. I forget about the spider for a while.

WHEN FALLON HAS WRUNG out an orgasm from me, I lie panting on the bed and throw an arm across my forehead. Fallon pulls me into his chest for a moment, then lets out a little grunt.

"What?" I ask, lids heavy as sleep threatens to pull me under.

"One sec." He pulls away from me, swinging his legs off the bed. Gulping down the rest of a glass of stale water by the bed, Fallon spins the cup in his hand and marches to the corner of the room. With lightning-quick movements, he places the cup upside-down on the floor, then stands up with a triumphant smile gracing his lips. "Got it."

I drag myself to the edge of the bed and peer over the edge only to see my friend Mr. Long-legs trapped under the glass. With a relieved sigh, I fall back on the pillows. "That perverted spider was watching us have sex!"

Fallon chuckles before ducking out of the bedroom.

This time, when he walks in—completely naked, mind you —I keep my eyes on the trapped spider. It's a difficult feat that requires a *lot* of concentration, especially when Fallon turns around and his glorious ass is there for me to ogle. He grabs my robe on the ground and tugs it on, tying it loosely at the waist.

Is it wrong that a muscular man in a very short robe is unbearably sexy to me? The paisley patterned silk hits him so high I can see the swell of his muscular butt as he grabs the dustpan and surveys the spider.

Before I can tell him about it, though, he starts the delicate process of shimmying the dustpan under the cup, then heads out to the living room. I hear the balcony door open and close again, and Fallon returns empty-handed.

"You released it outside?" I ask in a small voice.

"I did." He climbs back in bed and curls and arm behind my neck, tugging me tight to his body.

I let out a sigh. "Thank you. You're my hero."

"I saw Agnes on the road below the balcony," he tells me. "She waved right before she noticed what I was wearing." I can hear the grin in his voice. "Her scowl was legendary, but I will note she didn't look away."

I groan, rolling my back to him. "I'll never hear the end of it. The minute I head to Four Cups, I'll be hearing all about your dangly bits poking out from under my silk robe."

"She wasn't the only one ogling me."

I glare at him over my shoulder, and Fallon just laughs.

Despite my best intentions, my lips twitch. When Fallon tugs me closer and kisses me tenderly, I my heart goes soft and gooey in my chest.

"You do look good in paisley silk," I say between kisses.

"Maybe we can get matching robes."

I laugh. "Only if I'm the only one who gets to ogle you."

Propping himself up on his elbows, he ducks his lips to kiss the tip of my nose. "Deal. As long as I'm the only one who gets to save you from harmless spiders."

Tracing his features with my fingertips, I give him a quick nod. "I can agree to that."

The light catches the beautiful ring on my finger, and I can't help but admire it for a moment. Fallon catches my hand and kisses the diamond.

One day in the not-too-distant future, I'm going to be Fallon's wife. I'll live in the town I love surrounded by people who care about me because I'm me. I've got a man who thinks I'm cute and clever and sexy and irresistible, and he doesn't mind catching spiders for me first thing in the morning.

I'm the luckiest woman in the world.

ABOUT THE AUTHOR

Lilian Monroe adores writing swoonworthy heroes and the women who bring them to their knees. She loves making people laugh and is eternally grateful to have found people who share her sense of humor.

When she's not writing, she's reading (or rereading) a book, walking, lifting weights, or attempting to play the guitar with very limited success.

She grew up in Canada but now lives in Australia with her Irish husband. He frequently asks to be used as a cover model for her books, and she's not quite sure whether or not he's joking.

Dirty Little Midlife Dilemma

Dirty Little Midlife Drama

Dirty Little Midlife (fake) Date

Brother's Best Friend Romance

Shouldn't Want You

Can't Have You

Don't Need You

Won't Miss You

Protector Romance

His Vow

His Oath

His Word

Enemies to Lovers/Workplace Romance

Hate at First Sight

Loathe at First Sight

Despise at First Sight

Secret Baby/Accidental Pregnancy Romance

Knocked Up by the CEO

Knocked Up by the Single Dad

Knocked Up...Again!

Knocked Up by the Billionaire's Son

Yours for Christmas

Bad Prince

Heartless Prince

Cruel Prince

Broken Prince

Wicked Prince

Wrong Prince

Lone Prince

Ice Queen

Rogue Prince

<u>Fake Engagement Romance</u>

Engaged to Mr. Right

Engaged to Mr. Wrong

Engaged to Mr. Perfect

<u>Mountain Man Romance</u>

Lie to Me

Swear to Me

Run to Me

<u>Doctor's Orders</u>

Doctor O

Doctor D

Doctor L